BOTH SIDES OF THE VEIL

BOTH SIDES OF THE VEIL

by

RICHARD MARSH

Author of "The Beetle: A Mystery", "The Joss: A Reversion",
"Curios", "The Datchet Diamonds", "Philip Bennion's Death", etc.

𝕶𝖆𝖓𝖘𝖆𝖘 𝕮𝖎𝖙𝖞:
VALANCOURT BOOKS

2009

Both Sides of the Veil by Richard Marsh
First published by Methuen in 1901
First Valancourt Books edition, 2009

This edition © 2009 by Valancourt Books

Library of Congress Cataloguing-in-Publication Data

Marsh, Richard, d. 1915.
Both sides of the veil / by Richard Marsh. – 1st Valancourt Books ed.
p. cm.
"First published by Methuen in 1901"—T.p. verso.
ISBN 1-934555-50-9 (alk. paper)
1. Short stories, English. I. Title.
PR6025.A645B68 2008
823'.912–DC22

2008030323

Composition by James D. Jenkins
Published by Valancourt Books
Kansas City, Missouri
http://www.valancourtbooks.com

CONTENTS

AN ILLUSTRATION OF MODERN SCIENCE

"ARE you Mr. Dyke?"

Rising from his chair, Mr. Dyke confessed that he was.

"I want you to make my will."

Mr. Dyke surveyed the new-comer with amusement.

"Your will? I am afraid that is rather out of my line. It is a solicitor you want. I am a barrister."

"What a nuisance! Is it any odds? You're a lawyer, aren't you?"

She came right into the room. Perching herself on the elbow of an arm-chair, she rested the ferrule of her parasol against his writing-table. He was still more amused,—she really was so pretty! He endeavoured to explain the difference which exists between a barrister and a solicitor,—and endeavoured in vain. She preferred to be obtuse.

"Is it any matter? Can't any lawyer make a will? Pollie Pentagon said you were a lawyer. She sent me to you."

"Pollie Pentagon? Oh." He flushed,—though never so slightly. He was conscious that Miss Pentagon's own ideas were probably hazy on the subject of a barrister's status. "I am obliged to Miss Pentagon."

"Yes? It's good of you to be obliged. It's this way. I'm like a stranger over here. After last night, I said, 'This settles it! Before I go to bed again, I'll make my will. The only thing I want's a lawyer.' 'If that's all you want,' cried Pollie, 'I've just the thing you're wanting,—Ray Dyke. He's a special chum of mine, and ever so nice, and a lawyer too,—try Ray!' Then she gave me your address, and here I've come to try you."

She punctuated her remarks by making little dabs at the air with the end of her parasol. Mr. Dyke's flush had returned. He perceived that the service which was required of him was rather a friendly than a professional one.

"Surely"—he was aware, as he made it, that the remark was fatuous—"there is no cause why you should be in such haste to make your will."

"Isn't there! That's all you know. I'll be dead this time to-morrow,—that's the betting."

He looked at her for a moment, to see if she was serious. He had never seen anyone who looked less like dying. "You laugh at me, Miss"—

"Beaufie Buckingham,—that's who I am."

He bowed. He had been haunted by the feeling that he had seen her before, but then he had not realised that, as a matter of fact, the Buckingham could be so amazingly pretty. He owned that she was lovely on the stage. Clad in one of those marvellous costumes—which were rather *minus* quantities!—in which she thought proper to display her exquisite figure to superlative advantage, she was grace personified, and, after a fashion, beauty too. It was no wonder that men raved about her all the world over. But there is a difference between on the stage and off. Raymond Dyke was amazed to learn that this charming, piquant, innocent-looking, and—even more—fresh-looking damosel was Beaufie Buckingham. She was like something of Watteau's,—with an up-to-dateness which was all her own.

"I suppose you know I'm booked?"

He chose to misconstrue her meaning.

"I take it for granted that Miss Buckingham is booked, if she chooses to accept the bookings, for very many years to come."

"Not me. I'm booked, for an early date, upstairs or down."

Once more she illustrated her meaning with her parasol.

"You're laughing at me again."

"As for laughing, I laugh at everything,—that's me. But it's true. They've had two tries at me. The third time they won't fail."

"They? Who's they?"

"That's what I should like to know. There are so many of them who have sworn to have my life that I should be obliged if you could tell me."

A doubt crossed Mr. Dyke's mind as to whether the lady in front of him was perfectly sane. Some of the wild stories which had been told of Beaufie Buckingham recurred to his recollection.

Certain of the newspapers had been full, of late, of the sort of stories which are told of the women who call themselves actresses, and who, if they do not achieve fame, at least attain to world-wide notoriety,—only, in her case, they had been rather stranger, even, than they generally were. She fixed her pretty, laughing, blue eyes upon his face,—reading his thoughts aright.

"You think I'm cracked? I'm not, you bet! Whoever's seeking for sounder senses than those of mine will have to travel. Haven't you heard of what took place last night at the theatre?"

He remembered having noticed in his paper a paragraph headed "Extraordinary Occurrence at the Cerulean Theatre," but he had passed it by. He told her so.

"Ah, if you had you wouldn't have thought me cracked. There was a man got stung to death last night—in the band—instead of me."

"Miss Buckingham!"

"That's the second time I've been killed, by deputy. The next time there'll be no deputy about. The killed one will be me."

"I do not understand you."

"About last night? I'll tell you. I had been doing that dance of mine which I call 'Transparencies,'—you've heard of it?" He had. "There was the usual hubbub after I had done, and two or three bouquets were thrown upon the stage. Among them was one which, I believe, came from the side boxes. It fell right at my feet. I picked it up. It was covered with a sheet of paper. When I removed the sheet of paper, something sprang from the heart of the flowers right at me. I saw it coming just in time. I threw the bouquet from me.

It rolled into the orchestra. The something I had seen was some kind of a snake. I guess it was in a vicious sort of temper. It was only a little thing, but it bit the man that played the cornet on the face, and it fell down into the bosom of his shirt. In ten minutes he was dead."

"Is it possible? But who can have been guilty of such a diabolical action?"

"Perhaps you'll tell. I'd like to know. I'd soon cry evens if I did, though I'm small. You see all the people in the theatre were making a noise, and, I being hot and flurried, it made it hard for me to be certain. My impression was that the bouquet came from the balcony box upon my left. Now, that box was occupied by four of your very tallest aristocrats,—there was Lady Adelaide Frisborough and her husband, and Lady Mary Beaupré, and her father, the Earl of Glenlivat. They declared that they had thrown no bouquet, and how was I to prove they had? They said they fancied that a bouquet had come from a box above them. Well, the police kept everyone in their boxes till I had had a sight of them. I interviewed the entire shoot. They were all strangers to me, most of them were heavy swells, and they all swore they had thrown no bouquet. So there you are, you see!"

"I presume the matter is in the hands of the police."

"The police!" Putting the handle of her parasol to the tip of her nose, she gave it a twirl in the air. "They mean well, poor dears, but that's all they do do. I've two cousins in New York who are in the police themselves,—full-blown detectives, if you please,—the sort you read of in the thrillers! They may be ornamental, and they may do some good, to someone, sometimes, but they're no good to me. I knew that something was going to happen, because in the morning I got my notice."

"Your notice?"

"Half a sheet of paper, with, printed on it—printed, mind!—two words: 'Ce soir.' That's French. I daresay you know what it means as well as I do."

"But had you any reason to suppose that it pointed to the perpetration of such a crime?"

"Rather. I've had that notice before."

"Before! Do you mean to say, Miss Buckingham, that you have previously been made the victim of a similar outrage?"

"Don't I tell you?—it's the second time I've been killed by deputy! The first time was worse than this. I declare it gives me goose-flesh every time I think of it." In proof of her assertion, even as she spoke, a shiver went all over her. "That was in New York. I struck oil when I was at the Climax Theatre, and I stayed there for seven months,—became a regular fixture. I had a shower bath put into my dressing-room: dancing made me hot, and I found that, when I had finished, the splash of the cold water, immediately afterwards, did me good. One morning half a sheet of note-paper came to me through the mail, like the one I had yesterday. On it was printed, '*Demain!*'—and that was all. I knew that *demain* meant to-morrow, but what else it meant was more than I could say. You know we actresses get all sorts of rubbish sent to us, and I thought that this was some of it,—but it wasn't. That was Tuesday. On the Wednesday something was being done to Maud Lamont's dressing-room. Maud was one of the girls in the show, and a friend of mine, so I let her share mine. We were on the stage together, and we went off together, and when we got into my dressing-room she was the first undressed. 'Beau,' she said, 'I wish you'd let me try your shower bath.' 'You're welcome!' I told her; 'only go easy with the water, because there's only enough for one.' She hopped into the shower bath, and she pulled the chain. 'What's the matter with the thing?—it won't work,' she said. 'You don't pull hard enough,' I told her. So she caught hold of the chain with both her hands, and tugged at it with all her might, and"—

The narrator paused. For the moment she seemed unable to proceed. Covering her pretty face with her hands, she shuddered as with palsy. For some reason, Raymond Dyke felt that an uncomfortable sensation was stealing over him—a sensation which was accentuated when, on her removing her hands, he perceived the look which was on Miss Buckingham's face.

"She started yelling like nothing I had ever heard. I'm a cool hand, Mr. Dyke; but the noise she made, coming so suddenly,—she had been laughing only the moment before!—frightened me half out of my senses. I ran to her. 'Maudie!' I cried, 'what's wrong?' She was screaming like a lost spirit, and twisting herself into shapes which I never saw equalled by a contortionist, and I had just sense enough to see that she seemed to be turning black—and smoking! In my bewilderment I put out my arm to take hold of her, and"—She paused. As the man and the woman regarded each other it would have been difficult to say which face was the whiter of the two. "If I were to remove my bodice, you would see the scar there still. Something fell on my arm from the top of the bath which burnt me to the bone."

There was silence. Mr. Dyke's voice sounded a little husky. "What was it?"

"Well, some kind person had filled the reservoir of the shower bath, thinking that I was the only one who used it, with sulphuric acid instead of with water, and Maud had brought it all down upon herself instead of its coming upon me; and, when they got her out of it, no one but a doctor could have told that she ever had been a human being. Poor Maudie! Oh my God!"

Beaufie Buckingham broke into uncontrollable sobs. As he watched her, Mr. Dyke came near to crying too. Perhaps it was because he was tender-hearted, but it did not seem strange to him that the mere memory of so terrible an experience should have moved even a hardened woman of the theatre to tears. He turned away. He trifled with some odds and ends upon the mantelshelf. After some seconds he asked a question, gently,—

"But surely the wretch who did it was discovered?"

"Not a trace of him,—not one! I would have given every dollar I had to have found him, but they never did. It almost seemed as if some fiend had come straight from hell to do it, and then vanished into air. The bathman filled the bath with water in the early part of the evening, as he always did. My dresser was in the room at the time. The bathman had been in the theatre since he was so high." She held her hand a foot or so above the ground. "He went half silly when he heard what had happened. As for the dresser, she was my own aunt. I brought her with me into the theatre. I'll stake my life she had had no finger in such a pie."

"Then there was nothing to show how the vitriol got into the reservoir?"

"Nothing. You see, the room was empty a great part of the evening, because, whenever I was on, my dresser stood at the wings with a cloak ready to throw over me as I came off."

"How about the doorkeeper?"

"That was the man I'd like to have strangled. First of all he declared that no one had come into the place except those who were engaged behind. Then it turned out that, two or three times that night, he had toddled to a saloon which was across the road, and had a nip. Of course, the odds were that, one of those times, the sweet stranger who had business in my dressing-room just slipped in and out. That doorkeeper got the kick."

"And the half-sheet of paper?"

"They discovered no more about that than about anything else.

They did find out that it had been posted in a box on Madison Avenue, and then I suppose they were so struck at finding out that much that they rested from their labours."

"Had you yourself no idea who the sender might have been?"

Mr. Dyke, as he asked the question, eyed the lady closely. She met his glance with perfect candour. She evidently had nothing to conceal.

"Didn't I tell you that there were lots who'd like to have my life? Though, mind you, I did think that I owed one, for that, to Giulia Santimar."

"Who was Giulia Santimar?"

"She was a Spanish dancer—a gipsy, I think she was. She was starring at the Climax when I opened. I soon put her nose out of joint, so I told the boss that either she or I would have to go. He gave her her ticket,—then you should have seen how she let fly at me! The language which she used in English was enough to curl your hair, but I dare swear, by the sound of it, that it was nothing to what she said in Spanish. She swore she'd have my life, if she had to stew in purgatory for it for a million years. And she meant what she said. Then there was her husband. You see, her talking to me like that put my back up, so I took him from her."

"You took him from her?"

Mr. Dyke smiled, in spite of himself, impelled by the malicious laughter which was in the lady's eyes.

"You see, I didn't like to talk back at her,—that's not my way. I made love to her husband instead. He called himself August Rampini, and he was a dancer—a dry, shrivelled-up little chap, like whalebone set on springs. Whatever Santimar was, she wasn't pretty; he came to me directly I held up my finger. That didn't make her fonder of me." Leaning her dimpled chin upon the handle of her parasol, Miss Buckingham seemed to muse. "I never could make up my mind whether he did it, or his wife."

"Why should he have done it, under the circumstances you suggest?"

"You don't suppose I kept it up with him? I only did it all to spite her. Directly she had gone, I told him he might go after her. Then he let fly at me. I am inclined to think that he was quite as much in earnest as his wife,—he was a cross-grained little brute."

"Did you mention your suspicions of this man and woman to the police?"

"Of course I did. But it was proved that, when it happened, Santimar was dancing at Milan and Rampini was engaged at the Palais de Cristal in Marseilles. That didn't look as if they could have done it. And yet, somehow, I've always had my doubts. But if it comes to threatening to take my life, why, it was threatened only the other day by one of your own very biggest aristocrats."

"Indeed!" Mr. Dyke's lips wrinkled quizzically. "To whom do you refer?"

The lady's attitude was one of the most engaging frankness. Evidently, to her, nothing was sacred, or secret either.

"The Duchess of Bayswater. You know, her son, the Marquis of Paddington, wants me to be his wife; he's a nice boy, with a nice clean face, and a suit of clothes, and nothing else. He told me, the other night, when we were having supper—by way, I suppose, of encouraging me to take the plunge—that his mother had declared to him that, rather than he should marry me, she would take my life with her own hands. He seemed to know his mommie, and he seemed to think she meant it. But I can't go charging duchesses with attempted murder, can I?" She rose from her chair. She moved towards Mr. Dyke. "But about this will of mine, that's what's worrying me. It isn't what happened last night so much as that I have had another notice sent to me this morning."

He started. He stared at her. She did not seem to be at all discomposed.

"Miss Buckingham! Are you joking?"

"That's as you please. It came to me with this morning's letters. Here it is. You can have a look at it if you like."

She handed him an ordinary oblong blue envelope. He observed that the postmark was Camberwell. The address was not written, but printed. Inside the envelope was half a sheet of coarse letter-paper. On it was printed, in good, bold letters, one word—"*Aujourd'hui!*"

"Miss Buckingham! What does this mean?"

"I guess it means just what it says—'To-day.' It's my marching orders, that's what it is. There'll be no deputy this time. The killed one will be me. There's something here which tells me so,—I know."

She touched her breast with the tips of her fingers.

"Surely you will communicate with the police?"

"The police?—oh, bother your police!" She gave a little flourish with her parasol, expressive of contempt. "I am going to what you call communicate with the police when I leave you; but if two of them were tacked on to my skirts, one in front and one behind, they'd do no good. I'm booked."

He looked at her, feeling, with a sort of bewilderment, that she was beyond his comprehension. Her bearing suggested such absolute conviction, and yet such perfect unconcern—and she was so pretty with it all! Her every movement was the revelation of a further charm. Leaning against the edge of his writing-table, she looked up at him with the frank, almost childlike coquetry, which was evidently part of her being.

"And about that will of mine: you'll make it for me, won't you? Pollie Pentagon said you would. It'll be short and plain. I want to leave everything I've got to my sister Loo."

Mr. Dyke reflected.

"If you will accept my services as a friend, I shall be happy to draw up for you a simple form of will—if, as you say, you propose to make your sister sole residuary legatee."

"That's the time of day." She kissed her gloved hand to him. "My sister Loo is plain, and therefore good; her husband is honest, and therefore poor; they have five children, and I don't know how many more are coming along; and the wages of my sin will fall upon them like manna from the skies."

He sat down there and then, and drew up the simple form of testament she wanted, she furnishing him, from time to time, with the details he needed as she preened herself before his looking-glass. Between whiles she hummed to herself a little air. Lifting up the hem of her dainty draperies, she even practised a step or two of a dance upon the hearthrug.

"Will this do?"

He turned to her. She came to him, and, leaning her hand upon his shoulder, she read what he had written.

"First-rate. You're a trump." Without any sort of warning she stooped and kissed him on the lips. It was like the spontaneous action of a child. He laughed a little, and flushed still more. She seemed to be unconscious both of the laughter and the flush. "Where shall I put my name?"

"Your signature will require two witnesses. I have a friend in the adjoining chambers. If you will permit me, I will see if he is in. I think he may be willing to serve, with me, as one of them."

Gilbert Ellingham was in. He was willing to do what his friend required, especially when Raymond Dyke had poured into his ears a hurried résumé of the lady's curious story. Returning with him into his own chambers, Raymond Dyke introduced Mr. Ellingham to Beaufie Buckingham. Beaufie received him with eyes which were alive with laughter.

"You've come to see me sign my will? It's about time that my will was signed, because before to-morrow I'll be dead."

Seeing the lady laughing, Mr. Ellingham treated the whole thing as a joke. He affixed his signature, as witness, with a flourish.

"I hope not, Miss Buckingham. It will be very hard on me, since I have only just made your acquaintance."

Mr. Dyke turned to the lady, as he rose from having witnessed, in his turn, her hand and deed.

"I hope you will not think me discourteous, Miss Buckingham, but I have now to inform you that I do not intend to allow you to quit my sight until I have seen you place yourself in communication with the police. After what you have told me, whether you do or do not like it, I mean to keep watch and ward over you as if I were some sort of elder brother."

She laughed at him.

"You're welcome. I'll be delighted! If you care, you may act as guardian angel to me the whole day long." She pointed to the half-sheet of paper which lay upon the table. "But it won't be a guardian angel that will keep me safe from whoever it was sent that. It's in the betting that my checks will be called in underneath your very nose.—Have a candy?"

She held out a box of sweets to them. They declined.

"What a gorgeous box!" said Mr. Ellingham.

"Isn't it lovely? It's a present from someone, though I haven't the faintest notion who."

The box in question she had drawn from the pocket of her dress. It was one of those small but elaborate affairs, patronised by the manufacturers of bonbons, and by some of their customers, which cost so very much more than their contents. She took out from it a chocolate bonbon, holding the sweetmeat up for them to see.

"Isn't it a large one? I shall never be able to eat it in one mouthful. I shall have to bite it in two."

Suiting the action to the word, saucily enough, while they looked at her, she placed the bonbon between her beautiful white teeth and bit at it. And, instantly, there was a flash, a loud report, a blinding smoke.

"Good God!" exclaimed Mr. Dyke, who was standing farthest from the lady: "what's happened?"

Mr. Ellingham, holding his hands to his face, was staggering about like a drunken man.

"Ray!" he cried: "where are you? What devil's trick is this! I do believe I'm blind!"

His belief was a correct one. He was blind. With the physical eye he was never again to look out upon the world. For one reason it was as well that it should be so. Had he been able to see, in a mirror, what was left of his face, the sight would have been as much as he could bear.

"Gilbert!" said Mr. Dyke. He had not realised the situation. "Miss Buckingham!"

She was lying on the floor. He went and looked at her. "Help!" he screamed. He ran to the door, shrieking like a madman. The horror of it had unhinged his brain. And, indeed, he was destined to carry traces of the horror of it with him to his grave.

Help came in abundance. But it was no good. Beaufie Buckingham had been the subject of an excellent practical illustration of the progress of modern science. What had seemed a chocolate bonbon had been, in reality, some species of bomb, which had been constructed with such delicate, and withal such diabolical ingenuity, that it required but the pressure of a woman's teeth to explode it. She had applied the pressure. The explosion had ensued.

It was never discovered who had presented her with the bonbonnière. The rest of its contents were genuine sweetmeats. The donor had, apparently, taken it for granted that one specimen of the wonders of science would be sufficient. And his supposition had been justified.

There was a great crowd at the funeral. Among the "floral offerings" which were sent, as tributes of sympathy and of affection, was a large cross which was formed of Eudharis lilies, and which bore a card on which was inscribed in a large, dashing hand, the name "Giulia Santimar," and underneath, in a smaller hand, "Augoust Rampini," while in a corner was written, by a true artist in caligraphy,

"To sleep is best."

It might have been meant in irony. Who knows? The thing is true enough. At that time the husband and wife were together, and had been together for some weeks, fulfilling an engagement at the Opera House in Vienna.

GEORGE OGDEN'S WILL

CHAPTER I

THE WILL, AS IT WAS LEFT

GEORGE OGDEN died on Sunday, May 3rd, at half-past six in the evening. He was struck with paralysis on the preceding Thursday. Throughout the Friday and the Saturday he remained unconscious. Towards the evening on the Sunday there were signs of returning reason, but though he opened his eyes and looked at the faces of those who were leaning over his bed, and seemed to struggle to speak, he uttered no audible word until the end. He was buried on the Thursday following. On the return from the funeral his will was read.

There were present at the reading his three daughters, Mary, Ellen, and Elizabeth—Pollie, Nellie, and Lizzie,—and his two sons, John and James—Jack and Jim. The will was read by the dead man's solicitor, William Holmes. Mr. Holmes was a tall, thin man, who had something of the air and manner of a Dissenting minister of the stricter type. He produced a blue sealed envelope from a small leathern case.

"The will of the late George Ogden." Holding the envelope in both hands, he uttered these words as some men utter a grace before meat. "Shall I break the seal?"

Jack and Jim both nodded.

"Before I break the seal, one word. Of the contents of this document I have no more knowledge than yourselves. Your late father brought it to me at my office on the Wednesday preceding his attack—in fact, yesterday week. It is possible, if I may say so, that he had been forewarned, and had become all at once peculiarly conscious of the great truth how in the midst of life we are in death. Ahem!"

He broke the seal, using rather more deliberation than was absolutely necessary. It is not unreasonable to suppose that his fingers were guided by something of the instinct which, if we are to believe observers of the habits of the feline race, induces a cat to play with a mouse. From the envelope he produced what appeared to be a large sheet of ordinary letter-paper.

"This will is in your father's own handwriting. Shall I read it?"

Again a nod from Jack and Jim.

"'This is my last will and testament. I give and bequeath to my daughter Mary'—eh!" Mr. Holmes paused. He read the sentence again. "'I give and bequeath to my daughter Mary, to my daughter Ellen'"—Mr. Holmes paused again. "I—I'm afraid there—there's an omission."

"Omission?" said Jack. "What do you mean?"

"I will read the will through as it stands, and then you will see what is my meaning." Mr. Holmes appeared troubled. He was intently regarding the will, and was caressing his chin with a hand that was obviously nervous. "'This is my last will and testament. I give and bequeath to my daughter Mary, to my daughter Ellen, and to my daughter Elizabeth. My sons John and James have already had their portions. To each of them, therefore, I bequeath an equal share of what is left of my estate after the legacies to my daughters have been paid.'" Mr. Holmes ceased reading. "That is the will."

Silence, blank silence, ensued. Then Jack advanced to the table.

"Let me look at it?"

"Certainly. You will see that it is duly signed and witnessed, only in some unaccountable manner your father has omitted to mention what are the amounts which he leaves to your sisters. It is one more instance," added Mr. Holmes, with a little burst of severity, "of how indispensable it is in these cases to have the assistance of a properly qualified professional man."

CHAPTER II

THE WILL, AS IT WAS PROPOUNDED BY THE TESTATOR

ON the following Saturday there was a "friendly" meeting at Mr. Holmes's offices. The children met together in order that they might arrive at a common understanding of their father's will; or, if that was impossible, that they might at least arrive at a common agreement, which should, in some degree, give satisfaction to them all.

Mr. Holmes opened the proceedings with a piece of information which was not without interest for his hearers—

"I have endeavoured to arrive at an approximate estimate of the value of your late father's estate. Although he kept his affairs in very great order, it has not been possible, in so short a space of time, to enter into all the details. But I should say that the gross value is over, rather than under, one hundred and fifty thousand pounds. It would seem that he had clear intentions as to the disposition of this large property, but unfortunately these intentions he has not made plain. All we can do, therefore, is to endeavour to make them plainer. Have you, on your parts, any propositions to make?"

It appeared that some of them had.

"Share and share alike," said Jack.

"That's the fairest way," said Jim.

Their sisters said nothing. The lawyer looked at them, as if to elicit a remark. But they were still.

"I understand," continued Mr. Holmes, "that my position here is simply that of your common friend, and I repeat that what we have to do is to endeavour to comprehend what were your father's intentions, and, having arrived at such a comprehension, to proceed to carry them into effect."

"Excuse me," interrupted Jack, "but I do not see that that is the position at all."

"What then, from your point of view, is the position?"

"The position is that of a man who has died intestate."

"How so, when there is a will?"

"My father intended to make a will, but he failed to carry his intentions into effect. You are as well aware as I am that there practically is no will."

" "Excuse me, Mr. John, but you attribute to me knowledge which I do not possess. There is a will, only it requires propounding. It is quite clear that your father intended to leave the major portion of his property to your sisters. He says that you have already had your portions, and that, from my own personal knowledge, I know to be a fact."

Jim made a suggestion—

"Very well. You say there's a hundred and fifty thousand. Let them have a hundred thousand, and Jack and I have what's left."

"I'm not sure that I agree to that," said Jack.

"Let's hear what they have to say for themselves."

Jim turned to his sisters—

"I suppose you have something to say."

Mary said—

"I understood from a remark which papa made shortly before he was overtaken by his last illness that I was to have sixty thousand pounds."

"Sixty thousand pounds!" cried Jim. "That's good! And you, Nellie, were you to have another sixty?"

Nellie was crying, in a quiet, surreptitious sort of way.

"You know, Jim, that papa was always giving you money."

"That's very kind of you. Thank you for the information. I daresay you kept a keen eye upon his movements in that line. But that isn't an answer to my question."

"Papa never told me how much he was going to leave me, but I always understood that you had had your fortunes, and we were to have ours when he was dead."

"Did you, indeed? And pray, Miss Lizzie Ogden, what did you understand?"

Lizzie slightly blushed, but her tone was firm, as she replied—

"Papa told me that I should take a fortune to my husband."

"I suppose that means that Mr. Philip Cuddon is going to have his fingers in the pie."

"Philip Cuddon is at least an honest man."

"That means that I am not. Thank you, my dear."

Mr. Holmes interposed. He perceived that the dead man's mourning children showed a tendency towards exchanging civilities of an explosive kind; and he perhaps insufficiently realised the fact that the members of some families have a style of conversation which they reserve exclusively for use in the family circle.

"Permit me to hint that, standing, as we may almost be said to do, in the presence of the dead man whose grave has just been closed, it is our duty to lighten, and not increase, the burden which has been laid upon us."

Rising from his chair, Jim went and leaned his back against the mantelpiece.

"I've made a proposition. I don't know what else you expect me to do."

There was a pause. Mr. Holmes was holding the will in his hand.

He read and re-read it, with an expression of countenance which became more and more perplexed.

"Most unfortunate! Most unfortunate!" He solemnly shook his head. "How your father came to make the omission I confess I cannot understand. It would almost seem that he neglected to give a second glance even at his own will; but it appears quite clear to me that he had distinctly in his mind the exact amount which he intended to bequeath to each of his daughters, and that that amount, as a whole, comprehended by far the larger portion of his estate. This matter has of course not been submitted to counsel. I have no doubt that, by arriving at a private understanding among yourselves, you will obviate the necessity for such a course. But I venture to say that counsel's opinion would be this. He would say that the matter depended upon evidence which could be brought to throw light on the testator's intentions. Beyond doubt your father intended, for reasons with which we are all acquainted, to leave his estate practically to his daughters. I do not hesitate to say that that could be proved up to the hilt. I therefore very strongly urge you to arrive at a common understanding, with that fact as a basis."

"Mr. Holmes," said Jack, "you know that I have one virtue: I always mean what I say."

The lawyer made a sign that might mean anything.

"I'm quite willing to arrive at a common understanding. I'm the eldest son, but I waive that. Give me a fifth of the lot, and you may do with the rest as you please."

"It is quite clear that your father never intended that you should have a fifth."

"Thirty thousand pounds might set me on my legs again. Anything less than that would simply be food for the sharks."

"You have had, within my own knowledge, more than thirty thousand pounds within the last five years."

"Offer me less than a fifth and I will take the case through every Court in England. It's always well to know where we are, and that's where I am."

"In that case I doubt if you would get anything at all."

"Very well, my dear Holmes, don't get excited. I always have had a taste for long odds. So I'll go for the gloves."

Jack tilted his chair on to its hind legs. He thrust his hands into his breeches pockets. He even smiled at the lawyer's indignation. Jim made the next remark—

"If Jack has a fifth, of course I must have a fifth as well."

Jack turned to his brother—

"I don't know that that follows. You're not head over heels in debt, and you're not married."

"If you have a fifth, I have a fifth. You don't catch me napping."

As he said this Jim looked his brother full in the face. Jack met his glance with a smile.

"You can have a fifth, for all I care. Each man for himself, and the devil take the hindmost."

This was Jack's philosophy. The lawyer turned to the ladies—

"You hear what your brothers say? I am bound to observe that they appear to me to be endeavouring to take a wholly unjustifiable advantage of the position in which an unfortunate accident has placed them."

At this Jack laughed outright.

"Go it, Holmes!" he cried.

Mr. Holmes tried to wither him with his glance. But Jack was not to be withered, so the lawyer continued to address the ladies—

"It is with you that the decision lies."

Then Mary lifted up her voice—

"John has already made a similar proposition to me in private. I told him then what I tell him now, that I will never give my consent. I have heard my father often complain of his wanton waste and extravagance, and I have heard him say that the one end and aim of his eldest son seemed to be to ruin him."

"There spoke the virtuous sister!"

Mary turned to Jack—

"You know quite well that, to save you from prison, on one occasion alone father expended on your behalf nearly forty thousand pounds. You may think that I am not acquainted with all the circumstances of the case, but I am."

Mr. Holmes took a pen in his hand. He drew towards himself a sheet of paper.

"Do I understand, Mr. John Ogden, that you demand a fifth share of your father's estate?"

"I did demand a fifth; now my demand is for a fourth."

"A fourth!" Mr. Holmes looked up, apparently to see if the speaker was in earnest. "Monstrous!"

"Possibly if I am favoured with any more examples of Mary's eloquence I may go for a third."

But Mary was not to be cowed.

"I can easily believe that the man who robbed his father would rob his sisters too."

Jack flushed up to the roots of his hair. He rose from his chair and crossed to Jim. Mr. Holmes gave Mary a look which was intended to convey the suggestion that such a tone, if righteous, was, under the circumstances, perhaps unwise. Jack caught the look as it travelled.

"My dear Holmes, pray don't try to shut up Mary; she has only put the seal to a resolution that was already half formed. I will throw the estate into Chancery."

"Into Chancery? Come, Mr. John, be reasonable. Do I understand that you demand a fifth?"

"No, you don't."

"What, then, do I understand?"

"You understand that I intend to have the estate administered by the Court of Chancery."

"But what good will that do you?"

Jack shrugged his shoulders. Jim spoke—

"When you have all quite finished, perhaps you will allow me to say a word. It appears to me that I have something to say in the matter." He nudged his brother with his elbow. "Jack and I, each of us, require a fifth."

Jack was silent. Mr. Holmes made a note on the sheet of paper which was in front of him.

"That is your final determination?"

"That is our final determination."

Then Jack spoke—

"It's not my final determination. My final determination is to put the whole thing into Chancery."

Jim turned to him.

"In that case," he said, "you will have to reckon with me. I don't intend to allow you to play your favourite game of skittles with my chances in the world." Jim looked at Jack with a significance which caused an ugly expression to appear upon his brother's face. "You know what I mean," he added.

Possibly with a view of dispelling any doubt as to what it was he did mean, Jim leaned forward and whispered into his brother's ear.

As he heard Jack changed countenance. His lips twitched.

"You—you dare!"

"It is not a question of daring. It is a question of the nuisance it involves. One doesn't care to move against one's brother in such a thing as that. But that will be your fault, not mine."

The brothers surveyed each other. Suddenly Jack raised his hand. His fist was clenched. Jim never flinched, but it is possible that Jack intended to bring it down on him. If such was his intentions, its execution was baulked by an interruption which came from Lizzie.

"Jack," she cried, "there's father!"

The general attention was diverted, which, under the circumstances, was not unreasonable. Lizzie was standing by her chair. She was looking towards the door. They followed the direction of her glance.

There, looking as though he had just entered the room, stood an old man dressed from head to foot in black. His head was bald, but, as if to compensate for this, he had a fringe of white hair upon his upper lip and upon his cheeks. His chin was bare.

"Father!" Nellie stood up. "Father!"

Nellie advanced a step or two towards her father, who was standing near the door, and then was silent. They all were silent. It was as though a bombshell, and something worse than a bombshell, had been dropped in the room. Jack, his fist still clenched, stared, open-eyed and open-mouthed, at the old man by the door. Jim's attitude was expressive of as much amazement as his brother's. Nellie stood in the centre of the room, trembling visibly, her hands held out in front of her. Lizzie, her right hand grasping the back of her chair, pointed with her left at the new-comer. Mary sat as though rooted to her chair, her face indicative of a degree of bewilderment which, in its way, was comic. Mr. Holmes, risen from his seat, leant over his table. It was he who broke the stillness—

"Mr. Ogden!"

Then Nellie gave a great cry. She ran forward, throwing her arms wide open.

"Father!" she cried.

Raising his hands, the old man by the door motioned her away.

"Don't touch me! Don't touch me!"

The girl stopped dead. There was silence again, this time broken by Jack.

"What trick is this?" he asked.

No one noticed him. No one noticed his words at all. The old man looked at each one's face, a look of inquiry in his glance, as it passed from one to the other. Then he looked at Mr. Holmes.

"You know me, Holmes?"

"Know you? Of course I know you. It—it can't be an imposture."

Jack burst into a storm of rage.

"What is the meaning of this—shall I call it—unrehearsed effect? I suppose it is a little joke which you have arranged between you." He advanced towards the old man. "May I ask, sir, what purpose you proposed to serve by giving out that you were dead?"

The old man looked at the young one. He looked at him long

and earnestly. Yearning was in his eyes, and a look of pain upon his face.

"Jack, don't you understand me even yet?"

"I confess, sir, that I don't."

"Jack, don't you know why I have risen from the dead?"

Jack fell back. Mary covered her face with her hands. Nellie, falling on to her knees, burst into a passion of tears.

The old man went to her. He was evidently troubled.

"Don't cry, Nellie, don't cry. I—I can't touch you. It is for your sake I am come. But I would not have come could I have seen another way."

Jack turned to Mr. Holmes.

"Perhaps you will give me the answer to the riddle which it appears that my father declines to furnish."

The lawyer was silent. The old man answered for him—

"Jack, do you think that I am living? Do you not know that I am dead? For it was you who killed me." Going to Jack, the old man said something which the young one alone could catch. "When I heard that of my eldest son after all that I knew of him already, I knew that my time had come."

"It's—it's a lie!" said Jack.

"It is no lie. If you think so, give me your hand."

The old man held out his hand. The young one put both his behind his back. He crossed the room towards Jim. The old man's eyes followed him for a moment. Then he addressed himself to the lawyer—

"Holmes, my business is principally with you. It is about my will that I have come."

Mr. Holmes continued to lean over his table. He had never removed his eyes from his visitor.

"Ogden, I saw you lying dead."

"Now you see me dead."

The lawyer's attenuated visage assumed an extra sallow tinge. "What fiction of the brain is this?"

"It is no fiction of the brain. I am George Ogden, and I am a witness from the grave. When you have heard what I have to say, you will understand under what pressure I have come."

The old man paused. He looked round the room. No one

spoke. Then in a low, clear tone of voice he continued to address the lawyer—

"On Wednesday, April 29th—last Wednesday week—I received bad news." He glanced at Jack. "I was in my own private room. The news affected me to such an extent that I became insensible. When I recovered consciousness I knew that I had been attacked by a slight paralytic seizure. I was aware, from previous experience, that in my case a slight seizure was a prelude to one more serious. I had reason to believe that if I was again struck by paralysis the result would be fatal. I remembered that I had not made my will. I took a sheet of paper. I made it then and there. I had it witnessed by my butler, Charles Todd, and by my housekeeper, Mary Hawkins. I carried it at once to you. You remember that I brought it to you in a sealed blue envelope on the Wednesday afternoon?"

"I—I remember."

The lawyer's corroboration was given in a scarcely audible whisper.

"No sooner had I left it in your charge than I became impressed with the idea that about it there was something wrong. What it was I could not think. I tried to dismiss the idea as a mere fancy. But the effort was in vain. The seizure, slight though it was, had weakened me in a physical and in a mental sense. I could not collect my thoughts. I was bewildered. All night I lay in agony. In the morning, as I was dressing, I remembered I had forgotten to insert in my will the sums which I gave to my girls. The absence of specific mention would render the whole thing invalid. The discovery came with the force of a shock. The very act of recollection brought on a second seizure. I knew that my time had come."

The old man turned to his daughters. Tears were in his voice. His whole attitude was instinct with an exquisite pathos.

"You thought I was unconscious. I was not. Those three days I lay in agony. I knew that I had left you at the mercy of that man."

He pointed to Jack with a gesture which almost amounted to an imprecation.

"The latest discovery of his character was burning in my heart. It was he who had laid me there. How I struggled to speak! How I prayed that I might regain the power of speech only once before the end! Did you not see how I struggled?"

Mary replied to his appeal.

"Yes, father, I did. I leant over to hear what it was you had to say. I tried to comfort you. I kissed you. I thought you were in pain."

"In pain! What pain! My God! what pain! I died!"

His hands dropped to his sides. His head dropped. His bearing was indicative of extreme dejection. All in the room seemed to be holding their breath. His voice sounded like a low wail of woe.

"And I knew that what I feared would happen—had happened. The will was invalid—invalid!"

He raised his head. His eyes looked upwards.

"And in my grave I cried for help. And it came. I know not whence, but it came; and I am here."

He turned to the lawyer. His tone became easier.

"I have come, Holmes, about my will. I wish to rectify those omissions which I made in my haste. If you will take a pen and follow me, I will tell you what is the specific amount which I have designed for each of my daughters."

The lawyer hesitated.

"You wish me to take down certain sums at your dictation?"

"I do. And since, for all I know, my time is short, I desire you to use such expedition as you can."

Mr. Holmes sat down. He chose a pen and a sheet of paper.

"I am ready."

"To my daughter Mary I give sixty thousand pounds."

The lawyer noted the figures—

"Sixty thousand pounds."

"To my daughter Ellen, forty-five thousand pounds; and to my daughter Elizabeth, thirty-five thousand pounds. What remains of my estate, when those legacies are paid, is to be divided equally between my two sons, John and James."

"You are aware that the value of your estate is, approximately, one hundred and fifty thousand pounds—rather over than under?"

"I am."

Mr. Holmes made some notes upon his sheet of paper, then looked round the room.

"You are all of you witnesses?"

"Witnesses?" said Jack. "Of what?"

"Of your father's words."

"The essence of a farce is in its brevity. Don't you think that the curtain is a little overdue?"

"I don't understand you."

"Then you are not so keen a man as I supposed."

Jim spoke—

"I do not wish to infer any disrespect towards my father, but may I ask—and I do so without any sarcastic intention—are we supposed to be in the presence of a ghost?"

No one answered. Mr. Ogden looked at his son with reproachful eyes. Jim steadily looked at Mr. Holmes.

"I have not a dictionary at my fingers' ends, but I believe that a ghost is the soul of a man. Are we supposed to be looking at the soul of my father?"

Still none replied.

"Writers, who may be presumed to have studied these matters, tell us that there is something awe-inspiring in the presence of a ghost. I can only say that I personally am unconscious of any feeling of the kind."

Jim removed his glance from the lawyer. He fixed it steadily upon his father.

"So far from that being the case, my predominant feeling is a strong inclination to exclaim: 'My dear old dad, how are you? 'Pon my word, I thought we'd lost you!'"

Still no reply. Jim balanced himself upon his toes and heels. His air was one of serene enjoyment.

"By granting, for the sake of argument, that we are in the presence of a ghost, where are we then?"

"That's what I want to know," said Jack.

"If my father is dead, then all we have to do is to make the best of his last will and testament. I always supposed that in the eye of the law a will, as it came from the testator's hands, was sacred. All that remained was to act on its provisions. If a ghost has the power of revision, how far does that power extend? and how shall we attain finality?"

"Just so," said Jack.

The old man's eyes wandered from Mr. Holmes to his sons, and from his sons to Mr. Holmes. On him they rested. They seemed to supplicate an expression of opinion. Such an expression came—

"In the present case the terms of the will are indefinite, and need a definition. To supply that we require evidence."

"And a ghost is evidence?"

Mr. Holmes looked up at Jim. His tone was grave.

"To that question, sir, your own conscience must supply an answer."

The old man advanced towards his younger son.

"James."

"Sir?"

"Give me your hand."

"With pleasure."

Jim put his hand into his father's. As he did so a very curious expression began to come upon his countenance. It was an expression which it would have needed a physiognomist accurately to define.

"Is mine the hand of a living man? Is the life-blood coursing through my veins? Am I an impostor, Jim?"

"Have the goodness, sir, to release my hand."

"Is mine not the touch of the grave? Selfish you have always been—I have found all men selfish—but you are honest. Your father has come to you from the grave to ask you not to rob your sisters, Jim."

"Have the goodness, sir, to release my hand."

The old man sighed.

"Jim! Jim!"

And he withdrew his hand.

Jim took a handkerchief from his pocket, and with it he carefully wiped the hand which his father had held. He retreated a few steps as he did so. He left his father in possession of the hearthrug.

Jack, perceiving this action on his brother's part, made a detour upon his own account. Jim's face was white. It had a curious appearance of distension. There was a startled look in his eyes. When he began to speak it was with a little hesitation. That, however, disappeared as he went on.

"I think that you scarcely state the case quite fairly, sir. You ask me to acquiesce in my own ruin."

"Don't lie to me, Jim! You are not near ruin. You are too shrewd a man for that."

"At least you ask me to acquiesce in my own disinheritance."

"You have had your inheritance, Jim."

Jim said nothing. He continued to wipe his face with his pocket-handkerchief, and to look about him with his curiously startled eyes. But he held his peace. So Jack struck in—

"It would mean ruin to me."

"Ruin to you!" His father turned on him. "Everything means ruin to you. It is not money which can save you. You are one of those who are predestined to ruin. I come to save others from having to bear the burden of your crimes; yourself I cannot save."

Jack became a little savage.

"Do you think, sir, that I am likely to throw away thirty thousand pounds at the bidding of my father?"

"Not of your father—living, but of your father—dead!" The old man turned towards Jack. Jack made a rapid strategic movement to one side. "You fear me!"

For some moments Jack seemed to be in doubt as to whether he did or didn't. Then valour got the better of discretion. Advancing, he stood in front of his father.

"Fear you, sir? Why should I fear you?"

Stretching out his hand, the old man laid it upon the young one's shoulder.

"You fear me, Jack." Indeed, it was obvious that Jack was trembling. "You never were brave. You were a braggart, not a hero. In the presence of your dead father, he whom you so foully wronged, your heart dries up within you, Jack."

"I don't believe that you are dead. I believe that you are as much alive as I am."

"Look at me closer, Jack."

The old man placed his other hand upon Jack's shoulder. He advanced his face towards his son's. Jack put up his hands to veil his eyes. He staggered backwards.

"Don't, don't. I—I won't have it. It—it's some cursed trick."

He fell into a chair. He trembled as if with ague. The old man remained standing where his son had left him.

"Take my advice. Do not rob your sisters, Jack. Take the seriously offered advice of a father risen from the grave. Beware."

He raised his hand towards Jack with a self-supplicating, half-threatening gesture. As they watched him, with his hand upraised, he was gone. Jim commented on his departure—

"Gone, by gad. Quite a dramatic exit. You can look up, Jack; the dad's departed."

The tone was an attempt at joviality. The attempt was a failure. Jack looked up, his face a ghastly white.

"Has—has he gone? Tha—thank God. I—I don't feel well. Holmes, have—have you got any brandy?"

"No, Mr. John, nor do I think that yours is a case in which brandy would avail. Mr. John and Mr. James, I cannot doubt that we have had a visitation from the grave. I even think that, unseen by our mortal eyes, your father may be with us now." Jack perceptibly shuddered. "I therefore ask you, in his unseen presence, to give effect to your father's words."

"How did he say the coin was to go?" asked Jim.

Mr. Holmes referred to the memorandum on his table.

"Miss Mary is to have sixty thousand pounds, Miss Ellen forty-five thousand, and Miss Elizabeth thirty-five thousand."

"That leaves ten thousand between Jack and me. I am afraid I couldn't do it at the price."

"Mr. James!"

"Really, Holmes, I couldn't. Not even to oblige a ghost."

"Mr. John, may I hope that I shall have a different answer from you?"

"Damned if you will. I'm not going to be robbed. Where's—where's my hat? I—I'm going. I believe some cursed trick has been played, and I've had enough of it. May I ask, Holmes, if you have any objection to my lighting a cigar?"

Jack produced a cigar-case from his pocket, and from the cigar-case a cigar. This he proceeded to light, with, perhaps, a little show of ostentation. The process being concluded to his apparent satisfaction, he affably addressed the lawyer—

"Good-day, Holmes. Sorry you should be disappointed. But the legal walk in life, like other walks in life, is full of disappointments, is it not? Jim, if you are ready, we'll go together."

"I've been ready an hour ago," said Jim.

Without any further ceremony—such, for instance, as the

waste of valuable time which would be involved in saying good-day to their sisters—the brothers left the room.

CHAPTER III

THE WILL, AS IT WAS INTERPRETED IN COURT

Sir Raymond Braithwaite was the judge in "Ogden v. Ogden." This, in many respects, was fortunate. Braithwaite, for a judge, is peculiarly free from humbug. And then, what in the present instance is even more to the point, the interest he takes in psychical research is known to all the world. He does not pooh-pooh a ghost as a ghost. He inquires into such credentials as the spectre may be able to offer as to character. It is something, in these days, to find a man who will give a ghost the ghost of a chance.

Quince, Q.C., led for the Misses Ogden. Quince is dry, but sound. It was another score to have retained such a man in such a case. Quince is conscientious. He would not take up a ghost who was merely a spectre of the imagination.

The court was crowded when the case came on. Quince led off in his well-known style. He was rather inaudible, but that Quince always is.

"This, m'lud, is a singular case. I think it is the most singular case in which I ever held a brief."

They all say that, and so far Quince merely went with the ruck. Then he told his story: how George Ogden died, how his will was found defective, and how his clients proposed to supply its omissions. In the will, as he propounded it, one hundred and forty thousand pounds was left to the daughters. He pointed out that there was a large body of evidence which went to show that was the exact amount which the dead man intended to leave to his girls. This evidence was of various sorts, and among it was the evidence of the dead man himself. Here Quince gave a hitch to his gown.

"I will be frank with the court. My chief witness in this case is a ghost." The court smiled. "Yes, m'lud, a ghost." Quince looked round the court, as if he dared it to smile again. And it did. "I am aware of the opprobrium which attaches to a man who presumes, in cold blood, to argue as to the possibility of the existence of such a thing as a ghost."

"Not at all, Brother Quince, not at all," said m'lud.

"You are very good, m'lud. But I think, m'lud, that when I have put those witnesses in the box whom I intend to call it will be allowed, even by the most sceptical, that if evidence, unquestionable evidence, can prove anything, it proves my case."

"What is the nature of the evidence you propose to advance? Are you aware, Brother Quince, I take an interest in ghosts? For my part I shall be glad to hear their existence proved from the witness-box. The world has been waiting for such proof for a good many years."

"Just so, m'lud. I propose to show, m'lud, that George Ogden died on Sunday, May 3rd; that he was buried in the family grave in Brompton Cemetery on Thursday, May 7th; and that on Saturday, May 9th, he appeared to witnesses, who will be called, and then and there dictated to his lawyer—his lawyer, m'lud!—the terms of the will as we now propound it."

"If you prove that, you will prove a good deal."

The court smiled, but Quince was solemn.

"Call Stephen Cox."

Stephen Cox proved to be a doctor. He was George Ogden's medical attendant. He stated that he was present at the patient's death. It was he who had supplied the certificate of death.

We do not propose in this place to give a verbatim report of the case as Mr. Quince presented it. We are concerned principally with a particular part of it. The nurse was called, the servants who had seen their master lying dead, the attendants who had ministered to the corpse, the man who had measured the corpse for the coffin, the undertakers who had placed the corpse in the coffin, and, on the last day, had screwed it down. On that last day some of the older servants had taken a final farewell of their master as he lay in his narrow bed. The parson was called—George Ogden's own parson—who had ministered at the grave. Witnesses were called who testified of their knowledge of George Ogden's testamentary intentions. What they said went to show, more or less clearly, that the will as propounded by the daughters was the will as George Ogden would have had it.

Quite a cloud of witnesses had testified when Mr. Holmes came into the box.

Mr. Holmes began by explaining that he had been George Ogden's solicitor for over thirty years. He told the court what he knew of his client's intentions with regard to the disposition of his property. And then Mr. Quince gradually brought him down to the meeting at which George Ogden's children endeavoured to arrive at a common understanding as to their father's will.

"Tell the court what happened when they were unable to agree."

Then Mr. Holmes told the story of George Ogden's appearance. Nothing could have been clearer than the way in which he told it, and nothing could have been more obvious than the incredulity with which it was received. Even m'lud found the story too strong for his digestion. Indeed, his lordship subjected Mr. Holmes to a sort of cross-examination upon his own account.

"Were you in your usual health that morning, Mr. Holmes?"

Mr. Holmes said that he was.

"Are you subject to delusions, Mr. Holmes?"

Mr. Holmes said that he wasn't.

"What tests did you apply to your visitor?"

Mr. Holmes was obliged to confess that he had applied none. His lordship smiled. He turned to Mr. Quince.

"I am afraid, Mr. Quince, that to prove the supernatural you will require supernatural evidence."

"I submit, m'lud, that a fact can be established by the evidence of unimpeachable witnesses. Suppose y'r ludship were to die"—

"Thank you, Brother Quince."

"Or suppose I were to die, which would be much better, m'lud"—

"The court is with you, Brother Quince."

"And the fact of my death and burial were to be clearly proved, and that I was afterwards to appear to credible witnesses, I submit that, by their testimony, the fact of my appearance, and of what I did and said, would be established."

"I trust that, in the event of such an appearance, I may be one of the witnesses, Brother Quince."

"It is very kind of y'r ludship to say so. I trust that y'r ludship will allow me to express a similar wish the other way round?"

"Thank you, Brother Quince. Perhaps you will allow us to hear your other witnesses."

Mary Ogden was called, and Ellen and Elizabeth. They all proved themselves good witnesses. Each told her story with clearness and simplicity. It was impossible to doubt that they were stating what they believed to be the truth. And yet it was plain, from the manner in which their story was received, that, had those in the court been polled, the result would have been an almost unanimous vote of incredulity; and this even before Sir Hastings Skittles, who led for the other side, began his cruel work. The story was pathetic as told by the girls in their examination-in-chief; but as it appeared shaded by Sir Hastings, the pathos was not so marked.

The two brothers sat by the side of their counsel. It is to be feared that some of his questions were suggested by them. The whole thing assumed quite a comic aspect. Sir Hastings questioned them as to their knowledge of the laws which may be said to regulate ghosts. He was particularly pressing in his desire to ascertain if they knew a ghost when they saw one. He asked them if they had seen Pepper's Ghost, or the ghost of Benjamin Binns, who tells us, at certain marionette shows, that he is sent here—*i.e.* there—"all on account of his sins."

He became solemn when he asked them why they supposed that the whole body of laws which regulate the universe were to be disarranged for the sole end and purpose of giving them a few extra thousand pounds—why, in a word, a miracle was to be wrought for them.

When Sir Hastings sat down, the ghost-story, in a non-supernatural sense, looked a trifle blue. His lordship suggested as much to Brother Quince.

"You require," he added, "I fear, a ghost to prove a ghost, and then you will have to prove the ghost which proves the ghost. You will find, Brother Quince, that nothing short of that will convince the modern Briton. If, for example, you desire to prove George Ogden's ghost, it is necessary that George Ogden's ghost should be in court."

"He is in court, my lord."

His lordship was looking at Mr. Quince as he addressed him.

The retort came from someone at the back of the court. His lordship looked up with uncommon quickness.

"What's that?" he said.

"George Ogden's ghost is here, my lord."

The court rose—not in the ordinary, but in the extraordinary sense. Counsel, solicitors, clerks, officers, witnesses, even those most impassive of beings, the reporters, all stood up. The public craned their heads over the gallery railings. There was quite a scuffle.

"Who's that spoke?" demanded his lordship.

"I, my lord."

"And who is 'I'?"

"George Ogden."

It has to be chronicled that at this point the judge stood up—stood up, too, with quite a little jump. Putting up his spy-glasses, he peered across the intervening space.

"How dare you, sir, trifle with the court?"

"Order, order," cried the usher.

"Father," cried a voice.

It was Lizzie Ogden, who still was standing in the box.

"Silence," said the judge. He turned to the girl. His air was stern. He turned again to the person who was the cause of the commotion. "Bring that man forward."

Apparently the man who was thus referred to did not require bringing. Directly the words were spoken there was a movement at the back of the building. A man was seen threading his way through the little crowd. He advanced towards the solicitors' table. As he did so, someone else exclaimed—

"It's father."

"Silence," repeated the judge.

"But it's father."

Mary Ogden was standing up at the solicitors' table. Her hands were stretched out in front of her. She spoke in a loud, clear, ringing tone of voice.

"Order, order," cried the usher.

"If I cannot obtain silence," observed his lordship, "I shall clear the court." He turned to the cause of the commotion. "Who are you, sir? How dare you create this disturbance?"

"I am George Ogden, my lord."

His lordship looked a little bewildered. Counsel on both sides were conferring with their solicitors and clients. Sir Raymond addressed Mr. Quince—

"Mr. Quince, do you know this person?"

"I am informed, m'lud, that this is George Ogden."

"George Ogden! what do you mean? Are you propounding a will, the testator being still alive?"

"As I am advised, m'lud, the man is dead."

"Dead! What man?"

"Perhaps y'r ludship will allow me to put him into the witness-box."

"Put a dead man into the witness-box! Oh, do as you please. Only—only don't let's have any more of this sort of thing."

His lordship sat down, his plumes a little ruffled. The crowd parted—distinctly parted—as the newcomer moved towards the witness-box. The judge glanced at him as he stood there in an attitude of meek submission. His lordship questioned him.

"Now, sir, perhaps you will tell us who you are."

"I am George Ogden."

"George Ogden! Then what is all this we've heard about you being dead?"

"I am dead."

The judge's countenance assumed a ruddy tinge. It was marked by all the signs of irritation.

"The man's a lunatic," he said. "May I ask, Mr. Quince, what it is you propose to do?"

"I propose, m'lud, first of all to identify the witness."

The process of identification proceeded. He was identified by his daughters, by Mr. Holmes, and by others. His lordship interposed—

"I don't see what is the use of all this. Is the man's identity disputed by the other side?"

Sir Hastings conferred with his clients.

"With your lordship's permission, I propose to postpone any remarks until the case is a little more advanced."

"But if you admit the man's identity the case is finished."

Mr. Quince struck in—

"Y'r ludship will remember that y'r ludship observed that it would require a ghost to prove a ghost. Y'r ludship is now in the presence of a ghost, as I'm advised, m'lud."

The judge looked at Mr. Quince to see if he was in earnest. Then he looked at the occupant of the witness-box—

"So, you're a ghost, are you?"

Mr. Quince continued—

"With y'r ludship's permission, I propose to put some questions to the witness." Mr. Quince turned to the man in the box. "You are George Ogden?"

"I am."

"Are you living or dead?"

"I am dead."

The judge eyed Mr. Quince with much severity.

"Do you take this to be a burlesque theatre, Mr. Quince, or a court of justice?"

"M'lud, this is an unparalleled experience."

"So I should say."

"Have you any statement to make to the court, Mr. Ogden, which will explain your presence here?"

"I have."

"Then let us hear it."

Mr. Ogden repeated almost word for word the statement which he had made to Mr. Holmes at the family meeting. He spoke in a low but perfectly clear tone of voice, and with a degree of earnestness which could not fail to be impressive.

Whether they believed him or not, his hearers—judge, counsel, witnesses, all alike—hung on his words. Nor was his story without its pathos.

That a man, under pressure of paralysis, and of a sudden great fear for the safety of those whom he held dearest in the world, should have made his will, and then, in making it, have baffled his own purpose, this was in itself pathetic. But that in the very act of recollection he should have been struck by the final stroke, and, helpless, have died, knowing that what he had sacrificed his very life to prevent, because of that sacrifice, would happen!

As the story came quietly and simply from the old man's lips, they realised that they were listening to the basis of a tragedy; but when they were informed that the story was being told by a man who was dead, and heard the man who told the tale himself declare that he was not living—"Almost thou persuadest me," said Felix. But there was a chasm between the "almost" and the "quite."

"You have a remarkable invention, Mr. Ogden," observed the judge, when the old man ceased.

"Does your lordship doubt that I am dead?"

"The attitude of my mind, Mr. Ogden, would be inadequately described by such a word as 'doubt.'"

"Perhaps your lordship will give me your hand."

"Such a request is unusual as proceeding from the witness-box. May I ask why you make it?"

"Because then you will know that I am dead."

The judge smiled. He eyed the witness for a moment. Then he moved in his seat.

"If you will come up here I will give you my hand."

The old man left the witness-box. He went up to the judge's seat. He held out his hand. His lordship took it in his.

"Your hand is cold and damp and clammy, Mr. Ogden, but those are characteristics of some hands."

"Will your lordship grasp me firmly?"

"I will squeeze you if you like."

His lordship evidently increased the pressure of his hold. Mr. Ogden made a slight retrograde movement. An exclamation of horror burst from those who beheld. The old man left his hand in the judge's grasp. From the expression of his features his lordship was realising this with not unnatural surprise. The old man held up his handless arm.

The judge was silent; indeed, for some moments silence reigned omnipotent. As his lordship realised more and more plainly exactly what it was that had happened, his features betrayed a mixture of emotions. He looked at Mr. Ogden; then he looked at what he held. Realising what indeed it was, with an exclamation of disgust, he raised his hand, and dropped its contents on to his desk.

"Good God!" he cried.

The expression was not judicial, nor did it come appropriately from that seat; but there it was. He started to his feet; he glared at the old man holding up his handless arm.

"Can—can it be possible? Is there a medical man in court?"

Two or three persons rose to their feet Among them was the
Dr. Cox who had acted as George Ogden's medical adviser, and
who had appeared in the witness-box to prove his patient's death.

"Will one of you gentlemen step up here?"

As his lordship said this he had his eyes fixed on Dr. Cox. But
that gentleman declined.

"If your lordship will permit me, I should prefer to stand
excused."

"I should be delighted, my lord."

This answer came from a short, thick-set man, with a square,
resolute face. He went up to the judge's bench.

"You are a doctor?"

"I am Dr. Lees, consulting physician to the —— Hospital."

"Perhaps, Dr. Lees, you will be so good as to examine this hand."

The doctor took it up. He showed no signs of repugnance—
quite the other way.

"This is the hand of a corpse."

"Of a corpse!"

"And of a corpse which has been a corpse some weeks. Have I
your lordship's permission to examine this man?"

"I—I should be very glad if you would."

His lordship seemed a little bewildered.

Dr. Lees turned to Mr. Ogden.

"Have you any objection to my examining you?"

"None. My only desire is to establish the truth."

"Be so good as to unbutton your waistcoat."

"I cannot."

"Why?"

"I am dead."

"If you mean that you are incapable of independent action,
how came you to be able to do with your hand what we have just
now seen you do?"

"I cannot tell."

The words came from the old man wearily. It seemed as if he
had reached the last stage of physical exhaustion. Dr. Lees went
to him. He unfastened the top button of his waistcoat. As he did
so he gave a perceptible start. The old man stood quite still. The
doctor unfastened the waistcoat to the bottom. He threw it open.

He undid the stud at the neck of the shirt, and was about to thrust his hand into the bosom, when the old man spoke—

"Let me speak to the judge." The doctor stood aside. "My lord, if—if it be proved I am dead"—He paused. His lordship looked perplexed. The old man went on: "Let—let the girls have their own. Do—do not let them be robbed. I—I cannot—cannot come again."

"See to him, doctor; he is fainting."

The old man seemed to tremble. Dr. Lees advanced. He caught him round the waist.

"Steady. Keep up. Would you like a chair?"

The old man seemed to smile.

"I need no chair."

"I am only going to place my hand within your shirt to feel the pulsation of your heart."

The old man seemed to smile again.

"Lose no time."

The doctor did as he had said he would—he thrust in his hand. His face was turned away from the people, but as he did so his back was eloquent. Those behind him saw the muscles of his back working beneath his coat. A sound escaped his lips like a stifled cry. There was silence. All looked at the two figures which were in front of them. And, as they continued to look, the old man was gone.

His disappearance was so unexpected and so sudden, that the people in the court, not appearing to realise the fact of his departure, continued to stare in front of them as though he still were there. Then the doctor, drawing himself straight up with what seemed to be a convulsive effort, turned and faced them. His face was ashen pale; the muscles worked as though he were afflicted with St. Vitus' dance. He staggered against the railing which ran round the bench.

"He's—he's gone!"

The words seemed spoken not so much to others as to himself. The judge stared at him.

"Is—is it not possible, doctor, that we have been the victims of a trick?"

"He—he was dead."

"Are you sure?"

The doctor drew himself away from the railing; a ghastly smile lit up his face. He took out his pocket-handkerchief; with a trembling hand he wiped his brow.

"Possibly your lordship has never handled a dead man."

"But where has he gone?"

"Back to his grave."

"How came he here?"

"These, my lord, are questions which, if you require a satisfactory answer, you must address to a far wiser man than I."

His lordship was looking about him on his desk.

"Where—where is his hand?"

"I placed it on your lordship's desk."

"It—it has gone."

The doctor looked at the desk; he saw that there was nothing on it.

"My lord, we have seen strange things this day."

Silence again. The judge sat looking like a man who had received a great and sudden shock. It almost seemed, to judge from his appearance, as if he were not in full possession of all his faculties.

"Is—is it possible that—that we have been in the actual presence of a—of a ghost?"

Mr. Quince was still standing in his place; he took the question as being addressed to himself.

"I submit, m'lud, that y'r ludship is a better judge of such matters than I am. It is well known, m'lud, that on these subjects y'r ludship is a recognised authority."

"Yes, yes." His lordship seemed to find Mr. Quince's manner slightly irritating. "A man may be a recognised authority upon a subject, Mr. Quince, and yet know uncommonly little about it after all."

"Exactly, m'lud."

Mr. Quince's manner seemed to act on his lordship as an "eye-opener," as an irritant which forced him to realise the actualities of his position. He made an effort as if to pull himself together. He addressed the court.

"I crave forgiveness if I seem for a moment to have forgotten my position. In extenuation I would say that, if indeed we have been in the presence of a visitant from the unseen world, I, for one, am conscious that this is a solemn occasion."

His lordship paused. Mr. Quince took advantage of the pause to immediately strike in—

"That is my case, m'lud."

Mr. Quince sat down. Possibly because the tension in the court had hitherto been so great, there was an audible smile. His lordship's countenance alone remained unbending. As the smile died away—it had only been a little one—another sound was heard. It was the sound of sobbing. It was then perceived that Nellie and Lizzie Ogden were crying, and that Mary was whispering what were probably words of consolation into her sisters' ears. The judge sat and watched them. He said nothing, but he took a sheet of paper, and wrote on it a few lines. This he placed within an envelope. Calling an usher, he gave him the envelope. The usher gave it to the sisters.

In the meantime Sir Hastings had been conferring with his clients. Standing up, he addressed the judge—

"My lord, after what we have just witnessed, and the solemnity of which—if bonâ fide, and as to that I at this time say nothing—I am, with your lordship, fully conscious, any remarks of mine will be made at a disadvantage. I think it possible that your lordship will grant an adjournment. Before doing so, however, I would ask your attention to one point. Even granting what we have seen to have been an actual spirit—which just now I am not disputing—I submit that in a witness-box a spirit, as a spirit, has no locus standi."

Mr. Quince popped up.

"Evidence of intention, m'lud."

His lordship intervened.

"Let me understand your point, Sir Hastings."

"My point is very simple, my lord. It is simply this: that a dead man cannot testify."

Comment from Mr. Quince—

"I submit, m'lud, that I have shown that a man may be dead, yet living."

"Not, my lord, in the eye of the law."

His lordship's eyes began to twinkle. He scented the battle from afar.

"I see your point. But why did you not object at the proper time, Sir Hastings?"

"It was only after the evidence had been given that anything in the shape of proof was offered as to the spiritual nature of the witness. I was unprepared."

"That I can understand. I also was unprepared. What have you to say, Mr. Quince?"

"I have a great deal to say, m'lud."

There was a pause. His lordship spoke again—

"I am not inclined, neither am I ready, to give, at this moment, an opinion on the point which you have raised, Sir Hastings. As you have supposed, it is my intention to order an adjournment, and in so ordering I strongly advise a settlement among the parties out of court. It appears to me, to use the most moderate language at my command, to be pre-eminently a case for the adoption of such a course. And I may say that, entirely apart from the question of spiritual visitation, there is a strong body of evidence which goes to show that the will, as propounded by the daughters, is the will which the father had in his mind."

The several parties in the case acted on the advice thus tendered by the judge. When it was again called on an announcement was made that a settlement had been arrived at, the settlement being in the terms of the will as propounded by the daughters.

THE RING

I

I REALLY don't know what induced me to do it; it was done on the impulse of the moment—one of those impulses to which collectors, real collectors, collectors in the highest sense, are peculiarly liable; I know I am.

Pugh had left the room for a moment. I just opened his cabinet of rings. I glanced within. One of the rings particularly caught my eye. I just picked it up as he came in. Unconsciously—or *almost* unconsciously—as Pugh entered, I dropped the ring into my waistcoat pocket. It was the merest coincidence. Five minutes afterwards I went away.

As I was walking homewards it occurred to me that the ring was—where it was. The fact is that I slipped my fingers into my waistcoat pocket, and—found it there. It struck me that, as it *was* where it was, I might as well examine the thing.

I took it out. It was an engraved cameo, Italian, of about the middle of the sixteenth century; it was set in gold. I don't suppose it was of any value, either intrinsic or fanciful. It was merely a little curio—quite a commonplace affair—the sort of thing one might almost pick up in the street. But the odd part of the affair was that it was just the ring I wanted; that struck me then, and it strikes me now, as being, in its way, peculiar.

I have a few rings of my own—Pugh fancies his collection is better than mine, but then it is notorious that Pugh is simply a conglomerate mass of vanity and ignorance—but, strangely enough, I am particularly weak, as a collector, in Italian work of the middle of the sixteenth century. The coincidence, under the circumstances, of finding that identical ring in my waistcoat pocket, was, of course, surprising.

I examined the thing more closely. It was a large cream-coloured
ground, with the head of a woman cut in white relief. It was not
badly done—not at all. The more closely I looked into the thing,
the more clearly I saw that the cameo, for a cameo, was quite a
work of art. In *my* collection it would look uncommonly well. The
woman's head was beautiful; the face was perfectly exquisite. I
slipped the ring on to my little finger to study the effect.

As I did so I was just turning into the Edgware Road. As I
reached the corner I was seized with a sudden spasm of pain; it
was like a sudden constriction of the heart, or, better, an acute
attack of heartburn. At that moment who should come slouch-
ing along, with that habitual graceful slouch of his, but Martin
Brasher. I attempted to wave my hand to him; but so severe was
the spasm that I had to stagger against the railings to save myself
from falling. He pulled up in front of me.

"Are you ill?" he asked.

"Do you think I'm drunk?"

It was such an absurd question to ask a man who he saw was
almost fainting! Brasher's eyes began to wander all over me—he
was quite capable of thinking, in spite of visual evidence to the
contrary, that I was drunk! His gaze began at the soles of my boots,
and I knew that, in the course of ages, it would ascend to the crown
of my hat. I was aware that nothing would escape his glance; he
would be sure to perceive the ring. As the coincidence by which it
came into my possession was not one of those coincidences which
one is necessarily desirous of publishing to the world, I began fum-
bling at my little finger to get it off. Brasher immediately fixed me
with his eagle eye.

"What are you doing?" he inquired.

"Trying to stand," I said. "Brasher, would it be subjecting you
to too great an inconvenience if I were to ask you to turn round
and call me a cab?"

He hesitated; then, turning, he hailed a hansom. The instant his
back was towards me I replaced the ring in my waistcoat pocket.

The cabman drove me home. Directly I reached Randolph
Crescent I stumbled upstairs to my bedroom; I went straight to bed.
That scoundrel Bob was out, as usual, so I had to undress myself.
A pretty job I found it! That heartburn—I had never been subject

to heartburn, but if that was not heartburn I did not know what it was—had never for one instant ceased since it had first begun. Every vein in my body seemed to be throbbing at once. My head seemed to be on the point of splitting. I supposed that I was suffering from an acute attack of indigestion, though what I had eaten or drunk to give me indigestion was more than I could think. I mixed myself a strong sleeping-draught—I felt that if I did not go to sleep at once I should go mad—and, somehow, tumbled into bed.

II

"TRESS!" Someone seemed to be shaking me. "Tress!" Someone was shaking me. "Tress!" There could be no doubt about it, someone was shaking me to pieces. "Tress!"

I roused myself. I looked up. I found that I was lying in bed. Pugh was standing by my bedside, shaking me as though he were resolved to shake my body into its constituent parts.

"Pugh, is that you?"

"It is. You are a late sleeper, Joseph Tress. Do you know what time it is?"

"No."

"It is nearly noon."

Nearly noon! And I was in bed before nine o'clock the day before. I had been asleep for nearly fifteen hours, and still I felt unrested. It was that sleeping-draught had done it. It must have been too strong.

"I thought that you were never going to wake, upon this side, again—that you were in your long, last sleep. I shouldn't have been surprised."

I sat up in bed with some difficulty. I looked at Pugh. I noticed, for the first time, that his acidulated countenance was irradiated by what he, doubtless, meant to be a smile. It made him look as though he were suffering from an attack of jaundice.

"I had an attack of indigestion yesterday after I left you, and I took a sleeping-draught. I fancy the draught must have been too strong."

"After you left me? An attack of indigestion? I see. Is that all?"

"What else would you have had me have?"

"Ah!"

Pugh's "Ah!" was intended to convey a whole encyclopedia of meaning. What an idiot that man is! He drew a chair to the bedside. He sat down on it. He crossed his hands upon the handle of his stick, and leaned his chin upon his hands. He stared at me, like an owl.

"Tress, do you remember, yesterday, when I was showing you my cabinet of rings, noticing a cameo ring, cream ground, with a woman's head in white relief, of sixteenth century Italian workmanship?"

Now I knew why he had come. Up to that moment I had forgotten all about the ring, and the odd coincidence that I had found it in my waistcoat pocket. For the second I was taken aback. I did not know what to say to him. My head felt fuddled.

"A cameo ring, cream ground, with a woman's head in white relief, of sixteenth century Italian workmanship?"

"That's it, exactly. I see you noticed it."

I shook my head. I did not like to say, in so many words, I hadn't, being as fond of truth as most men.

"Why do you ask?"

"Because, when you went, the ring went too."

"What do you mean?"

"Nothing. Only, when you had gone, I found that the ring had gone. You are sure you didn't notice it?"

"Quite sure."

I was driven to a lie.

"That's odd, because I thought that I saw you pay particular attention to that particular ring—a cameo ring, cream ground, with a woman's head in white relief, of sixteenth century Italian workmanship. You are quite sure you didn't notice it—just think."

"I don't want to think; don't I tell you I am sure?"

What did the imbecile mean by making me pile lie upon lie? Pugh rose.

"That's odd, very odd. Well, it's gone. I thought I'd call and tell you, because"—what he meant for a smile grew more pronounced—"that ring is possessed of peculiar properties."

"Peculiar properties?"

"Some very peculiar properties indeed. A collector, ignorant of those properties, might not find it such an acquisition as he supposed. However, it is of no consequence, since you didn't notice it. Good-day, Tress. I hope your indigestion will be better."

He went. Directly he was gone I scrambled out of bed and locked the door. What an escape I had had! In the confused state of my mind, had he persisted in his questioning, I might have been worried into some fatal admission. I was in a fit state neither of mind nor of body to adequately cope with his impertinent prying.

And what did he mean by his mysterious allusions to the peculiar properties of his wretched ring? All bunkum, probably. Still, he had emphasised his words in a manner which seemed to suggest that he had intended them to mean something. An Italian ring, of the sixteenth century? I remembered, unless chroniclers lied, that certain rings of that period had been credited, in Italy, as being possessed of peculiar properties—as Pugh said, of very peculiar properties indeed.

When Brasher's back had been turned, at the corner of the Edgware Road, I had returned the ring to my waistcoat pocket. Having made sure that the door was locked, I took up my waistcoat and looked for the ring. It was strange. It wasn't there. I remembered, distinctly, putting the ring into the right-hand pocket. But as, then, there was no ring in that pocket I presumed that my memory betrayed me, and I had put it in the pocket on the other side. No, there was no ring in that one either. I couldn't have been such an ass as to have put it into my watch-pocket, and in fact I hadn't.

Then where was it? In the midst of my suffering I had torn my clothes off anyhow. It was possible that, unnoticed by me, it had found its way out of my pocket, and a refuge on the floor. I went down on my hands and knees. I peered under the bed, under the furniture; I minutely examined every square inch of the carpet. There was no ring there. It was possible that I might have lost the ring on my homeward way. I say it was possible, but it did not seem to me that it was probable. I began to be conscious of a feeling of irritation. When a collector so far yields to the enthusiasm of the moment as to borrow a specimen, he does not like to lose that specimen within half an hour of his having borrowed it. He feels that his collection has suffered a loss. Pugh had spoken of the peculiar properties of the ring. Was the act of self-abstraction one of them? Or—

A terrible suspicion flashed across my brain. Pugh, for all I knew, had shown himself into my room. He had found me asleep in bed—helpless! I knew the man. He was a man who, under certain circumstances, would stick at nothing; a man who would shrink from no trick because it chanced to be a dirty one; a man who was absolutely devoid of a sense of honesty. To add to that lot of trumpery which he calls his collection he would rob his friend. I had not the slightest doubt of it. I knew it as a positive fact.

On one occasion he had actually stolen my Sir Walter Raleigh pipe, a priceless relic, being the identical pipe which that great man himself had smoked. When he was taken, red-handed, in his crime, he had the audacity to pretend that he had slipped the pipe into his pocket by mistake, wrapped, as it was, inside his pocket-handkerchief. Such a man was capable of anything. It was quite within the range of possibility that he had come into my bedroom, found me wrapped in the slumber of unconscious innocence, and overhauled my clothing.

And then he had had the consummate hypocrisy to wake me, and to ask me, smiling all the time—I had observed his smile!—if I had noticed, in his cabinet, his wretched ring. And he had spoken of its peculiar properties! If, the next time I called at his house, he were to show me his cabinet of rings—which he would be sure to do!—and I were to see in it that ring, staring me in the face, I should feel demoralised.

The thing was to find out if he had shown himself into my room.

I rang for Bob. I rang once, I rang twice, I rang thrice; the third time I nearly broke the bell. Still no Bob. I went outside the bed-room door and bawled for him. By the time I had bawled myself hoarse, and was meditating descending to the kitchen in my night-shirt, and kicking him out of the house up the area steps, I heard, below, the sound of somebody stumbling up the stairs. Was it possible that, at that hour of the day, before I was dressed, the man was drunk? It sounded as though he was. Bump, bump, up he came; every moment I expected to hear him go bump, bump down again. At last he came blundering through the bedroom door.

"What on earth, you scoundrel, do you mean by getting drunk before I'm dressed? Do you know what time it is? It isn't noon!"

"I'm not drunk—I wish I were. I'm a dead 'un."

"You are drunk, sir! I tell you what it is, Bob Haines, I've had enough of your villainy, and I'll send you packing. Who showed Mr. Pugh up into my room?"

"Don't know."

"Of course you don't, you tippling fool!"

"I tell you I'm not drunk, I'm dying. Oh!—Oh!"

Leaning against the wall, he clapped his hand to his side, and groaned. I eyed him. He did not look as though he were drunk, and to do Bob Haines justice, although he has the most capacious and constant thirst of any man I ever knew, I never saw him exhibit any signs of having drunk too much. His is a thirst which nothing shall quench.

"What's the matter with you?"

"I've got a pain—here! It's heartburn! All my veins is bursting! So's my head."

Curious. From his words and his looks, he appeared to be suffering from an attack exactly similar to that by which I had been overtaken the evening before. I turned away.

"Bob, have you been in my room this morning?"

"Once. You was asleep."

Oh, I was, was I? Had *he* overhauled my clothes? What *were* the peculiar properties attached to that ring of Pugh's? I did not, in spite of the new and lurid suspicions which were darkening my mind, like to charge Bob Haines then and there with stealing from me the ring which I had borrowed from Pugh in the enthusiasm of the moment. Bob was an old and, comparatively, faithful servant, as servants go—they are all thieves. I did not like to blast his career, to charge him with an act of perfidy—that is, unless the evidence against him was undeniable, and—and until my mind was settled. I myself still was feeling queer. So I sent him out of the room.

"Go away; and, if you must die, die decently, without making all that noise!"

In spite of my command I heard him groan-groaning, as he went bump-bumping down the stairs.

Hardly had he gone than someone made a thundering assault

on the hall-door knocker. The door was opened. Someone entered—two persons, apparently. I heard them coming up the stairs. Not only did they come upstairs, but, without a with your leave or by your leave, or rapping at my door, or any sort of form or ceremony, they came into my room, just as I was putting on my trousers. It was that idiot Pugh, accompanied by that, if possible, still greater idiot, Martin Brasher.

"Hollo, Pugh, what have you come back for?"

"I have come back in consequence of a communication made to me by my friend Brasher, whom I chanced to encounter within a dozen yards of your doorstep. I should like to have, with your permission, five minutes' conversation with you, in the presence of Brasher. Take a chair, Brasher; sit down." Brasher sat down, on Pugh's invitation. Pugh sat down on his own.

"Mr. Tress, I should like once more to ask you—and before you answer I beg that you will bring your mind to bear upon the question—if, when yesterday I was showing you my cabinet of rings, you did not notice a cameo ring, cream ground, with a woman's head in white relief, of sixteenth century Italian workmanship?"

What did the fellow mean by pestering me with his ridiculous questions?

"I don't know, Pugh, what you're driving at. I can assure you that I haven't time, or inclination, to notice all your rubbish. I have told you, frankly, more than once, what is my opinion of that cabinet of yours."

Pugh waved his hands in the air.

"Quite so! Just so! We are quite aware that, as you say, you have more than once shown the extent of your connoisseurship. But that is not the point. The point is, that that particular ring is missing—missing, Tress. And a further point is, that that particular ring is possessed of—peculiar properties."

"My dear Pugh, I don't care about its peculiar properties."

"But I think it just as well that you should care, under the *special* circumstances. To begin with, that ring belonged to no less a person than Lucrezia Borgia."

"Lucrezia Jones!"

"Not Jones, but Borgia. Have you never heard of Lucrezia Borgia, Tress? She was a person of some notoriety, though possibly, and even probably, her name may not have come your way."

Confound his impudence; ignorant ass!

"Lucrezia Borgia, Tress, was a lady who had a partiality for getting rid of her friends, before she robbed them."

Pausing, Pugh looked steadily at me.

"That was an age of poisoners. In southern Europe they simply swarmed. Poison was Lucrezia's favourite method of disposing of her friends. Chroniclers tell us that, of all poisoners, she was the queen. She had as many ways of poisoning a friend as a modern *chef* has of cooking an egg. And one of her ways—Lucrezia's pretty ways—was by means of poisoned rings."

I could not help it, but I started. I know that Pugh observed the start, because he immediately indulged in his jaundiced libel on a smile.

"That ring, Tress, which was in my cabinet, and which now is missing, was one of Lucrezia's poisoned rings."

I turned away—I was compelled to.

"I don't know, Pugh, what all this has to do with me, though I, no doubt, ought to thank you for imparting such valuable information."

"Not at all, Tress, not at all. Permit me to continue. The way in which that ring works—in a poisonous sense—is by wearing it. Put it on your finger, you are poisoned."

I busied myself with the things upon the mantelshelf, being conscious of a sense of distinct discomfort. I was aware that Pugh was regarding me intently—with unqualified enjoyment—from behind, as, I make no doubt, was that addle-headed Brasher. The plague take Pugh's twopenny-halfpenny ring! I wished I had never seen it.

"The way in which the fair Lucrezia used to work the oracle was doubtless this: She used herself to put the ring upon the victim's finger, in that graceful way she had—the woman's head in white relief is Lucrezia's own likeness—and that same instant the recipient of the lady's generosity fell dead. The gift was probably presented in private. There was no eye there to see it given. It was slipped off the finger almost at the same instant in which the lady had slipped it on. It left no trace of its presence behind. The medical verdict was, no doubt, the contemporary equivalent for valvular disease of the heart. The victim had been slain as by a bolt from on high. That peculiarly active virtue which, if the chronicles are true, the ring once possessed, has been modified by time. Now, it does not kill—at once."

I should like to have thrown Pugh out of the bedroom window; he was simply playing on my nerves.

"Quite recently I have had that ring examined by an eminent toxicologist. The way in which it does its work, in this present year of grace, is this: You place it on your finger—as you, for instance, Tress, might do. That same instant you feel a pain in your side."

Almost without knowing it, I clapped my hand to my side.

"That pain is accompanied by a throbbing of all the veins in your body, and a feeling as though your head was about to split into pieces."

The man was simply brutal. I protest that, as he spoke, the symptoms he described returned to me with all their original force.

"You must own, Tress, that it was a little odd that I should have missed the ring directly I missed you. It appears that, as you were leaving my house, Brasher chanced to meet you. It is in consequence of a communication Brasher has made to me, referring to that chance encounter, that I have ventured upon this further interview. Brasher says—I believe, Brasher, that I am right in saying that when you encountered Mr. Tress he appeared to be suffering from indisposition?"

"He did."

"What appeared to you to be the nature of his indisposition?"

"He appeared to be suffering from a pain in his side. He was almost doubled up, and he had his hands pressed convulsively against the region of his heart."

"Did you notice anything else?"

"I did. I noticed upon the little finger of his left hand a ring."

"A ring? Can you tell us, Brasher, what kind of a ring it was which you noticed upon the little finger of his left hand?"

"I can. My eye was struck by it at once. First, because, although I have known Tress for many years, I never before saw him wear a ring. And, second, because the ring itself was a remarkable ring."

"Not the sort of ring which an ordinary English gentleman would be likely to wear during his walks abroad?"

"Certainly not."

"Describe it, Brasher."

"It was a large oval-shaped cameo. It had a cream ground, with a woman's head in white relief. It was set in gold, curiously chased. It struck me as being an antique, probably Italian, of the sixteenth century."

What eyes that Brasher has!

"You are quite sure, Tress, that when, yesterday, I was showing you my cabinet of rings you did not notice a cameo ring, cream ground, woman's head in white relief, of sixteenth century Italian workmanship?"

I sank down upon the bed. I was doubled up with pain—it had all come back again.

"Pugh, what's the antidote?"

"The antidote, Tress? To what?"

"To that confounded ring of yours!"

"Tress!" He pretended to be shocked. Rising from his chair, he let his stick fall to the floor with a clatter. "Is it possible that you—you! can have robbed your friend, the oldest friend you have in the world! I thought you capable of most things—of palming off the most trumpery rubbish as a priceless relic—but I never thought you capable of theft, from a friend! Oh, Tress! Tress! that it should have come to this!"

He groaned—the hypocrite!

"What's the antidote?"

"The best antidote I can recommend is, primarily, the return of the stolen property."

"I haven't got it!"

"Tress! Don't add another perjury—you, who are perhaps a dying man."

"I haven't! I slipped it into my waistcoat pocket by mistake."

"You slipped it into your pocket by mistake? I see. That explains how it was you didn't notice it. That also explains how it was you happened to be wearing it when Brasher met you in the street."

"It struck me senseless! I believe I'm dying now! I put it into my waistcoat pocket. When I looked for it this morning, it was gone. I thought—you had come in—when I was sleeping—found it—and taken it again."

"You thought! Tress, consider! Even now your moments may be numbered!"

"Oh-h! Ring the bell, and tell them to send me up some brandy!"

Instead of doing as I requested, and as common humanity directed, he began to preach at me to Brasher.

"Brasher, this man has been my friend for over thirty years. Look at him now, and ponder! I have helped him in his collection. You know my taste, what I may call my genius for the discovery of real antiques. If it had not been for me he would not have possessed the few articles of any value which his collection now contains."

Oh, if I had been sufficiently master of myself to kick him!

"And how does he show his gratitude? I will tell you. He breaks into my house like a highwayman, and ransacks all my most precious stores. He knows that I possess, for an amateur—a mere amateur, Brasher—one of the finest collections in Europe. He is green with envy, racked by covetous desires. He fixes his mind upon one of the finest gems in my collection, a relic for which crowned heads—crowned heads, Brasher!—might sigh in vain, and which none the less, so marvellously strong is my natural born instinct as a connoisseur, I picked up at a little town in Italy for less than fifteen shillings."

"More than it was worth."

"You hear him, Brasher, you hear him say that that was more than it was worth? But though he says it, he has sufficient knowledge, even in the midst of his wallowing ignorance, to be aware that it is of priceless value. But his knowledge goes no further. He does not know, what I, the true connoisseur, perceived at once, that in the hands of an ignorant man the ring would deal death and danger. So he steals it—from me, his friend! Within a very few minutes his misdeed finds him out. You saw him struggling with death—we see him struggling now! Brasher, look on him now, and ponder!"

"When you have quite finished, perhaps you'll ring the bell."

"I have not finished, but I will ring the bell. And when I have rung it, I will begin again."

"Oh!"

Brasher rang.

"Ring again."

He did.

"Smash the bell!"

He almost did.

"Bob's drunk."

Pugh turned to Brasher. He put his hands behind his back. He wagged his head.

"Like master, like man!"

"Go downstairs and kick him."

"No, Tress, I will not go downstairs and kick him. You hear Mr. Tress, Brasher, asking me to go downstairs to kick his servant? Unfortunately, that's the kind of man he is."

We waited; I expected I should have to go downstairs myself. Then there was a sound of somebody coming lumbering up the stairs; I knew it was Bob. At last he blundered into the room.

"Oh!" he gasped, and collapsed against the wall.

At that same moment a paroxysm overtook me too. Pugh addressed himself to Bob.

"Well, my man, I'm sorry to see you in this condition."

"Not so sorry as I am—I'm a dead 'un."

Brasher took Pugh by the arm.

"It's a curious coincidence, Mr. Pugh, but this person appears to be suffering in precisely the same manner as Mr. Tress was suffering when I encountered him yesterday evening at the corner of the Edgware Road."

Pugh turned to me; I was literally doubled up with pain.

"And as Mr. Tress is suffering now. I have it!" Pugh snapped his fingers in the air. "Tress, do you really mean that that ring is missing—that you don't know where it is?"

"I do."

"Then you have taken it!" Pugh turned to Bob. "So true is it that as the master so the man. You have stolen from your master the ring which your master stole from me!"

Pugh pointed his finger at Bob as if he—Pugh—were an accusing spirit. In the midst of his agony, Bob seemed to be taken aback.

"What d'ye say?"

"I say, and I say it again, that you—you too, have dipped your hands in crime. Fit associate of such a man!"

"Look here, Pugh, I wish you wouldn't speak of me like that to my own servant."

"But I will, Tress, I will. I will probe, at all hazards, to the bottom of this long-drawn-out crime." He returned to Bob. "Villain, confess your guilt. You have stolen from your master the ring of which he previously had plundered me."

"What are you talking about? I don't know nothing about no ring."

"Brasher, come here; look at this man. You know something of the working of—poisons."

"Poisons!"

Bob staggered back against the friendly wall.

"Look at this man's face—look at it closely. Do you not perceive, in the working of the muscles of his countenance, something strange and ghastly?"

"I do," said Brasher; "I see it most distinctly."

He would have been a fool if he didn't, considering the spectacle which Bob just then presented.

"Do you see a convulsive twitching?"

"I do."

"Do you see an ashen pallor?"

"Most undoubtedly."

"A startled look about the eyes?"

"I see all that."

"Man, the ring which you stole from your master's waistcoat pocket was"—

Bob gave himself away.

"What?"

"A poisoned ring."

Bob sprang at least six inches from the ground.

"If you put that ring on your finger, though only for an instant, you are doomed."

"Oh!" groaned Bob.

"Do you feel a pain in your side?"

Bob groaned again.

"Do you feel as if all your veins were filled with fire?"

Another groan.

"Do you feel as if your head were about to burst into a thousand atoms?"

Another groan, still louder than before.

"Wretched man, time is short. Tell us how long you wore this ill-fated gem, in order that we may, if possible, take measures to save you from the doom you have so justly merited. But first, before anything can be done, you must give me back the ring."

"I haven't got it."

"Where is it then?"

Bob drew himself upright, to the best of his ability, with his back against the wall. He looked round the room with ghastly eyes.

"I never see'd such a house as this in all my days."

"That I can easily believe, my man. And I trust that it may never be your ill-fortune to look on such another."

As he gave vent to this fervent desire of his heart, Pugh's eyes were fixed on me.

"I come up into this room this morning to see if master was awake. Cook had told me that he came in drunk last night."

"She lied!" I roared.

"It was a natural error," commented Brasher. "My own first impression, when I saw you yesterday evening at the corner of the Edgware Road, was that you were suffering from over-indulgence in strong drink."

Thus is a man robbed of his good name! Bob went on—

"He wasn't. He was sound asleep. I never see a man so sound asleep. I says to myself, 'He *must* have raised his elbow. *I* know what he can swallow.'"

"You hear, Brasher, what is the servant's opinion of the master?"

Only wait! I would have a settlement with Bob.

"There was his clothes littered all over the place. I sets to put 'em straight. As I picks up the waistcoat, something falls out of one of the pockets. It was a ring."

"A ring," said Pugh. "Just so—a ring!"

"It was a trumpery thing"—

"My man!" said Pugh.

"I picks it up and looks at it; it was a trumpery thing, not worth tuppence-hapenny!"

"Brasher, you hear this man—you hear him? My good fellow, that ring is a relic of the Borgias!"

"I don't know nothing about no boarders. I says to myself when I sees it, and I says to you, that I never see a commoner-looking article."

It sounds incredible, but I chuckled. I resolved to forgive him everything.

"The man's ignorance," cried Pugh, "is as colossal as the master's!"

"It was just a dirty white stone with another stone stuck on top of it, like a woman's head."

"So he describes one of the finest cameos that was ever touched by an Italian graver!"

"The ring itself was brass."

"Brass! It's the finest gold."

"Don't tell me! I know gold when I see it, and I know brass. I've seen heaps and heaps of rings like that, and better, at fairs; pay your penny and you takes your choice."

"Brasher, this man is like the ring—unique!"

"I takes a squint at it, and I sees it was a common-looking article, and I says to myself, 'This ain't worth nothing to nobody.' I was just going to put it back in the pocket, when it comes across me, sudden, 'This is the very ring for cook!'"

Pugh gasped.

"For cook?"

"For cook."

"And why—why for cook?"

"Well, I don't mind saying it, if I've got to say it." Bob looked determined. "I've been engaged to cook—nine years, *she* says it is, and I've never given her an engagement ring yet. She's always bothering me for one, so when I sees this ring wasn't worth nothing to nobody, I says to myself, 'This is the very thing for an engagement ring for cook.'"

Pugh took out his handkerchief. He wiped his brow.

"The very thing for an engagement ring for cook—that relic of the Borgias—the ring which was once the property of the fair Lucrezia herself! Brasher, don't—don't give way. Go on, my man, go on."

"I puts it into my pocket, and as I was going upstairs to my room, who should I see but cook. 'Cook,' I says, 'have you got half a crown?' 'What for?' she says. 'For me,' I says. 'No,' she says, 'I haven't.' 'Well,' I says, 'I don't quite like telling you, but the fact is, I've been spending a good bit of money on you lately, and it's left me rather short.'" Bob drew the back of his hand across his lips. "I never did like giving something for nothing, no matter to who it is. 'On me!' she says. 'I'll believe in your spending a brass farthing on anybody but yourself when I sees it.' 'Well,' I says, 'I've been buying you a ring.' 'A ring!' she says. She turned quite yeller."

Bob grinned. Pugh and Brasher didn't know what to make of it at all. I knew the blackguard.

"'Yes,' I says, 'I've been buying you one of the finest rings that ever yet you saw. Look at that now!' I takes it out of my pocket, and I holds it out in front of her. She didn't think nothing of it; I knew she wouldn't. She ain't such a fool as she looks. 'What, that dirty, tawdry, second-hand looking thing,' she says. 'Why, it ain't worth tuppence.' 'Ah, that's where you're wrong,' I says. 'That ring's worth a whole heap of money. If I was to tell you what I gave for that ring you wouldn't believe me. I only come on it accidental like. I calls it a handsome ring.' 'Well, I don't,' she says, 'I calls it hideous—I wouldn't be seen with such a thing on a finger of mine, not me!' 'Ah,' I says, 'wait till you sees it on the human hand.' And I slips it on the little finger of my right hand—just to show it off like. Oh, my crikey!" Bob doubled himself up in the middle. I was took with such a pain in the side I was obliged to holler. 'What's wrong now?' she says. 'Take the ring,' I says. And I takes it off my finger, I don't know how, and gives it her, and I makes straight for my bedroom, and I chucks myself upon the bed—I was that bad!"

Pugh looked at Bob. Then he looked at Brasher.

"Brasher, is it not strange, is it not more than strange, that in this age of so-called enlightenment there should exist in a civilised country such a master and such a man? Whether to blame more the master or the man it passes my wisdom to pronounce. It is true that the man is an ignorant creature, but then so also is the master. But it certainly, to me, does seem incredible that any creature having any pretensions, even the most shadowy pretensions, to even *legal* intellect, should present that priceless relic of the Borgias—Lucrezia's own ring—to a cook!"

"But how about the cook?" inquired Brasher. "If she puts"—

The room door was thrown wide open. Mary, the housemaid, came rushing in.

"If you please, sir, I believe that cook's a-dying!"

"A-dying, Mary?"

"She's been up in her bedroom ever so long, and I went up to see what she was doing, because there's nothing done for our dinner—no potatoes, nor nothing; and there she was lying on the bed, groaning awful. If you please, sir, I believe that cook's a-dying."

And Mary, who is a sensitive creature, at least so I should imagine, wept—I don't know why.

"It's the ring!" said Brasher.

We went up to cook in a body. First Mary, then Brasher, then Pugh, then me, then Bob—who apparently did not care to be left behind, though it was all that he could do to stagger. It was the ring, there was no doubt about it. That love-offering of the faithful Bob had all but done for her, if one might judge from the way in which she was behaving. I have seldom heard a woman make more noise; it had not deprived her of the use of her lungs. We heard her squealing as we came along the passage. When we entered the room her squeals redoubled.

"There is the ring!" said Pugh, pointing at her with his outstretched hand.

There was the ring, on cook's engagement finger, the third finger of her left hand—the love-token of a faithful heart, of a nine years' old engagement, the cameo ring, cream ground, with a woman's head in white relief, sixteenth century Italian workmanship, that relic of the Borgias, Lucrezia's pretty plaything. Finding herself in possession of that speaking symbol of Bob's fond love, she had been unable to resist the temptation of seeing how it really did look upon the human hand. She had put it on to see. The immediate result was that she was lying there upon the bed.

"Brasher," said Pugh, "if it is true that the dead are conscious of the acts of the living, how, at this moment, the great Lucrezia must be writhing in her grave!"

III

WELL, I survived, or I should not be telling this tale; and Bob survived, and cook. And I do not know that either of us is the worse for our experience of the peculiar characteristics of the fair Lucrezia's pretty plaything. Last week cook was married to Bob. A nicely assorted couple they bid fair to make.

Yet we might have been worse—much worse, easily. Pugh allowed me, in one of his rare moments of affability, to submit the ring to a minute examination, and I herewith acquit him of exaggerating its natural wickedness. He has his gifts in that direction; but no man could paint that diabolical illustration of mediæval fiendishness worse than it deserved, not even Pugh.

The ring itself was hollow. When you put it on your finger, directly it came into contact with the flesh, two minute needles were released, one on either side, which had sufficient penetrating force to introduce the poison, which was contained in the reservoir-like circlet, beneath the cuticle. This poison must, originally, have been of an extraordinarily active character, for, after the passage of probably more than three hundred years, it still retained sufficient of its force, so soon as the tiniest drop found its way beneath the scarf-skin, to impregnate the entire system, rushing through the veins with inconceivable rapidity, and instantly affecting the action of the heart.

In its youth it must have slain with lightning-like rapidity, since in its belated old age it could use folks as it had done Bob and cook and me.

The ring is still in Pugh's collection, what is left of it. By the exercise of great skill and care I succeeded in taking it to pieces—wonderfully ingenious mechanism had been contrived by its criminal constructor—but I was not so successful in putting the pieces together again. Pugh says that is my stupidity, which shows his ignorance.

However, there are the fragments. Should any person desire to learn what could be planned in the way of wickedness three hundred and fifty years ago, he had better give Pugh a call.

P.S.—I presented cook with her engagement ring. Bob and she seemed to have a vague impression that I ought to—so I did.

STAUNTON'S DINNER

I

WHEN Vane Staunton said to old General Ricketts, "I wish to be original," and the general replied, "Then be commonplace," it was difficult to deny, looking at things as they are, that the general had promulgated a not inexact recipe. So many people, quite commonplace folk, units of Carlyle's large majority, do try to be original, that originality has become a badge of mediocrity, not to use a "big, big D." And then all along Vane Staunton had been original—not socially insane, that is, but only legally. He had been almost engaged to Ermyntrude Bryant,—his aunt and her mother hinted that he had been quite,—and the Lady Ermyntrude was a pearl among girls, so pure—and so tasteless. And there were those who said he ought to have been married to Nora Cathcart—but he wasn't. She was a ruby, rather than a pearl, in vitality rich as ripe, red wine. Between these stools he fell—at least, so gossips say. Two laps spread out to catch him, and he fell down between. The result was, he disappeared. He was absent for more than a century—that is, for society's chronology is vague, quite a dozen years. They thought that he was dead. Some hoped that he was. For instance, his cousin, Horace Griffin, who had nine children,—seven in divided skirts,—and who was next heir. He was supposed to have taken with him about a thousand pounds, and he had never applied for a penny since. It was in Cairo he had last been heard of. In consequence, there were accumulations. Twelve years, fifty thousand pounds a year, at compound interest,—if you work that out you'll find it's just the sum you're wanting. It was just the sum which Horace wanted—and the nine!—with the seven in the skirts, and oh! so lean. But the mischief was that there was more than a presumption that Vane Staunton wasn't dead. They had heard of him last in Cairo, but they had heard *from* him every year. And the manner in which they heard was strange.

On the morning of the first of June of every year there was found on Mr. Tilley's desk—"Tilley, Foreclose, Charter, & Baynes"—a note. It was addressed "Walter Tilley," and it contained a sheet of paper on which were two words—"*Je suis.*" Old Tilley knew Vane Staunton's handwriting as well as he knew his own. He was prepared to swear in any court in England—and, in fact, did swear in at least one of them—that the address, and the two words, had been written by Vane Staunton.

The question was, how did that note get where it was—upon the desk. It had not come by post. The "laundress" had not seen it when she performed her early morning ministrations. None of the clerks had brought it in. Mr. Baynes, who had been in the room only a second or two before the head of the firm's arrival, was almost prepared to swear that it had not been on the desk when he was there. Yet, when the head of the firm did come, the first thing he saw was the note looking up into his face.

So it was when the note first came—that was three years after Vane Staunton had been heard of last in Cairo. On that first occasion the words, "*Je suis,*" were written with an abominable pen, with abominable ink, on an abominable sheet of paper,—Mr. Tilley had never seen its like before,—which was enclosed in another sheet of paper, of similar style and pattern, which was simply scribbled over, and sealed at the back with Vane Staunton's seal. On the second occasion the words were written on the office paper of the firm, and enclosed in one of their business envelopes.

When Horace Griffin heard of this, he raised a hue and cry. Where *was* Vane Staunton? It was ridiculous to suppose that he could use the office paper of the firm, and annex their envelopes, unless he was within easy reach of Lincoln's Inn. The idea that he could have taken the paper and the envelope away with him was exploded when it was discovered that they both belonged to a batch which had arrived in the office only the day before. Horace Griffin, to whom his cousin had been as good as a thousand a year, said all sorts of things. Somebody was playing him a trick,—and the look which he directed at Mr. Tilley sent the arrow home. The old lawyer tried to freeze this cousin.

"It is scarcely possible, Mr. Griffin, that your insinuation is intended for me."

Mr. Griffin leaned his elbows on the table and looked the lawyer in the face.

"Mr. Tilley, when did you see Vane Staunton last?"

Mr. Tilley looked at his partners, and round the room, as though he were appealing to the heavens *not* to fall.

"Mr. Griffin, you have seen Mr. Staunton since I did. On the last occasion on which you saw him you borrowed the sum of four hundred pounds. There is an entry in his diary to that effect. I last saw him the day before."

Mr. Griffin rose. Putting on his hat, he girded up his loins.

"I tell you candidly, gentlemen, that it is my belief—and the remark which I am about to make is not actionable since, at present, it is only my belief—that Vane Staunton is concealing himself, for purposes of his own, and that you are conniving at his concealment."

Then Mr. Griffin went,—and it was time he did.

The night of the thirty-first of May immediately following Mr. Tilley spent in the office, in company with Mr. Baynes. If that note *did* come they would see who brought it. Nothing happened during the course of the night, except, perhaps, that now and then they dozed; and there was still no note when the first post had come in on the following morning. If a trick had been played, it appeared that the trickster had been baffled. Mr. Baynes had left the office, Mr. Tilley, left alone, was wondering if Mr. Griffin would make another application to the court, also if he might venture to go home and make up for some of the sleep which he had lost, when, chancing to look down, he saw, lying on his desk, a note. He could scarcely believe his eyes, and indeed he rubbed them to make sure that they were giving evidence. His first impulse was to jump up and inquire if anyone had entered the office without his knowledge. But the absurdity of this struck him at once. If anyone had come in, if *he* had not been aware of it, who could have been? Mr. Baynes had not been gone out a minute, it was impossible he could have been to sleep, and yet that the note had not been there ten seconds ago he was prepared to swear, and, indeed, did swear when Horace Griffin put him to the testing-point.

It was a dainty thing, in a perfumed envelope, on the back of which was Vane Staunton's seal. Mr. Tilley thought that he had seen the counterpart of that envelope somewhere before, but, at the moment, for the life of him he could not think where. Ringing his bell he sent for Mr. Baynes. When the junior partner entered he found his senior in a state of excessive agitation.

"Mr. Baynes, a most extraordinary thing has happened. During your absence I—I have found this note upon my desk."

Mr. Tilley was, in general, the most precise old gentleman the world contained. Now he stammered and stuttered. Mr. Baynes stared,—as well he might.

"I am afraid I do not understand you."

Mr. Tilley explained; but the explanation did not make the matter much clearer to Mr. Baynes' understanding. The envelope was carefully opened. It contained a piece of perfumed paper, which matched the envelope. On it were written the old two words, in the well-known writing, "*Je suis.*" Mr. Baynes took from his pocket an envelope. It was so like the one which Mr. Tilley was holding in his hand, perfume and all, that if you turned them over, so as to conceal the writing, it would have been impossible to tell which was which. From the envelope Mr. Baynes took a sheet of paper. Here again the resemblance to the other sheet of paper was complete.

"Mr. Baynes," cried Mr. Tilley, thinking that here was an important clue, "where did you get that envelope and paper?"

"From your wife. I received them yesterday. Mrs. Tilley has been so good as to send me an invitation to dine."

Mr. Tilley was dumfounded. And yet, now that his attention was called to it, he recognised that the thing was fact. He himself had noticed the notepaper lying on his wife's writing table only a day or two before, and had spurned it, because to him all perfume was as an unclean thing.

Mr. Tilley himself knew that he had had no finger in this matter, that he knew no more of Vane Staunton's whereabouts than he knew of the dead. But even his partners seemed to doubt it,—at least, some of their suggestions nearly maddened him. And Horace Griffin!—It was currently reported that Mr. Griffin's proceedings broke the senior partner's heart. And when the next first of June came round the old man was dead,—his son, a second Walter, reigning in his stead.

On the evening preceding that first of June there was quite a "gathering" assembled in the office in Lincoln's Inn. Mr. Walter Tilley, the new edition of his father, Mr. Foreclose, Mr. Charter, Mr. Baynes, Mr. Horace Griffin, Mr. Muspeath, legally representing Mr. Griffin, and Mr. Allder, who, in a friendly way, was there for the court. Nothing took place in the night, and nothing came by the morning's post. About a quarter to nine Mr. Baynes took out his watch and laid it on the senior partner's desk.

"It was about this time last year that I left the room, and within a minute, Mr. Tilley assured me he saw the note upon his desk."

They sat round, in a sort of broken circle. All looked at the desk. Each man's countenance wore a different expression.

"It's almost like a spiritualistic séance," murmured Mr. Allder. He had a weakness in the direction of trivialities.

"It is." Mr. Griffin was nasty where the other was only trivial. "Like a séance at which the conditions are too stringent for the medium."

Hardly had he spoken than an odd thing happened. One moment there was nothing on the desk. The next, lying right in the centre, was an envelope. The oddity consisted in the two facts that no one was within reach of the desk, and that no one saw whence came the envelope, nor how. Indeed, so instantaneous was its appearance—right before their eyes!—that the assembled company, unable to realise that it had appeared, for a moment could do nothing but stare. Young Tilley broke the silence.

"You see, gentlemen, my father was right. He is avenged." Then, seeing that they yet were still, "I would suggest that Mr. Allder, as a third party, and without bias, takes up that envelope."

The suggestion was acted upon. Mr. Allder took it up. He read aloud what was written on the envelope.

"'To Walter Tilley's son, young Walter.' Shall I open it?" He opened it. "There are only two words written on this sheet of paper, 'Je suis.'"

He handed the envelope and the paper to Horace Griffin.

"It's deuced queer," Mr. Griffin allowed.

It was queer, but since it was admitted that, under the circumstances, the next heir had rights,—even to the extent of being allowed to live in the house in Grosvenor Square,—Mr. Griffin refrained from more than hinting that he had been the victim of an elaborate trick. The trick was repeated year after year, for five consecutive years, and then Vane Staunton returned to tell Mr. Griffin, if he chose, how the trick was done.

It was the beginning of the season, the Epsom Spring had just been finished, and the Griffins had been giving a dance. It was their "first small,"—as representing the head of the family Horace felt it his duty to go in pretty thoroughly for all that kind of thing. Besides, the seven in divided skirts were still unmarried. Four of them were hopeless,—barring always a special Providence,—but for three of them faint hopes still lingered. It was to make the running for this fatal three that the dance was given.

All was over, the guests had gone, the ballroom was a desert. Horace, who was a careful man, just looked in to see that all was right before the general extinction of the lights began.

"I shall require my room by Thursday evening next, at six."

So startled was Horace at hearing these words addressed to him that he clutched at the lintel of the door to save himself from falling. He turned his head in the direction of the speaker. At sight of what he saw his heart stopped beating; for this was Vane Staunton in the flesh. It was, and yet it wasn't. Yet,—*it was!*

There, at the other end of a room, on the opposite side, leaning against the wall, as a non-dancing man might lean, was Vane. God help poor Horace,—was it Vane? He could not even ask the question. He could only stand and stare.

"Do you not understand me? I say that I shall require my room by Thursday evening next, at six."

Vane, if it was Vane, repeated his observation as though it was the most natural observation a man could make after being absent, and taken for dead, for just about a dozen years. But Horace could not concede this point at all.

"Vane!—Staunton!—Is it you?"

"It certainly is I."

The voice was Staunton's, and the face, but the costume,—and something in his air! What Mr. Griffin saw was a tall, thin man. Vane always had been tall, but this man was so attenuated as to make one think of living skeletons outdone. He was dressed in a costume—if it could be called a costume, which Mr. Griffin felt it couldn't—which was in colour dirty, *very* dirty orange. His feet were bare, and so was his right shoulder. His head was not only innocent of any covering in the shape of a hat, but it was also innocent of any covering in the shape of hair. His scalp was as smooth, if not as shiny, as a billiard ball. Nor was there any hair upon his face. From the point of view of the "bald head" he left the prophet at the post. Vane Staunton had had a most beautiful moustache, and quite a barber's head of hair. As regards dress he had been the most fastidious of men. *Could* this be he? Horace, with presence of mind which did him credit, resolved to decline to admit, at a moment's notice, that it could. He advanced into the room, with legs which trembled, and with a heart which struggled not to sink. It was his intention to treat the case as an attempt at imposture.

"How came you into this room?"

His voice was as imperious as he could make it. But the man at the other end of the apartment gave no signs of quailing. Nor did he reply. Raising his right hand, he simply beckoned with his forefinger to Horace. To do him justice, Mr. Griffin had never been at the beck and call of any man. Yet he obeyed this little gesture with a promptitude which was quite surprising. He commenced running down the room as though he were starting for a race. When he reached the spot where the beckoner was standing, he stopped short right in front of him. He looked at the beckoner, and the beckoner, he looked at him. There was silence—broken by the man in the orange rags.

"I shall require my room by Thursday evening next, at six."

He said it, and was gone. Vanished, it seemed, into air. When Horace realised that he indeed had gone he staggered, and fell to his knees, and in that attitude he did what he had not done since he was a little child, he burst into tears,—crying as though his heart would break. His wife's voice roused him, addressing him from behind.

"Horace! is it you? What is the matter? Good heavens, what is wrong?"

Horace rose and faced her, his eyes swollen with weeping. With an effort he stifled his sobs.

"Agnes, Vane Staunton will be here on Thursday evening next, at six."

"Vane Staunton! Horace! are you mad?"

"We shall leave the house, all of us, at once."

"Leave the house! What do you mean?"

"At once! I do not think"—he stood in the attitude of one who listens—"no, not to-night, but"—he listened again—"yes, to-morrow we must go."

"Horace! you are ill!"

Suddenly his manner changed,—from bewilderment to sullen ferocity.

"Don't be a fool. I tell you that by noon to-morrow we must all of us be gone." Suddenly another change,—to bewilderment again. And again it was as though he listened. "That is, you understand, by noon to-day, for it is already nearly four."

Without another word he strode out of the room, leaving her to demand an explanation, if she wished it, from the vacant air. None the less what he said was done. By noon they were all gone—even to the seven in divided skirts. They were in hysterics, and in their dressing-gowns, folks *did* say. And on Thursday evening at six Vane came home. But this time the manner of his return was orthodox, inasmuch as he came in a hansom cab. They were prepared for his return, Mr. Griffin having informed the household he would come. So soon as his hand was on the knocker the door was opened—by the butler's own imperial hands. The butler was a stranger—to Mr. Staunton. So he announced himself.

"I am Mr. Staunton."

"Yes, sir. We are expecting you." Vane moved towards the library. The servants were drawn up in the hall in double lines. Vane passed down the avenue thus formed without paying the slightest heed to any one of them. The butler followed him. At the door of the library the great official paused.

"Dinner, sir, is ordered for eight, if the hour is suitable."

"I never dine," said Vane.

That was the first shock the butler had.

"He looks as though he didn't," said Mr. Reed when he got downstairs, and had amazed the cook—that *cordon bleu*! he had even made Lord Mulligatawny eat, so rumour said—with this astounding answer of their long lost master's. "He looks to me, without meaning anything disrespectful, like a walking suit of bones."

"And dressed all in black! Just like a mute! I never did!" Thus Mrs. Bean, who ruled the maids.

"And did you ever see such a head! It's like my face!" It wasn't, for Emma's face was pretty. But, like her cheek, Vane Staunton's head *was* innocent of hair.

Vane didn't dine—at least that night. The dinner which was meant for him was eaten by the cook—assisted by Mr. Reed and Mrs. Bean. And the cook swore—in French, which made it seem less strange. When Mr. Reed went to Mr. Staunton to get his instructions for the morning,—the returning wanderer having brought no servant of his own,—Vane said that they need not call him, for he never breakfasted.

Mr. Reed stared, but such was his good breeding that, so to speak, it was an inward stare.

"At what time, sir, do you require lunch?"

"I never lunch. In fact, I do not eat at all."

Mr. Reed was on the point of asking if he made up for it in drink, but he refrained.

"Shall I bring you something now, sir? A brandy and soda, sir?"

"Nor do I ever drink."

Mr. Reed was quelled. When he told the tale downstairs his cheeks were pale. And they trembled as they heard. A master who neither ate *nor* drank none of them had *ever* served before.

The thing was known all over town upon the morrow. Horace called, but got no farther than the door. Vane was not on view. Vane's aunt, that ancient Lady Dewsnap, followed hard on Mr. Griffin's heels. Her success was no better than his. The blow was dreadful. He, who had been to her as her own child,—he would not see her! "I don't believe it's Vane at all!" she said. Among the callers only one was admitted, and he was called. Young Walter Tilley found upon his desk an open sheet of paper, on which was scribbled, "Come to me at once in Grosvenor Square.—V. S." Mr. Tilley inquired how the message had arrived. No one appeared to know. It seemed to have been its own bearer through the air. But he obeyed the call, and called. He was closeted with Mr. Staunton an hour and more, looking, when he came out, well, *un peu dérangé*. But to this day no syllable of what transpired at that interview has ever crossed his lips.

It was understood that Vane Staunton was in town. Yet, as the days went, people began to regard the story of his presence as a sort of legend, for he was never seen, until one night. And then the legend took another form.

It was at the Duchess of Datchet's. All the world was there. A knot of men stood talking together. Among them was General Ricketts, now one of the oldest sinners left upon this side. Vane Staunton was the theme.

"I don't believe that he's come back," declared the general. Unbelief was about the only faculty which was left to him, in all its vigour. "I believe it's a put up thing."

"Hollo, there's Griffin," said one of the men.

Horace Griffin came strolling towards them.

"Mr. Griffin," inquired the general, "is it true that your cousin's in town?"

An odd look had been noticed of late on Mr. Griffin's face, almost like a look of fear. It was intensified just then.

"Yes, it is quite true," he said, and moved away without another word.

"I don't believe it," maintained the general stoutly.

"General, how do you do?"

He was obliged to believe it then, for Vane Staunton was standing by his side.

"Staunton! Goodloramighty!" cried the imperfectly bred old man. In a moment it was known throughout the building that Vane Staunton had arrived. "Where have you been all this time?" demanded the general.

"With the Brothers."

"With your brothers? I didn't know you had any. They must be on the wrong side of the blanket if you have." The veteran chuckled. Vane made no reply to this. He stood looking right in front of him, over the heads of the assembled crowd. Even in evening dress he presented a striking figure. So tall, and so phenomenally thin, his long bird-like neck projecting high above his low shirt collar; with his bald head and shaven cheeks and lips and chin, and that singular something on his face and in his eyes, which, even to look at, gave one a premonitory shiver. The general, peering up at him, perceived that his head was bald.

"Hollo! what's become of your hair?"

"The tonsure."

"The tonsure?" The old man stared. The crowd was staring too. A gentleman advanced towards Vane with outstretched hand. It was Colonel Austen.

"Vane, have you forgotten me?"

"Indeed, Philip, I remember you quite well."

"I am glad to see you. It is a dozen years ago, and we feared that you were dead. You look—forgive me if I seem impertinent, but you look as if you had joined some religious order."

"I am a Brother."

"A Brother?"

"But first I was a Mendicant."

"A Mendicant? Not a Buddhist, you don't mean?"

"That is what I mean. A follower of Gautama, who, latest, was a Buddha. Philip,"—he stretched out his hand with a curious gesture towards the colonel,—"I am an Arahat, I soon shall be Asekha, Nirvāna is at hand."

Such words were heard with surprise by the loungers in a London ballroom. The general touched him in the side. The old man was pointing to a woman.

"See her? That's the Countess of Staines, Ermyntrude Bryant that was. But she hasn't given Staines an heir."

Mr. Staunton looked in the direction referred to. There stood a tall, slender woman, with fair hair, and a composed, passionless face,—a face which was indeed almost sexless, so conspicuous was the absence of any species of emotion.

"She was my Great Renunciation," murmured Vane.

"You remember Nora Cathcart? She's skipped over the ropes, and got outside of the enclosure."

"She was my Bo-Tree," answered Vane.

Just at this moment there was a bustle in the crowd. It was the duchess herself, advancing to meet her unexpected guest.

"Mr. Staunton, this is indeed a pleasure." Vane Staunton bowed. "Where have you been this great, long time?"

"In Thibet."

"In Thibet? I should think you had become a Great Llama then by now."

"I have become a Mahatma."

"A Mahatma?"

"Yes, a Mahatma. Permit me to explain to you what is a Mahatma." He bent slightly forward. The duchess was holding a bouquet of flowers in her hand. But it was late in the evening,— their beauty was nearly gone. "Permit me to take your flowers."

"They are faded. I have used them cruelly. It is so hot," she said.

He took the bouquet in one hand. With the fingers of the other he lightly touched the flowers. In an instant their vitality came back to them, their brilliant hues were all restored, their beauty, and, indeed, their fragrance, was regained.

"That is to be a Mahatma."

As he returned to her the bouquet it was more beautiful even than it had been when it left the florist's hands.

"A Mahatma is a conjurer then?"

"He who conjures wisely. Permit me, duchess, to offer you my arm."

She took his arm. Together they advanced across the room.

"I don't know if it is imagination, Mr. Staunton, but as I touch your arm an electric shock seems passing through me. My pulses quicken."

He smiled at her.

"I am explaining, duchess, what is a Mahatma."

"Have you been all these years in Thibet learning how to conjure?"

"Learning to be wise."

"To be wise? But what is that?"

"Nirvāna."

"Nirvāna? I have often heard the word. As you use it, what does it mean?"

"How shall I tell you? How shall I put it into words? Yet I will try. It means extinction—the end of all—to be no more. It is, for me, quite close at hand. It is to attain Nirvāna I am home."

"You are a mystic, I perceive."

"Nay. I am no mystic. There *are* no mysteries for me."

"How lucky to be you! To me the world is full of mystery."

"Your world, not mine."

"Do you, then, live in a different world to me?"

"The same, and yet another."

"How can that be?"

"Why, easily. You live for the world. I live to be out of it. So long as, to you, the world is all, your eyes are blind. So soon as you begin to live to be out of it, then you begin to see. The world has many planes. You are in the depths. I upon the mountain-tops."

"Are you happy there?"

"My eyes can see."

"And you can conjure?"

"Duchess,—see!"

He held out his hand to her. The palm was as a mirror. She looked at it for some moments fixedly; then, with a sigh, she sank senseless to the ground. There was a great commotion. The people gathered round. He waved them back.

"It is nothing."

He stretched out his hand towards her. At the moment of contact her eyes were opened. She rose to her feet.

"Sir," she cried, "make me like you!"

"It is too late."

As Vane Staunton moved away, the duchess burst into tears. The sight of a duchess crying in the middle of her own ballroom is one not commonly seen. And this particular duchess was so popular! The public imagination was moved. Vane Staunton found his passage barred by the duke.

"Mr. Staunton, may I ask you to tell me what has happened?"

"The duchess has seen."

"Seen what?"

"Ah, that you must ask of her."

"Mr. Staunton, will you be so good as to step this way?" The duke led the way into a little room which was on the other side of the gallery. When they were in, his Grace of Datchet closed the door. "Mr. Staunton, you must allow me to say that your conduct is—eh—peculiar. You are here, I believe, without an invitation—which, however, is not of consequence, because, as you are aware, in this house you have always been a welcome guest. But, under the circumstances, I think I am compelled to ask what has passed between the duchess and you."

"The duchess has seen."

"Yes, sir; you said that before. But seen what?"

"That *Your* Grace must inquire of *Her* Grace." Datchet fidgeted. He looked as though he would like to say something, but couldn't quite make up his mind. "I will call the duchess. You will be able to put your inquiry at once."

"Call her! The duchess! Mr. Staunton!"

"See! She comes!"

Datchet stared. Mr. Staunton slightly raised his hand. There was a curious smile upon his face. Suddenly the door was opened, and Her Grace came hurrying in.

"What is it you want?" she asked.

Mr. Staunton turned to her.

"The duke desires to put to you a question."

"To me! A question! Oh, Datchet, don't!"

The duke beheld her with amazement. She, who was so famous for the "grand manner," united to that air of rare good nature without which we have not the real *grande dame*, was trembling with excitement, almost, it would seem, tortured by acute distress.

"I wish Your Grace good-night." Vane Staunton bowed.

"Mr. Staunton! Stay!"

"I will not stay."

The duke moved as if to bar his progress. On a sudden he stopped short, as if struck by a paralytic stroke. Mr. Staunton passed from the room without a word. When he was gone the duke turned to his wife with a startled air.

"Helen, what has taken place between that man and you?"

"Datchet, do not ask me!"

"But I must. Are you mad? There will be a scandal! Your behaviour will be the talk of all the town!" He advanced to her in anger. "Helen, tell me what has happened."

"If you insist upon my telling you, I will." She looked at him with a face of agony. "He has shown me what I am going to be!" To the duke's amazement, falling on her knees, she flung her arms about his waist and cried, "Oh, Datchet, do not let it come."

Of course, no one told the tale, yet it leaked out none the less. They always do, these sorts of tales. And the version which percolates is improved by percolation. They knew all about the scene between the duke and duchess. They could tell you, even to the

dotted i's, what words were said. As for Staunton, he had hypno-
tised the woman, that was plain. No wonder Datchet didn't like
it. Hypnotism is getting too much the rage; for married men it's
worse than the confessional. Besides, there was something between
them before Vane went away. In those days a good six inches of
the future duchess's black stockinged legs were visible beneath her
skirts. But what of that? We know the sort of lies which are told of
all good women in their turn.

But it was certain that Vane Staunton's fame filled all the air.
He had said, in the hearing of quite a crowd, that he had become a
Brother. First of all he had been a Mendicant, and had then become
a Brother. In Thibet too! Why, Madame Blavatsky was avenged,
and the colonel and Mr. Sinnett and all that faithful crowd. Or,—
was it all a tarradiddle? And this man a diddler too?

It has been aptly said that there are some people so constituted
that they will not believe in the impossible, even if you prove
it. Which is strange, yet true. So when it was known that Mr.
Staunton had openly declared that he had been to that monastic
haven in Thibet, and run up the chromatic scale, and become a
fully fledged Mahatma, the people who *knew* that that monastery
was where Alice went, Through the Looking-Glass, said, Another
outrage upon Common Sense,—he lies! Regular siege was laid to
the house in Grosvenor Square. The Theosophists camped on the
doorstep,—or would have done, if the policeman had not moved
them on. Letters were brought by an "extra" postman, specially
laid on, in sacks. But no one obtained a glimpse of the Mahatma
inside, nor is it known that among all that great multitude of letters a single one was read,—to put the question of being answered
entirely aside. Instructions had been given, it was understood, the
butler being the informant, to burn them as they came. To think
of that! How these later prophets do ill-use the world.

Other interesting scraps leaked out,—through the servants'
mouths, of course,—*they* were sociable enough. Mr. Staunton had
never had a meal served to him since he had been inside the house.
He had never once set foot outside the door; even on the night
of the duchess's party no one had seen him go. Once a day he
showed himself to Mr. Reed, and that was all that was seen of him
inside the house. He never slept inside a bed,—he never slept at all

for anything anyone could tell. He remained in his study day and night, and nobody had been inside that study door since the day he came. Yet, if the servants were to be believed, he *had* visitors at times. The sound of talking had been heard, sometimes of several speakers at a time. The voices were strange to them, and the tongue in which they spoke was strange as well. Whence did they come, these visitors? And why? And how?

Good-natured friends strongly recommended Mr. Griffin to apply for a writ *de lunatico*; or at least to insist on two medical men being sent to inquire into his cousin's state of mind. But to these recommendations Mr. Griffin not only turned a deaf ear, he even ran from them. At the dawn of the season he dragged his family out of town. They were known to have taken refuge in some obscure hole upon the Cornish coast. To those who knew Mr. Griffin, and who were acquainted with his creed that "dogged does it," this conduct on his part but made the wonder more. *What* was there wrong? Was it really Vane Staunton who had returned to life? Or was it, after all, only an impostor, through whose connivance Horace hoped to lay his hand on the estates?

In the midst of all these cross questions and crooked answers were issued the invitations for the famous dinner. When old Ricketts opened his, which he found waiting for him at the club, he almost swallowed his teeth in his surprise.

"Good-g-goodloramighty!" he stuttered. "W-will someone m-make out this for me?"

Someone did. In fact, a dozen did, and in less than no time. It purported to be an intimation of Mr. Staunton's desire to have General Ricketts's company at dinner in his house at Grosvenor Square, on the 5th of June, at half-past eight o'clock.

"But I—I t-thought he never dined," the general stammered.

"Perhaps it's a hoax," said someone standing by.

Just then Philip Austen entered the room. The veteran thrust towards him the card of invitation.

"Austen, look at that!"

The colonel did as he was told.

"I have a similar one myself," was the observation which he made.

"Is it a hoax?"

"Why should it be? It seems to me that it is the most natural thing that Vane could do. Possibly he intends it, in a sort of a way, to inaugurate his reappearance in the world,—as a hint that he intends to come among us in earnest again at last."

That was one way of looking at it. If it was the correct one, then the scheme on which the invitations appeared to have been planned was possibly on the whole a wise one. Certainly a heterogeneous gathering had been invited to assemble round the social board. The Duke of Datchet had an invitation. At first he was disposed to decline to accept it, but afterwards he changed his mind, and did. Hugh Sinclair had another. He had nursed Vane Staunton through the whooping-cough and chicken-pox, and was famous, in these later days, for being in the forefront of the medical phalanx which scoffed at the things which were strange, and new—to them. He was an "ancient" who declined, on principle, to accept the impossible, even though you proved it true. Walter Tilley had a card. Without hesitation he expressed his willingness to dine. When he was despatching his letter of acceptance he said to Mr. Baynes, in such a way that that gentleman could not make out if his words were meant for jest or earnest—

"I shall make my will before I go."

Mr. Baynes looked at the senior partner keenly. He would have liked to have asked a question,—but he didn't. He had, however, reason to believe that the will was made.

Another person who received a card was Horace Griffin. When at the breakfast-table, in his Fowey hermitage, he opened the envelope, and found what it contained, in the presence of his wife, and of the seven in divided skirts, he turned a "ghastly pale."

"What's the matter?" inquired Mrs. G.

"Nothing." Even as he said it his hands were trembling.

"Don't talk such stuff! I insist upon your telling me! Horace, why are all these mysteries?"

"If you must know what it is," rejoined her lord a little grimly, "it's an invitation from Vane to dine."

"Is that all? What is there to make a fuss about in that?"

Mr. Griffin rose from the table.

"Agnes," he said, in words which must, by this time, in a marital sense, be classical, "you're a fool."

And he went out. He was not addicted to pedestrianism as a rule, yet, on that occasion, he then and there took a twenty-mile walk, ten good miles out, ten good miles in. And all the way he told himself that he would not go—he would not go! He would not go to see that devil! "Devil" was the word he used. Yet, that same night he wrote a letter of acceptance, writhing as he wrote, and when he had written it, he sent it. And, daily, until the 5th of June, he faded visibly, before the naked eye, at the rate of quite two pounds a day. One might have thought that it was not dinner he was looking forward to, but execution.

In striking contrast to a well-known leading case, every man who received an invitation to that feast agreed to come, and, what is more, he came. It was not the dinner which was the attraction. Indeed, it was a matter of common notoriety that more than one of the invited guests had expressed a doubt as to whether there would be anything off which to dine. Mr. James G. Ruddock, the latest importation from New York, who, for some occult reason, had received a card among the rest, went so far as to call at the house on the morning of the day, and inquire of Mr. Reed as to whether any food was likely to be had. If there wasn't going to be anything to eat, he said, he would have his dinner before he came. But on this head the butler made his mind quite easy. A gorgeous feast had been commanded. The cook had been instructed to provide such a banquet as had never been surpassed, and which, in fact, should be unsurpassable. These tidings of great joy Mr. James G. Ruddock diffused around, and gentlemen were at least assured that it would be unnecessary to have their dinners before they went to dine.

The guests were punctual. As the hour of half-past eight approached a constant succession of cabs and carriages drove up to the house in Grosvenor Square. Their number was, indeed, surprising. It almost seemed as if a public banquet was being given within, and not a mere private dinner. One little incident took place. Two hansoms drove up almost at the same moment. Out of each of them a gentleman stepped. The one was Mr. Tilley, the other Mr. Griffin. Mr. Tilley stopped at sight of Mr. Griffin.

"Mr. Griffin! You don't look well."

"Well?—No!—I'm ill." Clutching the lawyer's arm he pointed

to the house in front of them. Mr. Tilley felt that the hand which held him trembled. "God help us when we get in there!"

The lawyer stared.

"I'm all right!" he laughed. "I've made my will."

Then they both of them went in to dine.

II

"GENTLEMEN, I am afraid that some of you perhaps think that I am mad."

They were waiting for dinner to be announced. Their host's remark was scarcely apposite.

"Not mad," murmured Jack Haines, who is one of those men who never can be serious, "but gone before."

Mr. Staunton paid no heed to him.

"I have asked you here to dine, and, after dinner, to say good-bye. You know I never eat." This was an encouraging remark for a host to make to a crowd of hungry men! "But there are some of you who are still the bond-slaves of your bodies."

He paused, and they were still. What could they say to a host who, while they waited and longed for dinner, talked seriously of their being the bond-slaves of their bodies? There were some who asked themselves, Why, before they ventured forth, had they not dined? Vane, leaning against the mantel-board, looked at his assembled guests with curious, smiling eyes.

"One other word I have to say to you, and it is this: I have attained to wisdom. I have acquired powers which will to you seem strange. For you, who think that you know all things, are indeed most ignorant. You are not even acquainted with the paths which, being assiduously pursued, will lead to the alphabet of knowledge. For me, the lesson has been hard and long, but now that it is learned Nirvāna is at hand. But before THAT comes, per-mission I have gained to show you certain of the things which may be learned, so that some of you, perhaps fired by example, may tell the tale abroad, seeking for yourselves THE PATH."

Was ever dinner-party prefaced by such words before? They looked at each other, telling themselves that it was evident the man was mad. But before they could proclaim the discovery in articulate language the welcome announcement was made that dinner was served. Mr. Staunton led the way across the hall. Then they halted in a crowd, and that for the sufficient reason that the room which he had entered was in pitch darkness.

"Enter! I will light it with my hand!"

It was his voice calling from within. They entered. There was Mr. Staunton standing in the centre of the room. He had his right hand raised, and from his hand there proceeded a pure white light of such effulgency that it dazzled all their eyes.

"What!" he said, on perceiving that at sight of this spectacle they had halted again. "Will you not dine by the light of my hand? Well, let it be!"

A huge candelabra was suspended from the ceiling. He touched each candle with his fingertip, and as each wick came into contact with his finger it at once sprang into flame.

"Dinner," he said, "will now be served."

They thought, perhaps, that it was time. But the peculiarity of the situation consisted in this, that there was nothing in the room, not even a table or a chair. Vane, moving from the centre of the room, slightly raised his head.

"Dinner."

That was the only word he uttered, but in an instant there was a massive table laid as for a feast, with spotless napery, adorned with flowers, with many servants standing round.

"I beg that you will take your seats!"

They took their seats. It was plain that they had come to dine! As they seated themselves Hugh Sinclair spoke.

"Vane, if this is an elaborate conjuring performance which you have prepared for our amusement, I hope that you will postpone further items of the programme till we have something solid in our insides."

Vane Staunton shook his head.

"Ah, doctor, but the time is short!" He turned to Mr. Reed. "Reed, we are ready." Then to his guests. "You need not fear that the service will be bad. The servants are under influence. They will not evince surprise."

"I wish I were under influence," whispered Jack to his next-door neighbour. "My appetite has gone already."

"But, Jack, it will return again." Vane spoke as though the other's words had been said aloud. Mr. Haines noticed this at once.

"You appear to have good hearing, Vane."

"Yes, I have good hearing. I can hear a whisper at a distance of a hundred thousand miles."

They were silent. None of them were prepared, at that early stage of the feast, to call their host a liar. The soup was served. Most of them did justice to it, but already, as Jack had said, one or two of their appetites had gone. Vane took nothing. He sat with his elbows resting on the table, his cheek resting on his hand.

"So you think, Sinclair, that I'm a conjurer?"

"I'm sure of it," replied the doctor. It was plain that he enjoyed his soup. Suddenly it was seen that at the end of each of Mr. Staunton's fingers was a little globe of fire. He advanced his hand towards Sinclair.

"See, doctor, electricity is life."

"Tell that to the marines!" The doctor gulped down his soup. "Or, better still, to Maskelyne and Cooke."

"Doctor, hold out your hand, or, stay, your nose will serve."

Mr. Staunton advanced his hand in the direction of the doctor's face. Immediately the five little balls of fire were transferred from his finger-tips, and ornamented the Æsculapian nose. The effect was comical,—you will see it produced by ventriloquists upon their talking figures if you choose to go and see. Hugh Sinclair sprang up in a rage. He tried to brush the shining globules off his nose.

"Confound it, Vane, what hankey-pankey trick is this?"

"It is an illustration of the volatility of electricity. Do you know, doctor, that if I chose to say the word those five small sparks would remain where they now are until you are what you understand by dead. But I see you do not like them, Hugh, so they shall come away at once instead."

He made a little movement of his hand,—the balls of light were gone. The doctor sat down to table with a ruffled air.

"I don't call it good form, Mr. Staunton, to play tricks with a man when you ask him to your house to dine."

Vane Staunton smiled.

"No, Hugh, I'm afraid I am not good form.—Reed, bring in the fish."

The soup plates were removed. Presently a dozen servants entered, bearing a huge glass tank which they placed upon the table. The tank was full of water. In the water there were fish. They proved that they were alive by swimming about merrily in all directions. The guests stared with wondering eyes at this novel method of serving up a second course. Jack Haines was frivolous.

"This is to be a feast of Barmecides, it seems."

"Nay, Jack, not so. Tell me, Jack, what is the fish, and what is the manner of its cooking, you would like."

"Grilled trout," said Jack.

Mr. Staunton waved his hand. There was a commotion in the tank. A fish leaped into the air. There was distinctly heard the sound of frizzling. Jack stared,—there was a grilled trout upon his plate.

"Might I venture to say encore?" said Jack.

"General, what may I offer you?"

"*Goujons à la caramel,*" rejoined the veteran. "I only had the dish once in my life, and that was at Amboise on the Loire."

"Then you shall have it for a second time to-night."

The experiment this time was quite a pretty one. A dozen little fish leaped out at once. One could see them going through some strange performance, with lightning-like rapidity, in mid-air. Old Ricketts dropped his pince-nez in his excitement,—and there were *goujons à la caramel* upon his plate.

"Now, duke, for you?"

The Duke of Datchet said that he would have sardines, just taken fresh out of the sea, and done upon hot coals,—and, behold, they were. Hugh Sinclair desired salmon cutlets. And then there was a sight! A kingly fish sprang into air, they saw him dismembered before their eyes—"Alas, poor Yorick!"—and in a trice the doctor had salmon cutlets, smoking hot, enough to feast a king. James G. Ruddock wished for buttered crab, with oyster sauce, and that he had. Those guests desired every kind of fish, cooked in every kind of way, and their wants were all supplied. Then the tank was removed the way it came.

"You do this sort of thing uncommonly well," admitted Jack, whose appetite had returned in sufficient force to enable him to eat his fish.

"The only question," said the doctor drily, "is how it's done."

"And yet it is the simplest thing!" This came from Vane.

"I do not doubt it,—I never did." The doctor was drier even than before. "All locks are simple, if the wards are oiled and you hold the key. There is no mystery in life and death. Shall I prove it to you? If you desire it I will. I have but to move my hand and you will all be what you understand as dead, and, being dead, I will bring you back to life again. What should you say if I were to slay you all with a movement of my hand?"

A cheerful question to be addressed by a host unto his guests! And they had come to dine. The Duke of Datchet took it upon himself to answer him.

"Excuse me, Mr. Staunton, but you frame your conversation on rather sombre lines. It has always been a maxim of mine that at the dinner-table the conversation should be light, so as to assist digestion."

"But what would you say, duke, if I were to slay you with a movement of my hand?"

"What should I say, sir! Why, good—good heavens! I—I should say nothing at all."

"I should say, why, here's my shooter!"

"Where?"

Mr. Ruddock's hand was travelling towards the pistol pocket in his trousers. But as Vane Staunton uttered his monosyllabic inquiry, it stayed.

"Well, it's in my pocket somewhere, but, in the meanwhile, there's something happened to my hand. It seems kind of stiff. I guess I've got the cramp."

"Yes, Mr. Ruddock, and now something is about to happen to you." Vane's arm shot out towards James G. Ruddock, as a boxer "let's drive" straight from the shoulder. "See, gentlemen, the man is dead."

That something very curious had happened to him was plain. Mr. Ruddock appeared to have been turned into a statue. His right hand appeared to have been paralysed as it was travelling towards his pistol pocket. In his left he held a fork. On the fork there was some fish. Hand and fork and fish were poised half-way between plate and mouth. Colonel Austen was sitting next to the "petrified American." He rose from his seat.

"Vane! What are you doing? Don't you think you may carry a trick too far?"

"A trick! You think it is a trick? Colonel Austen, hit Mr. Ruddock a crack on the head."

"A crack on the head?"

"Yes, with a decanter."

"With a decanter?"

Mr. Staunton had been speaking lightly. Now his voice assumed a "sweet severity,"—we have seen it written so.

"Colonel Austen, hit Mr. Ruddock a crack on the head with a decanter. Hit him with all your might."

Colonel Austen snatched up a heavy cut glass decanter which was in front of him. It was full of wine. Raising it above his head he gripped the neck with both his hands. Taking careful aim he brought it down with all his strength upon his neighbour's head. The decanter was shivered into fragments, Mr. Ruddock was laid upon the floor.

The "experienced novel reader" need not be told that this little performance of the colonel's occasioned surprise. Fragments of glass had been scattered in all directions, and so had the wine. And so, one might be disposed to lay "odds on," had been "samples" of the "gentleman's" brains. The room was in an uproar. Colonel Austen stood like a man in a dream, surveying the mischief he had done. Everyone knows that a kinder heart than his never beat in a brave man's bosom.

"You have killed him!" cried the duke. He seemed aghast.

"It's that devil!" Horace Griffin, standing up, pointed at his cousin down the table. "I knew there would be murder done."

Colonel Austen knelt beside the injured man.

"My God! He's dead! Staunton, if I've killed him I'll take your life for his! What is it I have done?"

Vane Staunton amidst all the tumult sat smiling in his seat, appearing not the least disturbed.

"My dear Philip, it is nothing! I only wish to show to you that it was not a trick. With Mr. Ruddock there is nothing wrong. See here!" Raising his hand he made some movements in the air. They watched him. "Philip, lift Mr. Ruddock up, and put him back upon his chair."

"I will not touch him."

"Obey me, Philip."

Again the change from lightness to that "sweet severity." Instantly the colonel put his long arms about the fallen man, and, lifting him with care, seated him again upon the chair.

"See, I said that there was nothing wrong."

Vane made another movement with his hand. Mr. Ruddock still had his fork in his hand, though the morsel of fish had vanished from the prong. He advanced it towards his plate,—this time the selected morsel had a safe passage towards his jaws.

"This is what I call a buttered crab," he said.

"I'm glad you like it," answered Vane.

"My God!" the colonel cried. "Mr. Ruddock! I hope I haven't smashed your head!"

"My head?" Mr. Ruddock looked up at him with inquiry in his eyes.

"With the decanter!"

"The decanter?"

Vane interposed.

"The decanter is in front of you, dear Philip. Fill yourself a glass of wine."

The colonel looked. There, in front of him, upon the table, was the veritable decanter he had smashed—and that upon his neighbour's head!—who now talked of buttered crab!—and it was full of wine! Beyond doubt a certain impression was created. Hugh Sinclair gave expression to it,—in his own peculiar way.

"Mr. Staunton, if you had invited us to witness an exhibition of the latest things in conjuring, we should have been prepared for the worst, but you invited us to dine. You may be a complete professor of hankey-pankey, but let me tell you that your behaviour this evening has not been what I understand as the behaviour of an English gentleman. I wish you, sir, good-night. I will never, willingly, take bite or sup again within your house."

"Doctor, eat what you have upon your plate."

"Sir!" Mr. Staunton waved his hand. The doctor had already moved from the table, with the apparent intention of making a "bee line" for the door. But at that mystic signal he resumed his seat with comical alacrity, and began cramming the contents of his plate into his mouth with a haste which was not only indecorous but absurd. "Confound you!" he cried, when the last scrap was bolted. He rose in a rage. But again Vane Staunton waved his hand.

"Doctor, just one word! Will you not bear with me a while?—I have so soon to go. You belong to that great multitude who say that there can be no new thing. Oh that foolish falsehood of the Western World! Though one rose from those whom you call dead you still would not believe that there are, let us say, forces in nature, whose very beginnings you do not understand."

"Mr. Staunton, I perceive that in your wanderings you have acquired the current slang of the day. You may have to an unusual extent what I believe nowadays is called the hypnotic power"—

"Is this an instance of hypnotic power?"

Vane Staunton was seated in the host's place at the head of the table. All their eyes were fixed upon him. In the full glare of the many lights, as he spoke, he was gone. There was his vacant chair.

"Gentlemen, which of you is Dr. Sinclair?"

Before anyone could inquire into the cause of Mr. Staunton's disappearance, this question was addressed to the company at large. With one accord all glances were turned in the questioner's direction.

Within a foot or two of where the host had just been seated stood a gentleman, who had certainly not been there a moment back. In stature he was above the average height, and he was broadly built. He was dressed as though he had just come from a journey. Under his arm was a case of polished wood, and he carried his hat in his hand. His costume was such as we know was worn by fine gentlemen in the first decade of the present century, whenever they chanced to journey far abroad. He repeated his inquiry.

"Gentlemen, which of you is Dr. Sinclair?" There was silence. "Perhaps it would be as well that I should present the company with my credentials." His manner was haughty, and a trifle stern. "I come, as one who has risen from what you call the dead, to bring you a message from the grave. I am John Winstanley."

"Permit me, Dr. Sinclair," interposed Philip Austen, "to say just one word.—Mr. Winstanley, I am Colonel Austen."

"Any relation to Denzil Austen, of Penshurst Priory?"

"He was my grandfather, sir."

"And my dearest friend. I left him not a minute ago."

"You left him not a minute ago! My grandfather has been dead these seventy years."

"Exactly,—that is what I say. I left him not a minute ago."

The colonel was still. Apparently he was trying to resolve a problem. The stranger smiled,—a curious, an enigmatic smile.

"Do you doubt, Colonel Austen, that I am dead?"

"I doubt it, sir." Mr. Winstanley turned. It was the doctor speaking. "In fact, I have no doubt upon that point at all. Go back to your confederate, who pays you for your services, and tell him that all his trickeries are thrown away on me."

"Do you doubt that I am dead?"

"Doubt, man! Do you take me for a fool?"

"Look at me now."

The doctor looked. In fact, so did they all. There was silence. The stranger stood at the head of the table, in the full glare of the lights, with his face turned towards the company. And, as he stood, a strange thing happened to him before their eyes. He, in some subtle way, had changed. The light had gone from his eyes; the colour from his cheeks; the sheen from his clothes; the polish from the box which was beneath his arm; the gloss from his boots, reaching to his thighs; the radiance from the sword which dangled at his side; his very hat and gloves, all at once, looked old.

"What think you now?"

Even his voice seemed changed. It seemed weak and worn and thin.

"Look at me still!"

They did not need his bidding. They never took their eyes away. As if fascinated, they all glared at him with one accord. He had changed again. His face had thinned, the bones peeped through his skin, his eyes were sunken, his jaw had fallen. His coat was shabby, it hung upon his attenuated frame as though it had been fashioned for a larger man. There was an indescribable look of age about his boots and hat and gloves, about his whole attire. The wood of the box beneath his arm had cracked, the thing looked musty, there was rust upon his sword.

"Now do I look dead?"

His voice was hollow. It sounded as though, borne on the winds, it had travelled from afar.

"You sound as though you were," said Jack.

"Look at me still!"

The flesh had vanished from his facial bones, the skin hung loose, his eyes were gone. His hands, just now so big and white and strong, were like two horrid claws, of a rank saffron hue. It seemed that his huge frame was fleshless; his clothes hung on him as you see them dangle on a scarecrow. They were all in rags. Huge rents were here and there, and through them peeped something white. His ancient boots stood up of their own accord about his shrivelled legs, as if to mock the man who fitted them. His hat was all in ruins, his gloves were relics. His sword was iron red with rust, you could see that the rust was eating the sheath away. The box beneath his arm was all in pieces; and a dry, earthy smell was in the room, such as you will detect if you put your nose into some long closed catacomb.

"Look at me still!"

The clothes were gone, except that here and there a tattered fragment of cloth seemed still to cling, a skeleton stood bare. As an example of articulation it might have been the pride of Mr. Venus, but in that place, crowning that festive board, it looked a trifle strange. Men's faces paled. Mr. Griffin began to cry. And as all that brilliant crowd of honoured guests leaned over the banqueting board, straining their eyes to see this thing, from the breast of many a one there came a sound which you might interpret to your fancy either as a sob or as a groan.

"Look at me still!" It was as though a voice spoke to them from the grave. "Do I look dead?"

Did he look dead? The mockery! There was a slight noise, the skeleton had gone, a little heap of bones lay on the floor. Each bone had parted from its fellows, only the head bones still were joined. The skull lay on its back. The gaping jaws, being upwards, seemed to grin. A strange object lay among the bones, which might have been a sword. There was a scrap or two of wood and two queer-looking things, which perhaps were pistols, of some antique pattern, once upon a time.

"Look at me still! Do I look dead?"

The voice seemed to issue from the grinning jaws. It was a horrid sound. As they heard it men caught at each other's arms, straining themselves to see. The bones were gone. Here and there little patches of what seemed dust obscured the pattern of Vane Staunton's carpet.

"Look at me still!"

The voice came from afar. Even the dust had gone. Nothing hid the carpet now.

There was silence. None seemed to care to move. Until someone, clutching a decanter, and filling a tumbler with the contents, drained the bumper at a draught. It was Mr. Ruddock. Then someone began to stagger from his place. It was Jack Haines.

"Let me get out of this before I go stark mad."

"Gentlemen, be seated, pray. I hope I have not kept you long."

They looked. There was Vane Staunton seated in his chair. But was it Vane? It surely was. Yet in what a garb! He was clad in what seemed a haphazard arrangement of yellow rags, which had been blown together, rather than sewn. They were none too clean, and his right shoulder was bare. It seemed that he was nearly naked, in such higgle-piggledy fashion, it appeared to them, was his disarray of rags put on. He was not a pleasing sight to look upon, with his shaven head and hairless face, and too prominent body, which was nothing else but skin and bones.

Yet they were compelled to look at him. There was something in his voice which lured them. And in his bearing there was a strange excitement, the meaning of which, as yet, they did not understand.

"Hugh!" He stretched out his arm to Sinclair. "Is it all a trick?" The doctor put his hand up to his face, as though he strove to shade his eyes. Vane addressed the company at large. "I told you that after dinner I should have to say good-bye. But I fear that you have badly dined. Finish the feast when I am gone. It is coming sooner than I thought it was. Nay, do not veil your eyes!" For some of them, following the doctor's example, were covering their faces with their hands. "Watch your old friend. For there is that within me which consumes. Nirvāna is at hand."

Suddenly he rose to his feet. His tall, thin figure, which seemed to them as though it were more than half unclothed, in its clothing of yellow rags, towered above them all. He held out his hands in front of him. Supplication was in his voice.

"Oh, seek THE PATH!"

And then he flung his hands above his head, crying, with a wild ecstasy of gladness, which made all their hearts seem out of tune—

"Nirvāna! Nirvāna!"

And then his arms fell to his sides, and his voice was soft and low.

"Good-bye!" he said. "Good-bye!" And then he stretched out his hands, in the attitude of one who bids his friends adieu. "Good-bye!"

As the word still trembled on his tongue, and as he still stood there, with his arms stretched out, the room was filled with an overpowering burst of light. It came from Staunton's person. For, as they gazed at him, amazed and speechless, a vivid flash burst from his breast, which was brighter than any flame which they had ever seen before. In an instant, and for an instant, they saw him standing, all bright with flame.

But only for an instant. The flame went as quickly as it came. And with it went their host. He had vanished as he was bidding them good-bye.

THE MATCH OF THE SEASON

IT was beastly weather. It had been raining, pretty well without cessation, for, I should say, quite three weeks on end. It was raining then; coming down in regular bucketfuls. And the ground! You should have seen the ground! Put one foot down, and lean all your weight on it for sixty seconds, and you wanted two strong men to pull you out again. But, you know, I don't call that a bad state of the ground for football—not for Rugby Union. Nobody minds a little mud; some men like it. Heavy forwards, for instance. The year the Pantaloons carried all before them—only lost one match—they owed it all to the mud. That was before the passing game came in. They had a lot of heavy men in front, regular weight-carriers. When they formed the scrummages—and they managed that there should be nothing else but scrummages—and they had their feet well planted in the mud, you couldn't move them. Upon my word, you couldn't. You might as well have run your head against the Monument. Even at the worst, mud *is* soft falling. When there's a frost, and you come down—you do come down. You're in luck if you don't get up in pieces.

I didn't play this year; it was a disappointment, I can tell you. Early in the season I had a bad eye. Poulter gave it me—in the Engineer match. The ball was near their goal. I stooped to pick it up. Somehow I tripped. Of course, Poulter didn't know what I was going to be up to. He kicked at the ball, and instead of the ball he kicked my eye. I was a sight! And then, hardly was I able to show again when, in the match with the St. Galen's men, Thistlethwaite, a great giant, over six feet high, picked me up when I was running, and pitched me on my head against one of the iron posts on which we hang the rope to enclose the ground. Of course he didn't mean it, but I thought that game had seen the last of me. It was all I could do, a month afterwards, to toddle down to the ground to

see the match with Biddleham. Play, worse luck, was out of the
question. My brother didn't play either. Miss Blake objected. She
used to be awfully fond of the game before she became engaged
to him, but since that event she seems to have cooled off a bit. She
says that when a man is going to be married she thinks he ought to
stop that kind of thing. There's something in it. Jack Hill, two days
before his marriage, got compound fracture in both his legs. It was
to be his last match—and it was. But the wedding was postponed.

I don't suppose there were more than five hundred people
there, all told. The weather kept them away. I've seen over ten
thousand on a sunny afternoon. But it isn't everybody who cares
to stand for a couple of hours in a shower bath, out in the open, in
the middle of January. They missed something, though, those who
didn't go. I never saw a better game of the kind. There wasn't any
science; when it was as much as a man could do to keep on his feet,
there couldn't be. And as for passing! When the ball is as heavy as
lead, and so greasy that you can't keep hold of it, you try what
passing comes to then. But there was pluck. Talk about "mimic
warfare"—there was precious little "mimic" about the "warfare"
there.

The Biddleham men kicked off. Ricketts, their captain, sent a
long rocketter flying into touch well inside our twenty-five. The
ball was dry, and it was about as good a kick as there was that
afternoon. But Gilkes, our right three-quarters, was on the ball. He
ran it down about a dozen yards, then punted it well back again.
One of their three-quarters had it, but muffed it rather, and was
downed. His was the first baptism of mud. Burrowes got behind
him, dropped him on to his face, and just fell down on the top of
him. You might have made a plaster cast of his figure in the place
on which he fell. I could see from the expression of his face—that
is, from what there was of it to be seen—that he didn't like it. He
seemed to think that Burrowes needn't have fallen all his length on
top of him. That was balderdash. But there are some men like that,
you know. I remember myself once, when I was playing against
the Finches—the Fulham Finches; the club is extinct now; they say,
as a joke, that the members all got killed—I knocked a man's two
front teeth right down his throat. He turned quite nasty. However,
I did hear afterwards that he also belonged to the engaged brigade;

and, no doubt, a man doesn't like to go toothless to meet his bride. Still, he ought to keep his temper, especially in the middle of a game.

Nowadays loose play is all the rage. I remember when they used to pack a scrummage, and keep it packed. Now the game is, directly a scrummage is formed, to break it up again. But that style of play don't pay always. Directly Burrowes had downed their man, a scrummage was formed.

"Play loosely! Play loosely!" cried Staines, our captain.

They did play loosely. The consequence was that they all fell flat, face foremost, in the mud. Before they were up, Staines was off with the ball. He passed the halves; the forwards were still making inquiries into the constitution of top soils. Then that man whom Burrowes had downed got hold of him. He must have been a vicious sort of chap. He ran at Staines just like a bull, sent him flying backwards, and fell bang on top of him. I thought the ball had burst, not to mention Staines. When the scrummage formed again he didn't say much about loose play. He seemed to want his breath to cool his porridge.

"Go it, Biddleham!" cried a man who stood by me. "You've got them now. Loose! Loose! Let them have another taste of their noses; then you'll be able to carry the ball right through."

That is the way in which some people talk at football matches. If I hadn't taken it for granted that he had paid his money at the gate, I should have asked him to leave the ground. But I could see at a glance that in the scrummages the Biddleham forwards were more effective than ours on ground like that. They were a heavy lot of men, and very fond of falling; and every time they fell they took care that our men were underneath to fall upon. It might not have been intentional, but it did look odd, for no man likes to be *always* fallen on, especially by a lot of fellows each of whom would turn the scale at a good twelve stone. I suppose they must have fallen on our fellows quite half a dozen times before the ball was brought into play again. Then they took it through with a rush, leaving our chaps staggering about as though they were stuck in the mud. Over went our halves like ninepins, and I thought they were going to take it right behind. But they let it get a little bit too far in front of them, and Gilkes had hold of it, and was off like a flash. He is a flyer—Gilkes. He ran through their forwards, and cannoned into Ricketts, letting him have the ball in the face—which, I should say by the look of it—the ball, I mean, not the face—was already beginning to weigh about a ton. Down sat Ricketts to think it over. But, before he began to think it over, he stretched out his arm and caught hold of Gilkes by the leg. And down went Gilkes. Possibly the ball was too greasy for anyone to get firm hold of it. Anyhow, when Gilkes went down, the ball went off in front of him. Crookshanks, their left three-quarters, got hold of it, and tried to pass to Knight, their centre. But by this time a lot of our men were up, and they sat down on Knight in a heap. This was hard on the beggar, for he had muffed the ball, and it had gone behind him. Their back had picked it up; and, while our men were still sitting upon Knight, he punted it into touch.

From the throw-out another scrummage was formed.

"Pack the scrummage!" I cried. "Don't let them rush it through."

But it was plain that in six inches of mud the Biddleham men were better than us at scrummages. Our men went in gamely, and they pushed. There is a lot of art in scrummaging. Watch an old hand, and see how he sticks to the ball, never letting it get six inches from his feet. I've seen a man screw through a scrummage single-handed. But to show that kind of skill there are two things needed. You want ground on which you can get some kind of a footing, and you don't want *all* the weight to be upon the other side. Those Biddleham men played a game of their own, and it was not a game which I should call good form. They gave way, judiciously, at unexpected moments, and our men fell down, and then, if the ball was underneath, they fell on top of them. You hadn't time to sing out "Man down!" before the Biddleham fellows were burying them in the mud. It was all very well to say it was accident, but after the first dozen accidents of that sort our men got wild. They lost their heads. They went in anyhow, having had about as much mud down their throats as they cared to swallow. And so the Biddleham men, who by that time had hustled the leather right down the field, rushed the ball clean through. Staines fell on it, or tried to; but, somehow, he just managed to miss it, and all he got was the mud. What made it worse was that one of their forwards, thinking that he hadn't got the mud, but the leather, plumped on top of him. I could see that Staines didn't like it at all. But it was no good saying anything, for Parker, our left three-quarters, had got the ball and tried to pass, and had passed to one of their men instead of to one of ours. And off went the Biddleham man like a bull of Bashan. You should have heard them screech! Before the ball was held he was within twelve yards of the goal line.

"Go it, Biddleham!" cried the man who had stood by me, and who had made himself obnoxious before. "One good shove, all together, and you're in."

And they were in, all in a heap, and the ball at the bottom. They didn't wait for our men to come up so that the scrummage might be properly formed, but rushed it in like blazes. And the touch was scored. Didn't they bellow! But one thing was certain, their men couldn't score a goal; they had touched-down close to the boundary. The man who could kick a goal at that distance against the wind, in a pouring rain, with the ground like a bog, and the ball as heavy as lead, has yet to be born. However, Ricketts had a try at it; but he got as near to the goal as he got to the moon.

"Play up, Biddleham!" I cried.

"They'll have to do a lot of playing first," said the man, who was still sticking himself beside me.

Of course I said nothing. A man who could make to a perfect stranger gratuitous remarks like that is a sort of man I never could get fond of.

Staines was on the ball before it had even got behind. He tried a drop. He might as well have tried to drop his head. The thing was waterlogged. From where I stood I could hear it squash as it touched his foot. It was an awful failure. The Biddleham forwards were down on him like a cartload of bricks. Then things grew lively. I couldn't follow the details, but, so far as I could judge, a faction fight wasn't halfway near it. Men were going down all over the place—singly, and in heaps. Scrummages were formed only to go to pieces. It was a regular riot. Suddenly someone broke away. It was Gilkes, with the leather tucked under his arm. Staines was after him, and so was Parker. Then we saw the first bit of play we had seen that afternoon. They closed on Gilkes, who passed to Staines, who passed to Parker. It was a beautiful bit of passing. Parker ran off to the left; Staines tripped in the mud. But Gilkes backed up in style. One of their three-quarters collared Parker, but not before he had passed again to Gilkes, who took it as well as ever I saw him take it yet. And there was nothing but the Biddleham back between Gilkes and the Biddleham goal.

Of course, under ordinary circumstances, he would have tried to drop it over. A better hand at a running drop-kick never lived than Gilkes. But let any man try to drop a ball which is full of water, and which weighs a ton. He seemed to think that there was nothing for it but to carry it in. I thought he had done it, too; and all that was left was the shouting. But the Biddleham back was a man named Ashton, and he is about one of the few backs who is a back. Instead of waiting, he went for Gilkes. Gilkes tried to dodge; but dodging is not easy in the middle of the mire. He almost pulled it off; but, just as he was past, Ashton spun right round, and caught him a back-hander which knocked him down as neat as ninepence. Our fellows claimed a foul, but I don't think rightly. Ashton tried to grab at him, but, missing, knocked him down instead. Anyhow, the claim was disallowed. But Gilkes was spun. Ashton had caught him fairly on the nose. The blood came out of him in quarts. He had to retire to see if he couldn't stop the bleeding.

In the scrummage which followed, the Biddleham forwards played the same old game. They kept the ball in scrummage, and they kept falling down on top of us. Some of our men got riled. Blackmore, whose temper is not to be relied on, pretty nearly came to fighting one of theirs. He said that the man did nothing else but fall on him, which, if true, was certainly not nice. But I do hate to see a man lose his temper in a game. Try how they would, our fellows couldn't get the ball into play. Scrummage followed scrummage, and they were still scrummaging when the whistle blew half-time.

"Play loosely! Don't form scrummages at all! Directly the ball is down, try to rush it through. Or, if you can't do that, make them rush it through at once. Let those behind have a chance. I should think you've had enough of the mud."

They had. Our blood was up. Well it might be! A more ragged regiment I never saw. There was scarcely a whole jersey among the lot, and they were so plastered with mud that I could hardly tell one from the other.

Directly ends were changed, there was a row—in consequence, I suppose, of our fellows' blood being up. Some people might have said there had been nothing but rows all through, and play had certainly been a little rough—but this was a regular row.

When the kick-off was returned, Blackmore, picking up the leather, tried a run. One of the Biddleham men, to collar him, caught him by the jersey, and, in so doing, ripped it off, and left Blackmore without a rag upon his back. That was not pleasant, and it is not supposed to be good form to try to collar a man by snatching at his jersey. Still, that didn't justify Blackmore in doing what he did. He went for that Biddleham man, and snatched at his jersey, and tore it off his back.

"There," he said, holding a fragment of the trophy in his hand, "I think we're even."

The Biddleham man didn't seem to think they were. He looked at Blackmore as though he would have liked to murder him. And his language, what I could hear of it, was not—I mean quite parliamentary. Of course play was stopped; and I thought that that would finish up the game as well. But Staines managed to smooth things over. Two fresh jerseys were brought, and play went on. But it didn't seem as though the incident had made either side much cooler—at least, so far as the lookers-on could judge.

Our men went in for loose play with a vengeance—I never saw much looser. Directly the ball was down they started kicking.

"No kicking in scrummages!" cried the Biddleham men.

"It's out of scrummage!" replied our fellows.

I didn't see myself how that could be, unless it was because it hadn't yet been in. But the Biddleham men didn't press the point, and nobody interfered. When they saw that our men *couldn't* be got to form a scrummage, they started free kicking too. To see the forwards on both sides hacking at the ball, and now and then at each other, anyhow, as they floundered about in the mud, gave the spectators an excellent idea of the science of the game.

Of course that sort of thing couldn't go on for long without there being another little shindy.

"You did that on purpose!" screamed out a voice. Play was stopped, and there was a Biddleham man nursing one leg and hopping about on the other, as though, instead of being stuck in the mud, he was dancing on red-hot plates. "He did it on purpose!" he yelled again.

He didn't say who had done it on purpose, but he pulled down his stocking and showed as pretty a leg as I remember to have seen. The skin had been scraped off, and the shin-bone all laid bare. He sat down in the mud to look at it, and the men crowded round to sympathise. The referee came up and spoke to them. I didn't catch what it was he said, but I suspect he dropped a hint that if there wasn't just a little less hacking he'd stop the game.

Then play began again. That man with the scraped leg must have been a game one. He just tied his handkerchief round the place, and pulled his stocking up, and went on playing as though that sort of thing was not worth mentioning. That's how I like to see a man behave, especially when he's playing a game.

The fresh start was followed by a lot more scrummaging—about as loose scrummaging as ever I saw. It was all inside their twenty-five. And talk about tempers! There's not a better-tempered chap in the world than our old Staines, but even he got riled when one of their men continued to sit on his head a good half-minute after the ball had gone away.

"I'll trouble you not to do that again!" he remarked, as he staggered to his feet.

"How was I to know the ball had gone away?" cried the Biddleham man. There was a thing to say!

"I don't know if you're aware," said Staines, who seemed half choked, "that you've made me swallow a peck of mud?"

The Biddleham fellow laughed.

"Never mind, old fellow, you'll get it out again."

But I could see that, if Staines didn't hate, quite as much as I do, to see a fellow lose his temper in a game, he would have set about that Biddleham beggar there and then. There can be no doubt that the play was rough—too much like the Cup Tie sort of thing for me.

Still, there were some lively episodes. And it isn't, necessarily, bad fun to look on at a row. Almost as good fun as being in it, if you listen to what some men say. And it certainly is the case that, since scientific play was out of the question on such an afternoon as that, there was some excuse for the fellows for trying to make things lively. When a man is tired of being trampled on, he's sure to try to trample on some other man, just by way of a little change. It's human nature. But I do hate to see men lose their tempers, even in a row. And a general row is what that game wound up with. I must own that I think the referee did let things go a little too far. Perhaps, since he saw that there was no chance of sport, he, too, had no objection to seeing a little fun. I don't say that it was so, but on no other hypothesis can I understand why he never gave the signal for the row to cease. But what annoyed me was this. After it was all over, and the match ended in a draw—for neither side scored more than the single try—as the men were going up to the pavilion I heard Blackmore say to the Biddleham man who had torn his jersey, "Next time you pull a man's jersey off his back, I hope that man will teach you manners."

The Biddleham man stopped short.

"You can have a try at teaching me manners now, if you like."

"Can I? Then, just to oblige you, I think I will."

And there was Blackmore making ready to fight the fellow there and then. Of course they interfered, and stopped the thing. But I do hate to see fellows lose their tempers, especially in a game.

I enjoyed that match uncommonly—almost as much as if I had played in it myself. No doubt there wasn't much science shown, if any. What could you expect with the mud six inches deep, and the rain coming down in waterspouts? But there was something almost as good as science, and that is pluck. But there are people who can see nothing in Rugby Union football at all; to discuss the thing with folks like that is simply to throw your time away.

A KNIGHT OF THE ROAD

I

It was in a house that stood close by the Cocoa Tree. They had been playing high. Nor had they spared the wine. Still there was not one there whose hand was not steady enough to rattle the box; and that however much his brains might reel. And as if to show that there is not of necessity virtue in the teaching which bids a punter keep his head both cool and clear, the heaviest loser was the soberest man. And yet, again, how much of temperament there is in this! Be it the stomach, be it the head, one man can drain the sea where another cannot drain his glass. Right from the first Mr. Lovell had drunk deep, deeper than them all, and yet, while it would have needed but the gentlest persuasion to have induced more than one to have taken up for the night his lodging on the floor, he was as much himself as ever he was. By all the rules of play this man had won. But, the plain fact was, he had lost. In that one sitting lost all he had.

Sir Will Pettifer challenged him, with a hiccoughing tongue and a murky eye.

"O-one m-more c-c-cast!"

"I thank you, Will,—not one."

He brushed a grain of snuff lightly, with his frilled handkerchief, from the collar of his coat. Then he addressed to the assembled company this little speech—

"Gentlemen, I am drained—dry. I go from here—a beggar. This morning I drew from my man of business the remainder of my fortune. Tonight I have divided it among this gallant company. 'Twas seventeen thousand pounds. One may divide seventeen thousand pounds in a many parts, yet have I divided it almost in two. You have near nine thousand, Will. Mr. Pacy, you have six. To the rest of the company I desire my apologies if the division seems unsociable."

Mr. Pacy was a big man with a red face—a country man. By him was a great heap of notes and gold. This he crammed into his pockets.

"Six thousand pounds! I'll with it to Hammersmith! I'll share it with Mistress Meg!"

When he heard these words Sir Will sprang to his feet and struck the table with his hand.

"Tha-at I've a m-mind to do!"

Mr. Pacy looked him straightly in the face. He bore his liquor with less ostentation than Sir Will.

"Then luck befriend the first!" he cried. And rose to go.

As he was going Mr. Lovell took him by the arm.

"To Hammersmith? That's a lonely road! With six thousand pounds! At this hour of the night! Have you a mind to carry the division further? To extend your charity to the gentlemen that ride the road?"

"Were there a thousand thieves that barred the road I'd ride to Hammersmith to-night! I have a mind to share my gains with Mistress Meg."

He was an obstinate man when the drink was out. When the drink was in an exposition of clear logic carried more meaning to a pig than it did to him. And where he was one fool, Sir Will, for very emulation's sake, made two. Besides, these were ancient rivals for the heart of Mistress Margaret Mathers. Mistress Mathers called herself a widow. God wot of whom! For they were many. So they rode off to Hammersmith. Mr. Pacy first, for his horse stood outside the door a-catching cold. Sir Will had none of his own. So he had to hunt for a steed to bear him to the fair. And since, in the middle of the night, horses are not to be had for whistling, it was a hunt which took some time.

Mr. Pacy went plodding steadily on. He rode fifteen stone, and perhaps a little more, so that it was not every beast that, with him on its back, went like the wind. Bruin—so he called the animal he rode that night—was better at weight than speed. Six miles an hour, with his master mounted, was all he cared to go. That night Mr. Pacy worried and hustled him until, at times, he rose to eight. The gentleman kept looking back, with his ears well cocked, to catch the first sounds of Sir Will following, like fate, behind.

To cheer the way he thought of his six thousand pounds, and of Mistress Meg in all her gorgeous array. Six thousand pounds! 'Twould make her sweet as honey and gorgeous as the god of day. But Sir Will had his nine thousand. If he were first upon the field Mr. Pacy feared that in the light of Sir Will's nine the glory of his six would fade away. So he did his best to induce Bruin to better his six-mile jog and make it eight.

At the turnpike the keeper, of course, was fast asleep. So fast indeed that Mr. Pacy had serious thoughts of putting Bruin at the gate to take it in his stride. But as Bruin made it clear that his thoughts were all the other way, he contented himself with battering and damning until the fellow was aroused from slumber and let him through. Then a lucky thought occurred to him. He gave the keeper a piece of gold to fall so fast asleep that he would never hear Sir Will until he had hammered at least a good half-hour. Then he rode on, congratulating himself that Sir Will's language would be at least as bad as his had been and worse.

He was nearing the hut in which lived the woman that was reported to be a witch, chuckling to himself, when something happened which drove all the chuckle out of him. All at once there stood a horse in front of him, his rider's hand was laid on Bruin's bridle, and, what was more, there was a pistol whose muzzle was within twelve inches of Mr. Pacy's nose. He had come so suddenly, this stranger, that Mr. Pacy did not understand whence he came, nor how. He was all bewildered.

"Stand and deliver!"

That was all the stranger said. He had a piece of crape before his face, and seemed indeed a most determined fellow.

"I have not a shilling," Mr. Pacy said. "I have lost it all at play to-night, and am journeying homewards to my wife."

Bang! whiz-z-z! The stranger had fired. The bullet grazed Mr. Pacy's cheek. Congratulating himself on what he supposed was his escape, he raised his hand to strike the other down. But, hey, presto! the pistol was dropped and there was another in the fellow's hand. It was like a conjurer's trick.

"That was for warning! This will hit its mark. Do you think that is the only one I carry? See here!"

The stranger undid his coat and disclosed a belt in which, in the dim light, for there was neither moon nor stars, there seemed a dozen pistols stuck at least. Mr. Pacy felt that it was time to treat.

"Sir, I do not think I have a guinea in my purse."

"You lie!"

The stranger's tones were clear and cold, and struck unpleasantly on Mr. Pacy's ears.

"You have won six thousand pounds this night at play. Such as I do not attack a bird if we are not sure he will be worth our plucking. Hand over the six thousand! And, because of the lie that you have told, every ha'porth that you have besides."

"I'll give you half."

"Nor yet three-quarters! I'll have the whole."

"'Tis very hard!" Mr. Pacy said. And "'Tis very hard!" he said again, when the stranger had bidden him a courteous good-night, and he was left to pursue his way alone. He hesitated as to what, in his sorry plight, it were best to do. To proceed to Mistress Meg without a stiver in his purse would be absurd. With the widow love meant money.

"Is there nothing left for me?"

As Mr. Pacy mused, all at once these words were spoken in his ears. He started as he had been struck. Then turned, and lo! there was another fellow with crape before his face and a pistol in his hand.

"'Fore God!" he cried, with a great oath. "This is a pleasant journeying."

This new-comer was of a different make to him who just now had gone. A small, mean man, that wore a hang-dog air.

"Sir," he inquired, "is there nothing left for me?"

"And that there's not! Not the value of a brass farthing's worth! Your friend has plucked me clean! It will hardly pay the cost of powder were you to put a bullet in my head."

"The greedy rogue!" exclaimed this second honest man.

"It was the devil!—or his friend!"

"Sir, it was a gentleman."

"A gentleman! By my life, but he is one now! It is with a good deal more than six thousand pounds that he rides away."

The stranger threw his hands up to the skies. There came from him a sound which was between and betwixt a gasp and a sigh.

"Ye saints in paradise! Sir, I have been upon the road these seven years! In all that time I have not earned the half of that. Yet here comes a gentleman who, just for a frolic, takes to the road but for a single night, and in one sweep doubles the earnings of my seven years. It is hard upon a persevering man. Sir, I have children and a wife to keep. It is not a thing I often do, but under the circumstances I entreat you will forgive me if I relieve you of your coat. 'Twill mean a morning's meal for my children, sir."

"My coat!" Mr. Pacy was aghast. "God's truth, it is a pleasant company one meets!"

And so he told himself again when the stranger, bearing his children's morning meal before him on his horse, had rode away. It was with a heavy heart that Mr. Pacy turned Bruin's head and, in his shirt sleeves, retraced his way. Adieu his dreams of gentle dalliance with Mistress Meg! Adieu his coat as well! As for the six thousand pounds,—God's curse go with the rogue who plundered him!

He hammered and hammered at the gatekeeper's house. It was with an added bitterness that he thought of the gold piece he had given him, and how he had paid the fellow to sleep sound. To think that he had paid a guinea to be kept shivering in his shirt sleeves all night!

"If I'd a match I'd set the place a-blaze!" Bang! Bang! Crash! He hammered with all his might upon the shuttered window-frame. "You fool! 'Tis not the other man! 'Tis I!"

But this was a deserving fellow that desired to earn his wage both faithfully and well. It was the full half-hour before he waked. When he showed his sleepy head, Mr. Pacy was well-nigh spent with rage. It must have warmed the cockles of the keeper's heart, the flood of oaths that poured from the belated traveller's scalding tongue.

They parted with a mutual malediction. Each felt himself aggrieved; though it is doubtless true that the coatless gentleman felt his grievance most. Because of his affliction Bruin suffered wrong. He pounded the poor beast until the creature felt that instead of fifteen stone it must be fifty which he bore upon his back. But still greater wrong awaited him before he saw his crib that night.

As Bruin toiled painfully, and Mr. Pacy furiously, on, suddenly a voice was heard from the roadside. It was a voice Mr. Pacy knew full well,—none other than that belonging to Sir Will. A figure rose from the bank that bordered the road. It was the gay young baronet. But in what a plight! Hatless, without his wig, as though he had been rolled in the mire and dust. Mr. Pacy was amazed.

"God's truth! It's Will Pettifer!" he cried.

"What's left of him." The baronet seemed quite sober now. Then he perceived that it was Mr. Pacy, and that it was in his shirt he rode. "Jack! Without a coat! Riding from Hammersmith, instead of to! What's happened now!"

With many curses Mr. Pacy told of the parting with the six thousand pounds, and then of the coat that went to provide the children's morning meal. The baronet was like a man who has heard the strangest thing that ever yet he heard.

"What! You too! Of all the pretty games that ever yet was played! Jack, as he came from robbing you, he robbed me too!"

"What! The rogue that took the coat?"

"No! He with the six thousand pounds!"

"God's truth!" was all that Mr. Pacy said. Then he added, as though lost in thought, "Not the whole nine thousand, Will?"

"The whole nine thousand! And not that alone. There was another thousand, and more, besides. Jack, between us he has rode off with seventeen thousand pounds!"

"If I knew the fellow I'd treat with him to marry Susan Anne." Susan Anne was Mr. Pacy's sister, a damsel that was past her prime. "It would be a great thing for the girl to get a husband with seventeen thousand pounds."

"You fool! Who was it told us he had lost seventeen thousand pounds to-night?"

"Where are you driving now? Why, 'tis just the sum that Gerard Lovell lost!"

"And won! He has lost and won seventeen thousand pounds all in a single night! Why do you stare? It is as plain as Jack of diamonds. 'Tis Lovell was the thief!"

"Will! God's truth! You don't mean that!"

"Upon my soul I do! 'Tis his revenge he's had. Mine is still to come. It was his voice!"

Mr. Pacy scratched his head.

"I thought that I had heard the voice before!"

"It was his horse!"

"I did not mind his horse."

"It was him, every inch! Besides, how came he to know I carried nine, and you six thousand pounds? How came he to name the very sum? Did he not know we rode to Hammersmith? Did he himself not warn us of the gentlemen upon the road? 'Tis he has done the riding, and, faith! he's ridden well; but I will cry him evens yet before the dawn."

Mr. Pacy still scratched his head.

"The fellow that took my coat said it was a gentleman that did the trick! But Lovell! God's truth! To think 'twas he!"

"What sort of beast is it you ride? I had my screw from Spavin, and when that villain threw me—'fore gad, it was the nearest thing! I know 'twas he from that; I've seen him do it in the wrestling ring—the three-legged brute went tearing off. Before now he's at home with Spavin in the yard. I am so sprained I could not walk to save my life. Let me get up behind. He'll take us both home, I'll swear."

And so it chanced that still greater wrong was done to Bruin. Before he understood that such villainy was even in the air, the baronet was on his back. And so he had to bear a double load. Of a surety that was the greatest wrong of all.

II

MR. LOVELL lived in Rider Street. It was very early in the morning when there came a clamouring at the street door. On the ground floor there lived a Captain Philip Ashton, that had fought in William's wars, and had left a leg in the Low Countries. When Anne came in, he came into a fortune, God alone knows how—unless he stole it, which was the most likely thing to happen with a Whig.

Since then he had set up as a gentleman that kept two rooms, and had increased in the art, to swear, since he had of necessity decreased in the art, to fight. Mr. Lovell had his rooms above the captain's, so, as was natural, 'twas the captain heard the clamour first. He put his head out of the window, all in his bedgown as he was.

"Who knocks so late?" And then came that eloquence of oaths for which he was famed almost more than any man in town. "Ods cannons rot you! 'Tis more than an hour ere the first cock shall crow!"

Then came an answer from the street.

"Sir, 'tis Mr. Lovell we desire to see. 'Tis a matter, sir, of life and death."

The captain saw there were two men and but one horse. And one of the men was without a coat, and the other was without a hat and wig. He that was hatless sang out—

"You know me, Captain Ashton, I'm Will Pettifer, and Mr. Pacy here is my good friend."

The captain strapped on his wooden peg and then stumped to the street door.

"Mr. Lovell is above," began Sir Will. "Captain Ashton, I desire that you will go up with us and be witness of what we have to say unto this gentleman."

So they all three went upstairs, a motley crew. Clatter, clatter went their steps upon the stairs, yet when they reached Mr. Lovell's room it would seem that the din had not awaked that gentleman from sleep. It was twice they knocked before from within there came a voice inquiring who was here.

"The scoundrel!" exclaimed Sir Will. "He pretends he is in bed! Was ever such hypocrisy before!"

Yet when Mr. Lovell undid the door it seemed indeed as though he were but just aroused from sleep, for his eyes were heavy and he was all undressed.

"Sir Will!—Mr. Pacy!—Ashton!—What frolic brings you here?"

His surprise, it seemed quite natural, and indeed his whole manner was of a man who is not yet quite wide awake. But Sir Will, with a certain roughness, pushed him aside and strode into the room, with Mr. Pacy and the captain following hard upon his heels.

"Thou prince of actors! Thou damned hypocrite!"

Sir Will stretched out his hand towards him with an unusual bitterness.

"Will!" he cried, like one amazed.

"Captain Ashton, you see this gentleman, you see the state his room is in, like one who has slept here honestly the whole night through. He does not look like one who has just returned from robbing of his friends! And that on the high road! And yet 'tis so! He has played the part of highwayman this very night, and robbed Mr. Pacy and myself of seventeen thousand pounds."

"Will!" cried Mr. Lovell, still as one amazed.

Sir Will was so enraged he sprang at Mr. Lovell and caught him by the throat.

"You thief! You gallows spawn! That was a scurvy trick you played! Had you not thrown me from my horse even now my sword had been sticking in your heart!" He threw Mr. Lovell from him with much force. "Jack, go fetch the constables. We should have brought them with us at the first. 'Tis only they can deal with such a knave."

Mr. Pacy turned to go. But Mr. Lovell stepped between the door and him.

"One moment, Mr. Pacy, if you please.—Sir William Pettifer, when I last saw you you were drunk. Am I to understand you are drunk still?"

"You thief!" Sir Will exclaimed. He would have been at Mr. Lovell's throat again had not the captain interposed. Mr. Lovell, in the face of all the other's rage, was both calm and cool, and the dignity of conscious rectitude was in his air in spite of his undress.

"Mr. Pacy, you seem calmer than your friend. What is it you charge me with?"

"You robbed me of six thousand pounds."

"I robbed you of six thousand pounds! How came I to do that?"

"That's what I want to know, whence you came and how. I know that you all at once were there, upon that barb of yours, with a piece of crape before your face and a dozen pistols in your belt, with one of which you scored my cheek—here is the place where it touched me now—and that you rode away leaving me without so much as a button that I might pawn."

"Captain Ashton, do I dream? or am I in fact awake?"

"You seem to me to be awake, that is if I'm not dreaming too, for it is the strangest tale that ever yet I heard, 'fore God it is."

"Sir William Pettifer, have I robbed you too?"

"Of ten thousand pounds, you knave! But I see plainly you would outbrazen hell,—I'll not contend! Jack, who'll fetch the constables? Is it you or I must go?"

Mr. Lovell drew himself straight up. He was very quiet and very stern.

"Gentlemen, in the presence of that God before whom we stand I do declare that I have never left the house this night—that is, since I parted with these gentlemen at the Cocoa Tree hard by. I am guiltless of this foul crime which, in my innocence, it seems to me that only madness can lay to my charge. I am willing to submit myself to the minions of the law whenever it shall please these gentlemen. But I would advise Sir William Pettifer of this, that sooner or later he shall render me satisfaction with his own right arm. And I would suggest to him that since he uses such bold words he should carry his boldness one small step farther, and submit this matter to the ordeal of the Most High God. Afterwards, there will still be at his service all the terrors of the law."

"Gentlemen do not fight with thieves," replied Sir Will.

"Then, Sir William Pettifer, hear this! While they go fetch the officers I will kill you with my own hands for the cur and coward which you are. That is the only crime with which they ever shall be stained."

"I think that you had better fight him, Will. Or if you shirk it, why then I'll take him on."

Sir Will turned on Mr. Pacy in a rage.

"Shirk it! Do you think I fear?"

"If you can, Sir William Pettifer, look me boldly in the face. Why, I am sure you fear. You dare not meet my eyes. I do believe it is some trick you try, and you yourself have played the thief!"

"That caps it!" cried Sir Will. "I'll fight him now!"

"Captain Ashton," said Mr. Lovell, "have you sufficient faith in the justice of my cause to be my friend?"

The captain was always ready to play the second if he could not be the first, and rather than not have figured on such a scene he would have played the second to Old Nick. So they went out to fight. Mr. Lovell and the captain put on their clothes, but Mr. Pacy and Sir Will went as they were. Sir Will was to have Mr. Pacy's sword, since his own had been snapped in two when he had fallen from his horse.

It was in Hyde Park they fought. In that part of it in which so many suchlike frolic games are played. Sir Will had his back towards the Cake House, and Mr. Lovell had his towards the Ring. It was an uncertain light, since the shimmerings of the dawn were only just beginning to be seen in the sky. Still it was light enough for two serious gentlemen, that meant business, to see the points of their swords.

Before they set to, Mr. Lovell said, and he spoke like a man who is very much in earnest—

"Captain Ashton, I desire you to understand that I am innocent of this crime that is laid to my charge, nor know I any reason why this gentleman should bear me enmity. I submit my cause to God. He shall adjudge the right."

Strangely enough, ere these words could have well ceased fluttering through the bars of heaven's gates, the thing was judged. Although there was no better swordsman in the town than was the gay young baronet, all at once his skill seemed to have deserted him. They all observed the confusion with which he handled his blade. While Mr. Lovell's was like an avenging sword. Hardly had the word been given than he ran Sir William right through the heart, so that he fell stone dead. Withdrawing his sword, Mr. Lovell bent over his fallen foe.

"God has judged!" he said. Then he began to mourn. "Oh, Will, my friend, what madness has overtaken you this night!" Then he stood straight up. "Gentlemen, I call you to witness that this was in fair fight."

Then he put on his clothes and wiped his sword, and went away, leaving the seconds to guard the dead.

It was now getting near the dawn. In the Park there it was light. And there was a fresh breeze that whispered among the grasses and rustled through the leaves. The sky was nearly clear, and there was a suspicion that at any moment, perhaps, the sun might burst in all his glory on the world. It bade fair, in fact, to be a beauteous morn. And Mr. Lovell walked over the grassy slope with his hands behind his back like a man who bears a conscience that is at peace with God and man. And yet there was something of sorrow in his gait—perchance it was sorrow for his friend.

But as he approached the road, more than once he paused, and looked round and stared and listened. And then seeing there was none in sight, went on again. And then again would pause, and go again through the same pantomime as he had done before. It was strange! It seemed to him that he heard footfalls which came close behind him on the grass. Yet when he turned, lo! none was there.

"It is a trick of the imagination!" he declared, and journeyed on. But no sooner had he started than there came the sound again, as of someone who stepped lightly on the grass keeping step with him a few feet behind. Yet when he turned again still none was there.

"It is an echo!" he observed. With his handkerchief he wiped his lips and went his way.

It was the strangest kind of echo that ever was. It kept pace with him all along the grass, seeming to mock his steps. The coolest gentleman was Mr. Lovell, yet this curious echo seemed to trouble him, for he kept giving furtive glances over his shoulder as he went. He went upon the gravel, and the echo went with him there. And when he got outside the Park there happened the strangest thing of all.

The echo quickened its pace, and came running after. Suddenly a hand was laid upon his shoulder, and Mr. Lovell turned, and behold! a gentleman looked in his face who had come God knows from where. And when he saw this gentleman all at once Mr. Lovell looked like a man who has received his death. God alone wots why! So for some moments they stood, face to face, neither speaking. It seemed as though Mr. Lovell had lost the power of speech. But at last there came, as it might be, a sort of frenzied convulsion of all the muscles in his face, which was horrible to see, and then he spake. But not in his usual clear, soft tones, but in a voice which had the hollow sound of a voice from the grave.

"Who are you that dogs my steps and intercepts me on the public way? I believe I do not know you, sir."

The strange gentleman smiled. That was all he did. Yet Mr. Lovell sank down on his knees, and covered his face with his hands, and was seized with a convulsive agony—there in the highway. The stranger stood and looked at the strong man trembling as with palsy at his feet. He touched him with his finger's tip and said—

"Rise up!"

It was as though he had weaved a spell. Mr. Lovell rose to his feet. The stranger passed his right arm through Mr. Lovell's left. A shudder went all over him, and then it was as though he were carved in stone.

"Home!" the stranger said.

Mechanically Mr. Lovell moved his feet, and looking neither to the right nor to the left he went straight on. The sun had just begun to rise. They met no passers-by on the way, yet all the air seemed filled with cries of pain. If Mr. Lovell heard he paid no heed, and for the stranger, he bore continually upon his countenance a smile of wondrous beauty, and yet one which in some strange way seemed filled with the intensest agony of pain,—pain which nothing human shall bear yet live.

When they reached Rider Street there still stood the patient Bruin where his master had tethered him in front of Mr. Lovell's door. But when he saw the stranger that came on Mr. Lovell's arm he gave the oddest cry that ever issued from a horse's throat, and broke his tether and tore off as for his life. He broke even his eight miles an hour record then. But neither Mr. Lovell nor the stranger paid the slightest heed. It might have been the commonest of things for a staid quadruped to go stark mad with fear.

They went up to Mr. Lovell's room. The stranger shut the door. Both were still. Mr. Lovell stood in the centre of the floor like, it might be, the husk of a man. The stranger held out his hand. It was the fairest, sweetest, daintiest hand that ever yet was seen.

"Friend!"

And like the sweetest music was the voice in which he spoke the word. And yet it was a music in which there were a thousand things. For in spite of its exceeding sweetness there was in it an unutterable agony of pain. Mr. Lovell covered his face with his hands. He was seized with the ague fit which had overtaken him at first. But he gave no heed to the outstretched hand. So the stranger spoke again.

"You know me, friend!"

With a frantic effort Mr. Lovell managed to get out the one word—

"No!"

It was a gasp, rather than a voice he said it in.

"Lies! To their father!"

That was all the stranger said. Yet Mr. Lovell fell flat upon the floor. The stranger advanced and stood right over him, looking down upon the quivering man.

"There is truth in the stories that are told. I come at times to men and women. To such as are after my own heart."

He paused. It was horrible to see how Mr. Lovell continued to quiver in every limb as the stranger with his wondrous smile, his wondrous voice, stood looking down. And it was all the time as though the whole air was filled with cries of pain.

"Friend, I bid you rise."

Mr. Lovell rose, mechanically, as he had done before.

"Give me your hand."

Mr. Lovell gave him his hand. As he did so he looked as we may conceive the lost spirits look in hell.

"You are my very child. Fair son! Thou dearest of them all!"

There was a silence. The sweat poured from Mr. Lovell's cheeks as in a sort of frenzy he kept his gaze upon the stranger's face. As if impelled by a fascination which he could not resist, he kept his eyes upon the stranger's eyes. And something that he saw in them he seemed gradually to be drinking in. Of a surety 'twas something strange, for he became transfigured as he gazed.

He lost first that look of a man who was stricken to his death. Then passed from him that look of anguished woe. Then fled from him that appearance of great pain. And last there vanished all signs of fear. It seemed, indeed, that he all at once began to find a pleasure in the presence of the stranger that stood there, and held him by the hand. He stood straight up, all bold, ay, bolder even than before. The transfiguration became indeed most wonderful, as wonderful as the transfiguration which had come on Mr. Lovell when he met the stranger first. And when at last the stranger said—

"It is a pact, thou son of my own heart?"

Mr. Lovell answered out both bold and clear—

"Use me as you will! Make me all yours! Give me the keys of the inner chambers of all sin!"

And the stranger answered, and it seemed as though the unutterable ecstasy of pain which, as it were, was hidden in his voice, acted on Mr. Lovell's veins as though it were the strongest wine—a stranger wine than ever yet was brewed by man.

"You shall be all mine! In my hands are not the keys of life and death, but I will be ever at your side. You shall know all the feverish delight of sin, and after all the mad delirium of unending pain."

Then Mr. Lovell cried, in a strange, wild voice—

"Father! Make me your son!"

And he leaped upon the stranger's breast. And the stranger folded him about with both his arms. And, behold! they kissed. And the effect of the stranger's kiss was to make Mr. Lovell drunker than ever man was made who had drunk more than his full, and that of the fiercest liquor.

III

IT was the next night in the house that stood close by the Cocoa Tree. Mr. Pacy was there, and Captain Ashton, and many more besides. And though to be there meant to play, yet it was not play alone which occupied their thoughts that night. There had been strange tales told in town all day, and it was these tales they spoke of now. Here were the two men that knew the truth, and it was the truth that the town was all agog to hear.

The Honourable Cleveland Sprague, that was a son of the Earl of Staines, drew his white buckskin gloves right up his arm. He had sworn to his maiden aunt, the last time she paid his debts, that he never more would touch a dice-box or a card. And so, to keep his vow, he always donned a pair of gloves that went right up his arm. It was they that touched the dice-box and the cards. 'Twas never he.

"So Will Pettifer is dead!" he cried. "Run to the heart! 'Twas not the first time his heart was touched. And I always told him that he had never caught the trick of the right counter-guard. Phew! How hot these gloves do make my hands! I think I might in honour wear a thinner pair."

"What is this tale they tell," asked Mr. Twentyman, that had killed his partner in a dozen duels, so they say, "of robbery and I know not what? Come, Mr. Pacy, all friends here—treat us to the tale."

But Mr. Pacy seemed not himself. He never had the clearest head even at the best of times. Now he seemed all muddled and bemused. The truth is, he had drunk half a dozen pots or so of good strong ale to sweep the tangle from his brain, and if they had swept it out they certainly had swept it in again.

"It is a sacred subject, Mr. Twentyman." And Mr. Pacy laid his hand upon his heart, and looked more solemn than a sexton's clerk. "The dearest friend I ever had is dead, slain by my other dearest friend, that robbed me of six thousand pounds. God's curse light on the rogue that robbed me of my coat besides! 'Twas my cherry coat that I'd had made to show myself to Mistress Margaret in."

"Lovell rob you of your coat! Good lack-a-day! Sure he has coats enough that he can call his own."

"Mr. Twentyman, it was not Mr. Lovell that robbed me of my coat,—it was his friend."

"His friend! Faith! it is fine company he keeps!"

"At least, I do not know it was his friend. It was the fellow that came after." Mr. Pacy leaned against the board, and raised his voice exceeding loud. "Mr. Twentyman, the fellow took my coat for his children's morning meal."

A sound that was very like a titter went round the room. But when they saw how fierce Mr. Pacy looked, the sound was hushed.

"Then it was Lovell robbed you of six thousand pounds?"

"Sir, I do not say 'twas he. I have no desire, sir, to affront a trusty friend. If I said 'twas he, he would feel affronted, Mr. Twentyman. God forbid that I should so affront the meanest rogue that breathes! 'Twas thus—'twas my dear friend, Will Pettifer, that said 'twas he."

"Did Will Pettifer then see it done?"

"Do you think Will Pettifer 'd stand by and see me robbed? God forbid that I should so affront the dead! Sir, Will Pettifer was a good two miles away."

"As you tell the tale, Mr. Pacy, 'tis like a puzzle, as I live. Let me ask you, was it Will Pettifer that Mr. Lovell robbed?"

"Sir, he said it was,—it was for that he died. It has misgiven me a dozen times that Sir Will was wrong."

"Because he died?"

"Yes, sir, because he died. For, sir, 'twas thus. Mr. Lovell declared his innocence with as fine an air as ever yet I saw,—Captain Ashton will bear me witness that he spoke as would an honest man. And further he declared that he left his cause unto the God of battles,— Captain Ashton will proclaim if they were not solemn words. Sure, had he been guilty 'twas Mr. Lovell, sir, had died."

Mr. Twentyman snuffed, and then the box went round. Only Captain Ashton had a mixture of his own, which made him sneeze.

"Hum! How much had this incognito from you, and how much from Will?"

"More than six thousand pounds from me, and more than ten from Will. Together, the villain rode away the richer for seventeen thousand pounds."

"Seventeen thousand pounds! Odd! The sum which Mr. Lovell, standing there where you are standing now, declared that he had lost."

There was silence. Each man occupied himself with his own thoughts. Then they began to play. But Mr. Pacy, he stood out.

"I am drained dry. Until my rents come in I shall have to be in debt even for the things I eat. And but this morning Mistress Meg writes entreating the loan of a hundred pounds. It is, I think she says, to pay her glover's bill. It goes to my heart to say her nay, but when one has to go in debt for the ale one drinks!—Sandy, bring me a jug of wine!"

"Why don't you go upon the road?" asked Mr. Sprague. "'Fore God, I have a mind to challenge fate myself. 'Tis a good haul, seventeen thousand pounds. If I but saw a chance of it I'd rob a hundred men, and still swear black was white. 'Twould pay my debts, or some of them, and still there'd be a trifle left for my true love besides."

"Ay, but he that took my coat said that he had not gained the half of it in seven years. It is not every night one pouches seventeen thousand pounds."

"It is not every night one meets so prime a pair of fools." This, or something like it, was what Mr. Sprague observed beneath his breath.

"Sir, I desire to be informed, sir, what it is you say beneath your breath. It is not a seemly trick to whisper in good company."

"Sir, I will tell you straight. Mr. Pacy, you are my dearest friend; I had rather I had lost these six thousand pounds than you. I beg that I may drink with you."

"Sandy," Mr. Pacy cried, "another jug of wine." It was a good hour after that Mr. Lovell came. By that time the most of the company were too busy with the dice to concern themselves with other things. Yet when he came you might have sworn a little breeze blew through the room so that each man shivered as with cold. With one accord they all looked up, even to the croupiers and the men that served, and there was Mr. Lovell at the door.

It was strange to see how all that company so suddenly was still. Yea, and how all stared. It was as though Mr. Lovell had the power of the loadstone to draw their eyes to him like magnets, as it were. They paused, and he. For the space of thirty seconds there was such silence that it seemed that none there breathed. Then, with that grace which was notoriously his, he took off his hat and made to them the fairest sweeping bow that ever was.

"Unto all this gallant company,—service!"

When he spoke a curious expression flitted across the countenance of each one that heard. For it seemed to them that his voice was not the voice of the Mr. Lovell they had known. It had a bolder, richer, acuter tone. It seemed to ring out through the room until the very lustres were set tinkling. And this rare gentleman was scarce the ruined gambler of yesternight. That was cool and easy, yet, withal, a trifle stern. This held himself more bravely than a king. He had grown taller, as it were. On his face there was a radiance that made it strangely beautiful. Yet, as you regarded it, it seemed as though it had the power of communicating to your heart a quaint consciousness of pain.

None returned his salutation. All, as it seemed, even unconsciously to themselves, refrained from speech. With one accord they kept their eyes fastened upon his radiant countenance. But he seemed in no way concerned at the strangeness of their bearing. He came into the room with a buoyant lightness that was glorious to see.

"Jack!" he cried, when he perceived Mr. Pacy standing at his side, "I hope fortune has used you well since yesternight!"

But Mr. Pacy was in a solemn humour still.

"Mr. Lovell, God give you a good greeting."

It was curious to observe how Mr. Lovell was affected when Mr. Pacy spoke those simple words. He grasped the back of a chair with both his hands. A sort of convulsion passed all over him. His face became hideous all at once with its grins and its grimaces. They stared at him amazed.

"It—it is a spasm—of the heart—that sometimes—overtakes me." The words came out as though they rattled in his throat. "Give me—give me some brandy—a tumbler full."

They brought it him. A good half-pint at least. He drank it at a single draught.

"How long have these spasms troubled you?" asked Mr. Twentyman.

"Oh, ever since I was so high,—not higher than that glass is now." He dashed the glass out of his hand so that it was shivered to fragments on the floor. "But I interrupt your play! It should be a more serious person than I that did that! Who holds the bank, and what's the stake?"

He advanced to the table. He thrust his hands into his pockets and drew them out crammed full with notes and gold. And all this wealth he threw upon the board. At sight of it Mr. Sprague cried out—

"It would seem, Mr. Lovell, that you had come into another fortune since you lost your first last night."

"Nay, this is not mine." And Mr. Lovell chinked perhaps a hundred guineas in his hand. "It's the devil's own."

"Why, then, upon my word, I would the devil were at hand with its fellow one for me."

"What!" And Mr. Lovell drew himself straight up and his voice rang out so that it seemed to shake the very walls. "You wish the devil were at hand!" And he leaned forward on the board, and stretching out his hand, stared at Mr. Sprague with an intensity which made them more and more amazed. "Even at this moment the devil looks you in the face."

"Upon my word, Mr. Lovell, I do protest that there is something in your eyes which makes me feel quite strange."

"In my eyes! Oh, but what is there in his! If you could only see! But come, play! play! Let the game go round! We but stand idly here!"

But though they began to play it was not with the zest with which they were wont to pursue that great business of their lives, but in a nervous, fitful fashion, as though their thoughts—if not their hearts—were otherwise. Mr. Lovell played wildly, with no sort of care or skill, and kept losing all the time. Suddenly he cried—

"See, here's a guinea piece, it shall be staked alone, it may chance to turn my luck, for you see it is a lucky coin."

"'Fore God! It's mine!"

Mr. Lovell was seized with the same convulsion which had over-taken him before, and he grasped the table as it seemed to help him stand. And, indeed, he needed some support. For Mr. Pacy pushed rudely by him and snatched the guinea piece out of his hand.

"It's mine!" roared Mr. Pacy, with the bellow of a bull. "It's mine!"

Before they knew what it was he would be at, he had begun to overhaul the heap of gold which Mr. Lovell had placed upon the board. From it he drew two guinea pieces which were exactly like the first.

"They're mine!" he roared. "As I breathe, they are my lucky three!" Then he turned on Mr. Lovell like a wild animal. "You damnedest rogue! You were the robber all the time!"

But Mr. Lovell stood straight up as calm and easy as ever yet he was.

"Pray, Mr. Pacy, why do you meddle with my money? And why this sudden rage? Have you gone mad? Or are you only drunk—the sequel of last night?"

"Your money! Sure, Mr. Lovell, since I know you I never will believe that ever a lie blasted the liar's throat or you had died the day that you were born. Sirs, I beseech you to observe these coins. In each of them three holes are drilled with a peculiar tool. I did it when I was a boy. They were fastened to a ribbon which hung out of my fob last night when I was robbed even to the buttons that were in my shirt and sleeves. And now Mr. Lovell, that so lately was a ruined man, throws them upon the board with other wealth of notes and gold that he so rightly calls the devil's own."

They all were still. There stood Mr. Pacy, suddenly clear witted as it seemed, the three curious pieces held in his great open palm. It was Mr. Sprague that spoke first. He took the guineas and examined them closely one by one. The whole company looked on.

"It is certainly a little curious," he said. "One would suppose that the man who made these marks could scarcely mistake his work if he came on it again."

"Perhaps the pieces in very truth are Mr. Pacy's own."

It was Mr. Lovell's voice. He seemed no whit abashed. He still held himself quite straight—more bravely than a king. There was still that strange resonance in his voice which made the lustres ring. There was still that radiance in his eyes and on his face, which made those who regarded him the most, most conscious of a sense of pain.

"Suppose they are his own,—what then?"

As he spoke he seemed to increase in radiance and beauty before their very eyes. And with it, too, increased their consciousness of pain.

"I say—what then?"

His voice increased until it became a very ecstasy of song.

"Because I stole them? Why, yes—I did! I lost my money and regained it with my own hands. You see that I am not ashamed."

They saw it very plain. He held himself as though he were the fabled hero of some glorious deed.

"Still less am I afraid. No, of nothing that may come. Sir Will is dead. I slew him with my own hand. Here is the self-same sword which finished him. Mr. Pacy, are you afraid?"

"I am not afraid," Pacy said, "of you."

And in his stolid bearing there was a certain glory too.

"I think you are. You dare not meet me boldly like Sir Will. After all, there was a man. Although he knew me for what I am, he never feared to meet my sword. But you! oh, you will say you do not fight with thieves! And I believe it too! You would far rather run away."

"I will not run away from you."

"You'll fight me then?"

"Yes, you thief, I'll fight you to the death."

"Now?"

"Ay, and even where you stand."

"Nay, the Park will serve—where I fought Sir Will until he died. Captain Ashton, may I again entreat you to be my friend?"

But Captain Ashton turned away, a great oath upon his lips. Even his strong stomach could not swallow that. He might stand for Old Nick, but for this brazen gentleman, not he. Mr. Lovell, still unabashed, but smiled at him.

"Am I then to fly in the face of all rules? To fight without a friend—because I am a thief?"

"You shall always have a friend in me!"

It was the strangest voice that spoke the words, stranger than Mr. Lovell's even—ay, stranger far. A voice of the most wondrous music. You knew that he whose voice that was could keep no company with fear. It was like the clarion note that loves to defy the world. Yet in it there was something that spoke of hopeless pain,— pain which no man shall live and know.

And when they heard it each man there, down to the very croupiers even—they that have no souls—was seized with a strange sort of fear. And the fashion of their faces changed. It was as though each man had suddenly grown old. Only one man there was who was the same, and that was Mr. Lovell. There never was a gladder man than that man then, he held himself so very proudly, and his face was all radiant with such a radiancy of light. But all those that were about him shrank shudderingly away.

And, behold, a gentleman advanced towards Mr. Lovell. They know not to this day whence he came, nor how it was he was found so suddenly amongst them in that room. Sure, there never was one finer yet. He bore himself with a most marvellous grace. He was exquisite in each detail of his dress. He was still young,—a wondrous youth, and withal most beautiful. There was upon his face a most enchanting smile. Yet when they saw it there broke from each man there a little cry of pain. It was as though he smiled in a wild, mad ecstasy of pain.

He advanced towards Mr. Lovell, and took him by the hand. And as he did so it was as though Mr. Lovell was transfigured. It was as though he became the counterpart of the gentleman who had come to be his friend. They were a wondrous pair. And yet all the company shrank tremblingly away, and the fashions of their faces changed, so that it seemed that they had suddenly grown old.

But Mr. Lovell, with the gentleman's hand still linked in his, turned to them, and said—

"This gentleman will be my friend."

And his voice, albeit it seemed that he spoke low, rang through the room with a resonant power that was indeed most wonderful. And yet—yet there was in it that note of pain! Then, perceiving that Mr. Pacy leaned with one hand against the wall, with something greenish about his face and in his eyes—

"Ah, Mr. Pacy, I think that now you are afraid."

It was with a sort of struggle that Mr. Pacy seemed to get the answering words to issue from his lips. Yet after his fashion he was game.

"I'm not afraid of you. I'll fight you now!" Then, with a supreme effort he broke, as it were, into a spasmodic rage. "Fight!—I'll fight you until you die."

The gentleman that had come to be Mr. Lovell's friend regarded him with his fair smile. And beneath his gaze Mr. Pacy seemed to shrink and shrink, and to become every moment a meaner man. The gentleman said—

"Bravely spoken! I would you also were my friend—even as my friend here. But come! Let us all go out to fight."

Holding Mr. Lovell by the hand he led the way out of the room, and like a flock of sheep all followed him, even to the croupiers and the serving men. Down the stairs went he, and after him went they, and out into the night. It was a strange sight to see that gallant company. All held their peace, and all seemed to wear so curious an air of decrepitude and age. There were there some of the bravest and the prettiest men in the town. Youths, some in the prime of life, and others that were old. Some of England's purest blood was there, some of the finest fortunes in the land, some of its most glorious names. Yet never was seen such a hang-dog crew! They went like a pack of beaten curs, a set of mongrels in whom either life and spirit had never been, or from whom for certain it was ever gone. And the strangest part was that all at once they all seemed to have grown meanly old.

There was a moon that night. Through the moonlit streets they all went after Mr. Lovell and the gentleman that was come to be his friend. And to see the contrast that there was between those two and the sorry set that followed as their tail! The rich dresses of this mangy crowd made them seem a still sorrier set, their gait was in ill accord with the clothes they wore. And all the way they went the air seemed filled with wails and cries of pain.

Into the Park they went, and so across the grass, and still not any spoke a word. They were a silent crew! So that when the strange gentleman stopped short, and turning said to Mr. Lovell, who still had his hand—

"Here is where you killed Sir Will!" His sudden speech woke all the echoes of the night. It was as though they were echoes that they heard—wild cries of anguish from afar. And all the gallant gentlemen shivered, and seemed to grow still older and more mean,—they alone knew why.

"Here I will kill Mr. Pacy too. That is, unless Mr. Pacy is afraid."

And Mr. Lovell turned towards Mr. Pacy with his sweet smile. But it seemed that Mr. Pacy was the only one that had a spark of spirit in all that gallant company. With a sort of dreadful energy he drew his sword out of its sheath, and that as awkwardly as though he had never unsheathed a sword before. Holding the naked blade in his great hand, he went and stood in front of Mr. Lovell, where the moonbeams shone upon his face. He was a great shambling fellow, a man of inches and of breadth, a good head taller than Mr. Lovell, yet now as he stood in front of him he seemed to be a smaller man. Yet, in his own peculiar way, it was plain that he was game.

"Pray, Mr. Pacy, are you in the plight I was—without a friend?"

One sneaked out from amidst the crowd. It was Mr. Twentyman, so famed in the duello. He never spoke a word, but went and stood by Mr. Pacy's side. 'Tis true he helped him to remove his coat and vest, and clumsy enough they were the pair of them, but beyond that he never raised a hand or did a thing. And he so famed in the laws and niceties of the duello! It was Mr. Lovell's friend that did it all. And indeed he did it with the rarest grace, as though he loved the work right well. And all the gallant company, in their rich clothes, like a crowd of toothless, shivering curs, stood by.

When all was ready for the fighting to begin it was very strange to look on the opposing pair. The one in all his radiant strength, bearing himself as in a wild maze of joy. The other in the dogged abandonment of a mean despair. Yet was Mr. Pacy game, as they soon saw when the swords were crossed. Never was a more awkward fencer seen. Yet it seemed as though he were consumed with a sullen internal rage, and he had so strong a wrist that it was not easy to turn aside either his defence or his attack. More than once he thrust nearly home, and followed up his thrust with such fierce determination, that had not Mr. Lovell's agility and skill been marvellous alike, it had gone hard with him that night. And, in truth, it was wonderful to see him fence. In the moonlight his blade moved with the speed of a flash of lightning, here, there, and everywhere at once. Soon it was evident that Mr. Pacy saw that it was vain to fence against this wondrous man. Such skill was never seen. Although it was plain that he perceived that the thing was vain, his determination became more dogged even than before, and he rushed on Mr. Lovell with the rage of a wild beast.

And that instant he was killed. With a most exquisite grace Mr. Lovell thrust him through the breast right to the heart. And with a dreadful suddenness he fell back upon the ground stone dead.

The gentleman that was Mr. Lovell's friend bent over the dead man as he lay upon the ground, and lightly cried—

"You have killed Mr. Pacy as you killed Sir Will."

And then he stood straight up and stretched out his hand to Mr. Lovell. And Mr. Lovell, still with his bloody blade in his right hand, took it with his left. And then he glided between his arms, drawn as it were by something he drank out of the gentleman's bright eyes, and he was folded to his breast, and their lips met in a long, long kiss. And all that gallant company looked on.

And suddenly was heard a wild, hideous, anguished, ear-splitting scream, the like of which God grant no human ever heard before. And all that gallant company cried out in an extremity of terror and of pain. It was a dreadful sound to hear.

And, when they looked again, the gentleman that was Mr. Lovell's friend had gone, and Mr. Lovell himself had fallen all in a horrid heap upon the ground. And when those that were most courageous went to look at him, they found that he was dead. And there was so awful a look upon his face that they shuddered and turned their eyes away. And one with his handkerchief covered the dead man's face.

THE "*MIGNONETTE*"

To spend your summer holiday in, there is no place like a house-boat. If you have not tried one, do. I have.

Faulkner—Reggie Faulkner—came into the office to me one day, and said—

"Lane, where are you going to spend your holiday?"

I did not know. I told him so.

"Then you're the very man I want. And I have the very thing you want."

I asked him what that was.

"The *Mignonette*," he said.

"The *Mignonette*! What's that?"

"What's that! Why, it's a house-boat. Fancy asking what that is. There is scarcely a man between Putney and Oxford who doesn't know the *Mignonette*."

I confess I was not greatly impressed. Nor did I see that the *Mignonette* was just the thing I wanted. But Faulkner is such an eloquent man.

"House-boats are all the rage. Everyone has a house-boat."

I did not see that that was an attraction; but I did not tell him so.

"If the thing goes much further, both banks will be lined with them, from the mouth of the river to the source. They're splendid fun. If you're fond of boating"—

"But I'm not fond of boating," I suggested mildly. "I don't mind, on a fine day, sitting in a boat and messing about with the oars—with the stream. But playing the amateur galley-slave I leave to other men."

"That's what you say. But wait till you find yourself in a boat, and then you'll show us how it's done. Why, you're just the build for an oarsman."

I felt, nay, I knew, that this was an outrage upon truth. I am short, and full in the waist. If that is just the build for an oarsman, then I have still some things to learn. Yet his eloquence prevailed. I allowed him to persuade me that the *Mignonette* was just the thing I wanted. It was to be had for a song—forty pounds for a month. I did not see that that was much of a song; but he assured me that it was.

"In August, sir; the month of the year. And furnished—plate and all—down to the linen. And such a boat! and only done up the other day. It is the cheapest thing upon the river."

There were to be four of us: Faulkner and I, and two other men. I asked him who the two other men were to be.

"They'll be all right," he assured me. "Trust me. I'll get two of the jolliest fellows going."

I trusted him. We were to share expenses. They also, Faulkner declared, would be a song. But I had an intuitive suspicion that he had his idea of songs, and I had mine.

My holiday began on the Wednesday following. In the interim Faulkner was to arrange all details, and on the Wednesday morning we were to go down together from Paddington. By the first post on the Wednesday there came a note from Faulkner. It seemed that he was detained in town, but I was to go down by the train agreed upon, and he was to follow with the other two men later in the day. On no account was I to delay my departure. Everything on board the *Mignonette* was in apple-pie order, and if no one put in an appearance at the time agreed upon, they—he did not say who—but they would think there was something wrong. My first impulse was to let them think. It was cool of Faulkner to leave me in the lurch like that. I had half a mind to pack my trunks and start at once—for Norway, say. But second thoughts prevailed. I was to book for a Berkshire station, and, on arrival, I was to inquire for the *Mignonette*. Anyone would tell me where it was.

I followed my part of the programme to the letter. I booked to the Berkshire station, and I inquired for the *Mignonette*; but no one could tell me where it was. The more inquiries I made, the less information I obtained. One thing I did learn, and that was, how wanting was my knowledge of the geography—and of the railway systems—of my native land. It was only on my arrival that

I became aware—Faulkner had not hinted at such a thing, perhaps he thought I knew—that that Berkshire station was, some said three, some said four, some said five miles distant from the riverside. I chartered a fly; the driver solemnly assured me that the river was nearly six miles off. When I arrived at the stream—it seemed a very short six miles, I must allow, unless the horse went very fast, which, as it only had three sound legs to go upon, I scarcely think it did—no one knew anything about the *Mignonette*. I was beginning to wonder if Faulkner had been having a joke with me—the thing was scarcely credible, yet I had some acquaintance with his character, and he might have been—and I was just going to instruct the flyman to drive me back that phenomenally short six miles of his, at the rate of a shilling a mile, and something for the driver—with a view of inflicting on Faulkner some severe bodily injury on my return to town, when help arrived. It came in the shape of a small boy. There was a house-boat moored off Mr. Coningham's fields. He had seen it there that morning.

"What's its name?"

Small boy didn't know. It was a house-boat—that was all he knew. To him, apparently, all house-boats were the same.

On this meagre information I ventured to act. I dismissed the flyman—in whose mind, all at once, the six miles seemed to have swollen into seven—and saddled the boy with my Gladstone bag. He went in search of the house-boat he had seen.

It was the *Mignonette*. There was the name painted in letters so large that he who ran might read. It was moored close into the bank. I paid the boy, and went on board. From what Faulkner had said in his note I supposed that I should find somebody awaiting my arrival. But that was a mistake of Faulkner's, and not his first, nor his last, by any means. The boat was quite deserted.

I had never been on board a house-boat before. I was at once struck by the fact that the *Mignonette* offered scanty accommodation for four grown-up persons. There was but one apartment, and that was certainly no larger than a state-room on board a liner. Behind it was a sort of cupboard, which was apparently intended to serve as a kitchen, for it contained a stove, and some pots and pans. Possibly my little adventures in search of the *Mignonette* had given my mind a jaundiced tinge; but certainly, the idea of four men living, eating, drinking, sleeping, "cribbed, cabined, confined," for four weeks, during the hottest season of the year, in such a "parlour," the thought was horrible.

There was another thing. Faulkner had mentioned—as a recommendation—that the *Mignonette* had just been done up. It had so recently that it reeked of paint. If there is one thing to which I do object, it is the smell of paint. I merely mention this to show how brightly things were promising. Faulkner had also mentioned that the *Mignonette* was furnished—down to the plate and linen. I did not go then into questions of plate and linen; but so far as I could discover there was a camp-stool on board, and a deck-chair, which required mending. There was no table, nor did I see where they could put it if there had been. Certainly not in the cabin—or whatever they called the solitary apartment—unless we were to keep outside. A cursory examination induced me to believe that that camp-stool, and that deck-chair, which required mending, was all the furniture the *Mignonette* contained. If the presence of those two articles realised Faulkner's ideas of "furnished," then I felt that his ideas were vague.

One more point. Faulkner had mentioned—always in his note—that I should find everything in apple-pie order. Among other things I expected to find was something to eat. He had undertaken to see to all the details. Considering that we had arranged to stay for a month on board, one would have supposed that such an item as provisions would have come among the details. But, if the "naked eye" could be trusted, assisted by an inquiring pair of hands, this was a delusion of mine. I had to begin my month's sojourn on board the *Mignonette* by tramping back to the village—a better six miles than the flyman's—in search of food. I found it at the inn. It took the shape of cold beef and pickles. On the bill this repast figured as "Luncheon, three-and-sixpence." I could have had the same quantity and quality of provisions, at a City luncheon bar, for sixpence. Even then I doubt if I should not have preferred my sixpence.

After "luncheon," I walked back to the *Mignonette*—I am not fond of walking, but that is by the way. When I reached it, I perceived an old gentleman was standing on the bank. He eyed me, as I thought, rather aggressively, as I boarded the craft—I am not sure if a house-boat is a "craft," but my knowledge of nautical terms is not to be relied on. Directly I was on board, he—well, shouted at me, is the only expression I can use.

"You, sir!"

I turned, and looked at him. He was a tall old gentleman, about fifty-five years old—with, I should judge, a temper somewhat older. Something seemed to have displeased him.

"I beg your pardon—did you speak to me?"

My inquiry was at least a courteous one, which his reply was not.

"Confound your impudence!" I put up my eye-glass. I thought the man was mad. "What the something are you doing there?"

"I am afraid I don't understand you."

I didn't.

"Oh yes you do, you Cockney tailor."

He looked a gentleman. I felt that no gentleman would use such language towards a perfect stranger without having some shadow of reason on his side.

"May I ask, sir, what it is that I have done?"

"You know well enough. If you don't clear out of that within an hour, I'll cut you loose."

He shook his stick at me, and went striding off at a good four miles an hour. What he meant I had not the least idea. Who he was I didn't know from Adam. A horrible fear came over me. Had I blundered on somebody else's house-boat by mistake? There might be a dozen *Mignonettes*, or a hundred, for all I knew. Certainly that particular *Mignonette* fell very short of the picture which Faulkner's eloquence had suggested to my imagination. I felt that discretion was the better part of valour, and that it would be advisable to leave it before I was turned out by force, and taken up for trespassing, or burglary, or something. In that case, it would be prudent to return to the station and await Faulkner's appearance on the scene, so that I might learn from his own lips where I was to spend my holiday.

The only reason which deterred me from pursuing such a course was a simple one: I couldn't. I had already, I reckoned, walked twelve miles. On the top of those twelve miles the prospect of another pedestrian feat was more than I could stomach.

Better wait where I was, trusting to the soothing effects of well-worded explanations when the moment of trial came. I waited. While I waited I fell asleep. I was roused from slumber by a hand being laid on my shoulder, and a familiar voice sounding in my ears—

"Hollo, old chap, haven't you got dinner ready?"

I looked up. There was Faulkner standing by my side. With him were two men. One was a stranger to me; the other was Philip Aitken: the only man with whom I am not on good terms in all this wide, wide world.

"Dinner!" I stammered.

The sudden sight of Aitken had made me feel quite queer. I had refused countless invitations to avoid running the risk of having to meet that man.

"Yes, dinner. Do you know what time it is? It's nearly eight o'clock."

"Nearly eight o'clock!"

I had been asleep four hours.

"We're starving."

"But dinner? I don't understand you, Faulkner. How was I to get your dinner when there was nothing to eat for miles?"

"Nothing to eat for miles? You don't mean to say that you have got us nothing to eat?" I suppose my face was a sufficient answer. He went on: "Why, I told you in my note to get something for dinner."

"Excuse me; but you did nothing of the kind."

He protested that he had. It was only when I showed him his own note that he discovered that he had intended to tell me, but had stopped short at the intention.

"Well, this is a go!" he said

I felt myself that the position was a pleasant one. I drew him aside.

"What is that man doing here?" I asked.

He glanced over his shoulder.

"What man? Aitken? That's one of the fellows I told you about. Let me introduce you to him."

"Thank you. Spare yourself the trouble. I know him; or, at least I did—once. Do I understand that Mr. Aitken is going to spend four weeks with me on board the *Mignonette*?"

"Of course he is. What's the matter with you, man?"

I did not tell him; at least, not then. The situation might have its comic side; but it was all tragedy to me. To think of all I had done to avoid encountering that man, and yet I had condemned myself to spend my summer holiday with him, shut up in a cabin twelve feet square!

"I suppose this is the *Mignonette*?" I hazarded a moment after.

"Of course it is the *Mignonette*. Lane, old boy, don't you feel well?"

"I only asked the question because an old gentleman has been conducting himself in a fashion which is, perhaps, peculiar to the natives of these parts. He seemed to more than think that I had no right on board."

"Some old lunatic, I suppose. But, I say, this question of food is serious. I've had nothing to eat all day; I'm starving."

The stranger spoke—

"Let us draw lots, and he on whom the lot shall fall shall be killed and cooked and consumed for the benefit of his fellows."

When the man said that, I knew, from the way in which he said it, that he was a funny man. That was the final straw. The sooner I fell overboard the better. Faulkner seemed to think that the man was humorous.

"None of your jokes, Beadle!" Beadle! What a name! "The thing's too serious. I told Metcalf to see that the *Mignonette* was moored in a nice, quiet part of the stream—I know that you like quietude, Lane—and he has. But too much quietude has its draw-backs, don't you know."

We were relieved from the food difficulty in an unexpected way. While we were debating the advisability of tramping back to the village, and adjourning to the inn for the night, we were hailed from the river. A boat was approaching us, with four men on board. Faulkner seemed to know them.

"Hollo, Metcalf!" he cried. "Here's a pretty go! We're starving, and there's nothing to eat in the place."

"That's all right," rejoined someone in the boat—who I after-wards learned was Metcalf—"we've come to dine."

"No! Not really?"

"Really. We've brought our dinner with us, too." They had.

Sorrow was turned into joy. "We thought you'd be a bit short, as this was your first night in quarters—fellows always do begin with a muddle—so we've brought enough to feed an army."

We had a sumptuous meal on the roof of the cabin. I don't enjoy picnics as a rule, but I did that one—thoroughly. Before we had finished, "the shades of night were falling fast."

"Let's light up downstairs and have a hand at nap," suggested Metcalf.

The suggestion was the cause of a discovery. There was a lamp in the cabin—but no oil.

"You're supposed to supply your own oil," said Metcalf.

It was as well to learn it—then. Faulkner ought to have been aware of it before.

"No one got a candle?" No one had. "Then it will be a case of early to bed, my boys. Unless you care to come back with us, and allow us to provide you with light, as well as food."

We thought it would be better, on the whole, to decline their invitation. Metcalf and his friends got into their boat, and pulled off through the gathering gloom. When they had got clear of us, they stopped.

"I say, Faulkner," sang out Metcalf, "I think I'd better mention it. I don't know if you're aware that you are trespassing?"

"Trespassing? No! What do you mean?"

"You told me to see that the *Mignonette* was moored in a quiet place, and I saw she was. You're moored off Coningham's meadow."

"Well, what then?"

"Nothing; only Coningham is a riparian owner, and objects to the presence of house-boats on his land. If he discovers you in the middle of the night he'll cut you loose. Ta-ta, dear boys; the stream runs our way. See you in the morning."

And Metcalf went off through the night.

"I suppose that was Coningham who slanged me," I remarked, when Faulkner had partially exhausted his vocabulary of bad language. "He said he would cut us loose. I didn't understand his meaning then. I understand it better now."

Faulkner went off again at this. All I cared for was to turn in. I hadn't felt so tired for years. I mentioned this to Faulkner. His rejoinder startled me—

"I suppose you saw that there were beds on board?"

"You suppose I saw there were beds on board? Faulkner, I don't understand you. What have I to do with all these things? You said that you would see to the details."

"So I did. I told Metcalf to see that things were right."

"You call that seeing to the details? Then next time you say that you will do a thing, I shall understand you to mean that you will tell somebody else to do it—or, you won't. As Metcalf has seen so well to the mooring of the boat, I expect he has been equally careful of the beds and bedding."

What I expected was the case. There was nothing in the shape of a bed—not even a sheet—on board.

"How about the plate and linen?" I inquired.

We had routed out two knives and three forks to help us eat Metcalf's food; but that was all the plate and linen we could find. Fortunately, I had brought a rug and ulster with me—for, even in August, I decline to blindly trust the English climate—or I should have had to sleep, uncovered, upon bare boards. The others had to. They had left their luggage in the village, with instructions to send it up in the morning. There was some talk about walking to the inn. But, in the first place, they were tired; then, for those parts, it was late; and, in the third place, it was doubtful if, when they did get there, they would find a bed.

"The place is always crammed to the roof this time of the year," said Faulkner.

So they resolved to bear the ills they had, rather than fly to others which they knew not of.

It seemed to me that I had only just closed my eyes when I opened them again. Yet it was broad daylight. I looked at my watch. It was a few minutes past five. I had been sleeping on the roof of the cabin; its interior I had left to Faulkner and his friends. They were rugless. Moreover, I felt persuaded that with three inside, the cabin would have as much as it could hold. Never in my life had I slept in the open air before. When I found myself awake, I also found that I was shivering. Moving, I discovered that one cause of this was that the rug which covered me was sopping wet; it was soaked with dew. So were the boards on which I had been lying. I sat up when I realised these little facts, sat up with a groan, for

I was stiff and sore, and my limbs ached as though they were a "mask of bruises." Apparently, like the paths of glory, my holidays bade fair to lead me to the grave.

As I sat, wondering whether my money might not be as profitably spent on doctors' bills as on the *Mignonette* and on Aitken's sweet society, I became aware that something was happening on the bank. It was, doubtless, that which had roused me. I got up, with difficulty, to see what it was.

There were three persons on the bank. One was the old gentleman who had insulted me yesterday, and two were evidently his myrmidons. He was superintending their operations. One of them was carrying a pole, and the other was doing something to the moorings of the *Mignonette*. Suddenly the house-boat gave a lurch. The old gentleman said something, as though, now, he were pleased.

"That's right! She's adrift! Now, Gale, give her a shove with the pole!"

Gale gave her a shove with the pole, so violent a shove that he all but heeled us over. I thought, for a moment, that he had done it quite.

"Good gracious, man! What are you doing?"

My exclamation caused them to be, for the first time, conscious of my presence. The old gentleman looked at me, and smiled.

"So it's you, is it? I hope you enjoy drifting with the stream. Both together, my men, pole her clear."

Both the myrmidons took hold of the pole, and poled her clear. I thought that my latter end had come. If she had gone over, chilled as I was to the bone, and hampered with my clothes, I knew I should have been unable to swim.

"If I find you here again," shouted the old gentleman, "I'll not only cut you loose, but I'll prosecute you as well."

He might. If he ever found me there again I gave him leave to work his wicked will. Apparently the misadventures of the *Mignonette* had not aroused the slumberers below. I went down to supply this slight omission. Opening the cabin door somewhat suddenly, it struck against something hard. The something hard proved to be Aitken's head. He was lying on the floor in such a position that whoever opened the door was bound to hit him.

"Faulkner!" I cried. "Wake up!"

He woke up.

"Hollo, Lane, is that you? By Jingo, aren't I stiff!"

"So am I; but that's a trifle. We're not only stiff—we're adrift as well."

"Adrift!"

Faulkner sat up, rubbing his eyes. Aitken sat up too—rubbing his head.

"That old gentleman who slanged me yesterday has cast our moorings loose, and had us shoved into the centre of the stream."

"No!"

But a momentary examination showed that it was Yes. We were drifting down the stream, broadside on, at the rate of about a mile an hour. Faulkner roused himself to a sense of the situation.

"We shall have to get into the boat, and tow the whole thing down to the village. Coningham's a beast, I've heard of him before; but I'll be even with Metcalf for playing us this trick."

A pair-oared skiff was attached to the *Mignonette*. Into this we had to get, two by two, and strain ourselves, with a view of towing the *Mignonette* against the stream. My companion in the boat was Beadle.

"I don't know if you are aware that I am doing most of the work," he said. I thought, on the contrary, that that was very possible.

"I shouldn't mind if you did it all," I owned. "This sort of thing is not my line."

"Perhaps not. Nor is it mine. But it has to be done."

He was not a funny man just then. After we had towed the *Mignonette* about six yards—and she had to be towed six miles!—I stopped pulling; not that my ceasing to labour made much difference to our rate of progress, but I did.

"I have had enough of this. I don't see that it has to be done. If it has, I don't do it. I decline to pull another stroke."

There was a wrangle, but I didn't mind. I had my way. The *Mignonette* was allowed to drift from the village, instead of towards it. Presently a tug came along, with a couple of barges in tow. To the tail of one of the barges we were allowed to attach ourselves, for a consideration. And the tug towed us towards the village. On the way I had a little talk to Faulkner.

"I don't know, Faulkner, if you are aware that I am on my holiday."

"Of course I am. What do you mean?"

"Nothing. Only I am waiting for the holiday to begin."

"It's beginning now."

"Is it? I'm glad you told me."

"Have a little patience, and we'll soon get things in shape. By the way, I've been drawing up a list of some of the things we'll have to get. We'd better buy them. It's cheaper than getting them on hire."

He handed me a list. It contained knives, forks, spoons, glasses, a dinner-service, a tea-service, carpets—"just a little Turkish carpet or two to put about the place"—said Faulkner; chairs, all sorts of chairs, apparently, perhaps wanted for the same purpose as the carpets, "to put about the place"; tables, curtains, beds, bedding, blankets, sheets. In short, all the furniture required to furnish a "bijou residence," and, when furnished, a jewel it would be. I handed him back the list.

"You don't seriously mean to say, Faulkner, that you expect me to join you in buying all those things?"

"Why not? It's cheaper than getting them on hire."

"Possibly. But I would point out to you that we are supposed to have got them on hire already. You told me that we were to have the *Mignonette* for a month for forty pounds—furnished."

"Just so. Furnished as it is. You don't suppose we were going to find a lot of costly fittings on board for forty pounds? Why, the things on some of the house-boats cost thousands."

"Exactly. Now I understand you. What you meant was, that we were to enjoy the use of the *Mignonette*, furnished—as it isn't. Thank you, Faulkner. I am obliged to you for your list; but I am afraid I must ask you to allow me to stand excused. You shall have my share of the forty pounds, and, for my holiday, I will go elsewhere. If nothing else swayed me, the presence of Mr. Aitken on board the *Mignonette* would be sufficient reason. Under no circumstances could I consent to associate with Mr. Aitken. It is, perhaps, a prejudice on my part; but there it is."

"That's odd. Aitken says just the same thing of you. He says if you don't go, he will."

"That renders the matter delightfully simple. I will go."

I did. Faulkner, in a half-hearted sort of way, tried to induce me to stay. He assured me that when they had got things in shape—and purchased the furniture of that "bijou residence"—the *Mignonette* would be a paradise on earth. I didn't see it. I have seen something of house-boats since then, and I see it less than ever. Every man and every woman has his and her own ideas of enjoyment. Some men go to the North Pole—for pleasure! I believe some of them would walk there if they could get the chance. I prefer to stay at home, within easy distance of Pall Mall. I enjoyed my holiday immensely—upon the shady side.

A SET OF CHESSMEN

I

"BUT, Monsieur, perceive how magnificent they are! There is not in Finistère, there is not in Brittany, nay, it is certain there is not in France so superb a set of chessmen. And ivory! And the carving—observe, for example, the variety of detail."

They certainly were a curious set of chessmen, magnificent in a way, but curious first of all. As M. Bobineau remarked, holding a rook in one hand and a knight in the other, the care paid to details by the carver really was surprising. But two hundred and fifty francs! For a set of chessmen!

"So, so, my friend. I am willing to admit that the work is good—in a kind of a way. But two hundred and fifty francs! If it were fifty, now?"

"Fifty!" Up went M. Bobineau's shoulders, and down went M. Bobineau's head between them, in the fashion of those toys which are pulled by a string. "Ah, mon Dieu! Monsieur laughs at me!"

And there came another voluble declaration of their merits. They certainly were a curious set. I really think they were the most curious set I ever saw. I would have preferred them, for instance, to anything they have at South Kensington, and they have some remarkable examples there. And, of course, the price was small—I even admit it was ridiculously small. But when one has only five thousand francs a year for everything, two hundred and fifty being taken away—and for a set of chessmen—do leave a vacancy behind.

I asked Bobineau where he got them. Business was slack that sunny afternoon—it seemed to me that I was the only customer he ever had, but that must have been a delusion on my part. Report said he was a warm man, one of Morlaix's warmest men, and his queer old shop in the queer old Grande Rue—Grande Rue! what

a name for an alley!—contained many things which were valuable
as well as queer. But there, at least, was no other customer in sight
just then, so Bobineau told me all the tale.

It seemed there had been a M. Funichon—Auguste Funichon—
no, not a Breton, a Parisian, a true Parisian, who had come and
settled down in the commune of Plouigneau, over by the *gare*.
This M. Funichon was, for example, a little—well, a little—a little
exalted, let us say. It is true that the country people said he was stark
mad, but Bobineau, for his part, said no, no, no! It is not necessary,
because one is a little eccentric, that one is mad. Here Bobineau
looked at me out of the corner of his eye. Are not the English, of
all people, the most eccentric, and yet is it not known to all the
world that they are not, necessarily, stark mad? This M. Funichon
was not rich, quite the contrary. It was a little place he lived in—the
merest cottage, in fact. And in it he lived alone, and, according to
report, there was only one thing he did all day and all night long,
and that was, play chess. It appears that he was that rarest and
most amiable of imbeciles, a chess-maniac. Is there such a word?

"What a life!" said M. Bobineau. "Figure it to yourself! To do
nothing—nothing!—but play chess! They say"—M. Bobineau
looked round him with an air of mystery—"they say he starved
himself to death. He was so besotted by his miserable chess that
he forgot—absolutely forgot, this imbecile—to eat."

That was what M. Bobineau said they said. It required a vigor-
ous effort of the imagination to quite take it in. To what a state
of forgetfulness must a man arrive before he forgets to eat! But
whether M. Funichon forgot to eat, or whether he didn't, at least
he died, and being dead they sold his goods—why they sold them
was not quite clear, but at the sale M. Bobineau was the chief pur-
chaser. One of the chief lots was the set of ivory chessmen which
had caught my eyes. They were the dead man's favourite set, and
no wonder! Bobineau was of opinion that if he had had his way he
would have had them buried with him in his grave.

"It is said," he whispered, again with the glance of mystery
around, "that they found him dead, seated at the table, the chessmen on the board, his hand on the white rook, which was giving
mate to the adversary's king."

Either what a vivid imagination had Bobineau, or what odd

things the people said! One pictures the old man, seated all alone, with his last breath finishing his game.

Well, I bought the set of ivory chessmen. At this time of day I freely admit that they were cheap at two hundred and fifty francs—dirt cheap, indeed; but a hundred was all I paid. I knew Bobineau so well—I daresay he bought them for twenty-five. As I bore them triumphantly away my mind was occupied by thoughts of their original possessor. I was filled by quite a sentimental tenderness as I meditated on the part they had played, according to Bobineau, in that last scene. But St. Servan drove all those thoughts away. Philippe Henri de St. Servan was rather a difficult person to get on with. It was with him I shared at that time my apartment on the *place.*

"Let us see!" I remarked when I got in, "what have I here?"

He was seated, his country pipe in his mouth, at the open window, looking down upon the river. The Havre boat was making ready to start—at Morlaix the nautical event of the week. There was quite a bustle on the quay. St. Servan just looked round, and then looked back again. I sat down and untied my purchase.

"I think there have been criticisms—derogatory criticisms—passed by a certain person upon a certain set of chessmen. Perhaps that person will explain what he has to say to these."

St. Servan marched up to the table. He looked at them through his half-closed eyelids.

"Toys!" was all he said.

"Perhaps! Yet toys which made a tragedy. Have you ever heard of the name of Funichon?" By a slight movement of his grisly grey eyebrows he intimated that it was possible he had. "These chessmen belonged to him. He had just finished a game with them when they found him dead—the winning piece, a white rook, was in his hand. Suggest an epitaph to be placed over his grave. There's a picture for a painter—eh?"

"Bah! He was a Communist!"

That was all St. Servan said. And so saying, St. Servan turned away to look out of the window at the Havre boat again. There was an end of M. Funichon for him. Not that he meant exactly what he said. He simply meant that M. Funichon was not Legitimist—out of sympathy with the gentlemen who met, and decayed, visibly, before the naked eye, at the club on the other side of the *place*. With St. Servan not to be Legitimist meant to be nothing at all—out of his range of vision absolutely. Seeing that was so, it is strange he should have borne with me as he did. But he was a wonderful old man.

II

WE played our first game with the ivory chessmen when St. Servan returned from the club. I am free to confess that it was an occasion for me. I had dusted all the pieces, and had the board all laid when St. Servan entered, and when we drew for choice of moves the dominant feeling in my mind was the thought of the dead man sitting all alone, with the white rook in his hand. There was an odour of sanctity about the affair—a whiff of air from the land of the ghosts.

Nevertheless, my loins were girded up, and I was prepared to bear myself as a man in the strife. We were curiously well matched, St. Servan and I. We had played two hundred and twenty games, and, putting draws aside, each had scored the same number of wins. He had his days, and so had I. At one time I was eleven games ahead, but since that thrice blessed hour I had not scored a single game. He had tracked me steadily, and eventually had made the scores exactly tie. In these latter days it had grown with him to be an article of faith that as a chess-player I was quite played out—and there was a time when I had thought the same of him!

He won the move, and then, as usual, there came an interval for reflection. The worst thing about St. Servan—regarded from a chess-playing point of view—was, that he took such a time to begin. When a man has opened his game it is excusable—laudable, indeed—if he pauses to reflect, a reasonable length of time. But I never knew a man who was so fond of reflection before a move was made. As a rule, that absurd habit of his had quite an irritating effect upon my nerves, but that evening I felt quite cool and prepared to sit him out.

There we sat, both smoking our great pipes, he staring at the board, and I at him. He put out his hand, almost touched a piece, and then, with a start, he drew it back again. An interval—the same pantomime again. Another interval—and a repetition of the pantomime. I puffed a cloud of smoke into the air, and softly sighed. I knew he had been ten minutes by my watch. Possibly the sigh had a stimulating effect, for he suddenly stretched out his hand and moved queen's knight's pawn a single square.

I was startled. He was great at book openings, that was the absurdest part of it. He would lead you to suppose that he was meditating something quite original, and then would perhaps begin with fool's mate after all. He, at least, had never tried queen's knight's pawn a single square before.

I considered a reply. Pray let it be understood—though I would not have confessed it to St. Servan for the world—that I am no player. I am wedded to the game for an hour or two at night, or, peradventure, of an afternoon at times; but I shall never be admitted to its inner mysteries—never! not if I outspan Methuselah. I am not built that way. St. Servan and I were two children who, loving the sea, dabble their feet in the shallows left by the tide. I have no doubt that there are a dozen replies to that opening of his, but I did not know one then. I had some hazy idea of developing a game of my own, while keeping an eye on his, and for that purpose put out my hand to move the queen's pawn two, when I felt my wrist grasped by—well, by what felt uncommonly like an invisible hand. I was so startled that I almost dropped my pipe. I drew my hand back again, and was conscious of the slight detaining pressure of unseen fingers. Of course it was hallucination, but it seemed so real, and was so expected, that—well, I settled my pipe more firmly between my lips—it had all but fallen from my mouth, and took a whiff or two to calm my nerves. I glanced up, cautiously, to see if St. Servan noticed my unusual behaviour, but his eyes were fixed stonily upon the board.

After a moment's hesitation—it was absurd!—I stretched out my hand again. The hallucination was repeated, and in a very tangible form. I was distinctly conscious of my wrist being wrenched aside and guided to a piece I had never meant to touch, and almost before I was aware of it, instead of the move I had meant to make, I had made a servile copy of St. Servan's opening—I had moved queen's knight's pawn a single square!

To adopt the language of the late Dick Swiveller, that was a staggerer. I own that for an instant I was staggered. I could do nothing else but stare. For at least ten seconds I forgot to smoke. I was conscious that when St. Servan saw my move he knit his brows. Then the usual interval for reflection came again. Half unconsciously I watched him. When, as I supposed, he had decided on his move, he stretched out his hand, as I had done, and also, as I had done, he drew it back again. I was a little startled—he seemed a little startled too. There was a momentary pause; back went his hand again, and, by way of varying the monotony, he moved—king's knight's pawn a single square.

I wondered, and held my peace. There might be a gambit based upon these lines, or there might not; but since I was quite clear that I knew no reply to such an opening I thought I would try a little experiment, and put out my hand, not with the slightest conception of any particular move in my head, but simply to see what happened. Instantly a grasp fastened on my wrist; my hand was guided to—king's knight's pawn a single square.

This was getting, from every point of view, to be distinctly interesting. The chessmen appeared to be possessed of a property of which Bobineau had been unaware. I caught myself wondering if he would have insisted on a higher price if he had known of it. Curiosities nowadays do fetch such fancy sums—and what price for a ghost? They appeared to be automatic chessmen, automatic in a sense entirely their own.

Having made my move, or having had somebody else's move made for me, which is perhaps the more exact way of putting it, I contemplated my antagonist. When he saw what I had done, or what somebody else had done—the things are equal—St. Servan frowned. He belongs to the bony variety, the people who would not loll in a chair to save their lives—his aspect struck me as being even more poker-like than usual. He meditated his reply an unconscionable length of time, the more unconscionable since I strongly doubted if it would be his reply after all. But at last he showed signs of action. He kept his eyes fixed steadily upon the board, his frown became pronounced, and he began to raise his hand. I write "began," because it was a process which took some time. Cautiously he brought it up, inch by inch. But no sooner had he brought it over the board than his behaviour became quite singular. He positively glared, and to my eyes seemed to be having a struggle with his own right hand. A struggle in which he was worsted, for he leant back in his seat with a curiously discomfited air.

He had moved queen's rook's pawn two squares—the automatic principle which impelled these chessmen seemed to have a partiality for pawns.

It was my turn for reflection. I pressed the tobacco down in my pipe, and thought—or tried to think—it out. Was it an hallucination, and was St. Servan the victim of hallucination too? Had I moved those pawns spontaneously, actuated by the impulse of my own free will, or hadn't I? And what was the meaning of the little scene I had just observed? I am a tolerably strong man. It would require no slight exercise of force to compel me to move one piece when I had made up my mind that I would move another piece instead. I have been told, and I believe not altogether untruly told, that the rigidity of my right wrist resembles iron. I have not spent so much time in the tennis-court and fencing-room for nothing. I had tried one experiment. I thought I would try another. I made up my mind that I would move queen's pawn two—stop me who stop can.

I felt that St. Servan in his turn was watching me. Preposterously easy though the feat appeared to be as I resolved on its performance, I was conscious of an unusual degree of cerebral excitement—a sort of feeling of do or die. But as, in spite of the feeling, I didn't do, it was perhaps as well I didn't die. Intending to keep complete control over my own muscles, I raised my right hand, probably to the full as cautiously as St. Servan had done. I approached the queen's pawn. I was just about to seize the piece when that unseen grasp fastened on my wrist. I paused, with something of the feeling which induces the wrestler to pause before entering on the veritable tug of war. For one thing, I was desirous to satisfy myself as to the nature of the grasp—what it was that seemed to grasp me.

It seemed to be a hand. The fingers went over the back of my wrist, and the thumb beneath. The fingers were long and thin—it was altogether a slender hand. But it seemed to be a man's hand, and an old man's hand at that. The skin was tough and wrinkled, clammy and cold. On the little finger there was a ring, and on the first, about the region of the first joint, appeared to be something of the nature of a wart. I should say that it was anything but a beautiful hand, it was altogether too attenuated and clawlike, and I would have betted that it was yellow with age.

At first the pressure was slight, almost as slight as the touch of a baby's hand, with a gentle inclination to one side. But as I kept my own hand firm, stiff, resolved upon my own particular move, with, as it were, a sudden snap, the pressure tightened and, not a little to my discomfiture, I felt my wrist held as in an iron vice. Then, as it must have seemed to St. Servan, who, I was aware, was still keenly watching me, I began to struggle with my own hand. The spectacle might have been fun to him, but the reality was, at that moment, anything but fun to me. I was dragged to one side. Another hand was fastened upon mine. My fingers were forced open—I had tightly clenched my fist to enable me better to resist—my wrist was forced down, my fingers were closed upon a piece, I was compelled to move it forward, my fingers were unfastened to replace the piece upon the board. The move completed, the unseen grasp instantly relaxed, and I was free, or appeared to be free, again to call my hand my own.

I had moved queen's rook's pawn two squares. This may seem comical enough to read about, but it was anything but comical to feel. When the thing was done I stared at St. Servan, and St. Servan stared at me. We stared at each other, I suppose, a good long minute, then I broke the pause.

"Anything the matter?" I inquired. He put up his hand and curled his moustache, and, if I may say so, he curled his lip as well. "Do you notice anything odd about—about the game?" As I spoke about the game I motioned my hand towards my brand-new set of chessmen. He looked at me with hard suspicious eyes.

"Is it a trick of yours?" he asked.

"Is what a trick of mine?"

"If you do not know, then how should I?"

I drew a whiff or two from my pipe, looking at him keenly all the time, then signed towards the board with my hand.

"It's your move," I said.

He merely inclined his head. There was a momentary pause.

When he stretched out his hand he suddenly snatched it back again, and half started from his seat with a stifled execration.

"Did you feel anything upon your wrist?" I asked.

"Mon Dieu! It is not what I feel—see that!"

He was eyeing his wrist as he spoke. He held it out under the glare of the lamp. I bent across and looked at it. For so old a man he had a phenomenally white and delicate skin—under the glare of the lamp the impressions of finger-marks were plainly visible upon his wrist. I whistled as I saw them.

"Is it a trick of yours?" he asked again.

"It is certainly no trick of mine."

"Is there anyone in the room besides us two?"

I shrugged my shoulders and looked round. He too looked round, with something I thought not quite easy in his glance.

"Certainly no one of my acquaintance, and certainly no one who is visible to me!"

With his fair white hand—the left, not the one which had the finger-marks upon the wrist—St. Servan smoothed his huge moustache.

"Someone, or something, has compelled me—yes, from the first—to move, not as I would, but—bah! I know not how."

"Exactly the same thing has occurred to me."

I laughed. St. Servan glared. Evidently the humour of the thing did not occur to him, he being the sort of man who would require a surgical operation to make him see a joke. But the humorous side of the situation struck me forcibly.

"Perhaps we are favoured by the presence of a ghost—perhaps even by the ghost of M. Funichon. Perhaps, after all, he has not yet played his last game with his favourite set. He may have returned—shall we say from—where?—to try just one more set-to with us! If, my dear sir"—I waved my pipe affably, as though addressing an unseen personage—"it is really you, I beg you will reveal yourself—materialise is, I believe, the expression now in vogue—and show us the sort of ghost you are!"

Somewhat to my surprise, and considerably to my amusement, St. Servan rose from his seat and stood by the table, stiff and straight as a scaffold-pole.

"These, Monsieur, are subjects on which one does not jest."

"Do you, then, believe in ghosts?" I knew he was a superstitious man—witness his fidelity to the superstition of right divine—but this was the first inkling I had had of how far his superstition carried him.

"Believe!—In ghosts! In what, then, do you believe? I, Monsieur, am a religious man."

"Do you believe, then, that a ghost is present with us now—the ghost, for instance, of M. Funichon?"

St. Servan paused. Then he crossed himself—actually crossed himself before my eyes. When he spoke there was a peculiar dryness in his tone.

"With your permission, Monsieur, I will retire to bed."

There was an exasperating thing to say! There must be a large number of men in the world who would give—well, a good round sum, to light even on the trail of a ghost. And here were we in the actual presence of something—let us say apparently curious, at anyrate, and here was St. Servan calmly talking about retiring to bed, without making the slightest attempt to examine the thing! It was enough to make the members of the Psychical Research Society turn in their graves. The mere suggestion fired my blood.

"I do beg, St. Servan, that you at least will finish the game." I saw he hesitated, so I drove the nail well home. "Is it possible that you, a brave man, having given proofs of courage upon countless fields, can turn tail at what is doubtless an hallucination after all?"

"Is it that Monsieur doubts my courage?"

I knew the tone—if I was not careful I should have an affair upon my hands.

"Come, St. Servan, sit down and finish the game."

Another momentary pause. He sat down, and—it would not be correct to write that we finished the game, but we made another effort to go on. My pipe had gone out. I refilled and lighted it.

"You know, St. Servan, it is really nonsense to talk about ghosts."

"It is a subject on which I never talk."

"If something does compel us to make moves which we do not intend, it is something which is capable of a natural explanation."

"Perhaps Monsieur will explain it, then?"

"I will! Before I've finished! If you only won't turn tail and go to bed! I think it very possible, too, that the influence, whatever it is, has gone—it is quite on the cards that our imagination has played us some subtle trick. It is your move, but before you do anything just tell me what move you mean to make."

"I will move"—he hesitated—"I will move queen's pawn."

He put out his hand, and, with what seemed to me hysterical suddenness, he moved king's rook's pawn two squares.

"So! our friend is still here then! I suppose you did not change your mind?"

There was a *very* peculiar look about St. Servan's eyes.

"I did not change my mind."

I noticed, too, that his lips were uncommonly compressed.

"It is my move now. *I* will move queen's pawn. We are not done yet. When I put out my hand you grasp my wrist—and we shall see what we shall see."

"Shall I come round to you?"

"No, stretch out across the table—now!"

I stretched out my hand; that instant he stretched out his, but spontaneous though the action seemed to be, another, an unseen hand, had fastened on my wrist. He observed it too.

"There appears to be another hand between yours and mine."

"I know there is."

Before I had the words well out my hand had been wrenched aside, my fingers unclosed, and then closed, then unclosed again, and I had moved king's rook's pawn two squares. St. Servan and I sat staring at each other—for my part I felt a little bewildered.

"This is very curious! Very curious indeed! But before we say anything about it we will try another little experiment, if you don't mind. I will come over to you." I went over to him. "Let me grasp your wrist with both my hands." I grasped it, as firmly as I could, as it lay upon his knee. "Now try to move queen's pawn."

He began to raise his hand, I holding on to his wrist with all my strength. Hardly had he raised it to the level of the table when two unseen hands, grasping mine, tore them away as though my strength were of no account. I saw him give a sort of shudder—he had moved queen's bishop's pawn two squares.

"This is a devil of a ghost!" I said.

St. Servan said nothing. But he crossed himself, not once, but half a dozen times.

"There is still one little experiment that I would wish to make."

St. Servan shook his head.

"Not I!" he said.

"Ah but, my friend, this is an experiment which I can make without your aid. I simply want to know if there is nothing tangible about our unseen visitor except his hands. It is my move." I returned to my side of the table. I again addressed myself, as it were, to an unseen auditor. "My good ghost, my good M. Funichon—if it is you—you are at liberty to do as you desire with my hand."

I held it out. It instantly was grasped. With my left hand I made several passes in the air up and down, behind and before, in every direction so far as I could. It met with no resistance. There seemed to be nothing tangible but those invisible fingers which grasped my wrist—and I had moved queen's bishop's pawn two squares.

St. Servan rose from his seat.

"It is enough. Indeed it is too much. This ribaldry must cease. It had been better had Monsieur permitted me to retire to bed."

"Then you are sure it is a ghost—the ghost of M. Funichon, we'll say?"

"This time Monsieur must permit me to wish him a good night's rest."

He bestowed on me, as his manner was, a stiff inclination of the head, which would have led a stranger to suppose that we had met each other for the first time ten minutes ago, instead of being the acquaintances of twelve good years. He moved across the room.

"St. Servan, one moment before you go! You are surely not going to leave a man alone at the post of peril?"

"It were better that Monsieur should come too."

"Half a second, and I will. I have only one remark to make, and that is to the ghost."

I rose from my seat. St. Servan made a half-movement towards the door, then changed his mind and remained quite still.

"If there is any other person with us in the room, may I ask that person to let us hear his voice, or hers? Just to speak one word."

Not a sound.

"It is possible—I am not acquainted with the laws which govern—eh—ghosts—that the faculty of speech is denied to them. If that be so, might I ask for the favour of a sign—for instance, move a piece while my friend and I are standing where we are?"

Not a sign; not a chessman moved.

"Then M. Funichon, if it indeed be you, and you are incapable of speech, or even of moving a piece of your own accord, and are only able to spoil our game, I beg to inform you that you are an exceedingly ill-mannered and foolish person, and had far better have stayed away."

As I said this I was conscious of a current of cold air before my face, as though a swiftly moving hand had shaved my cheek.

"By Jove, St. Servan, something has happened at last. I believe our friend the ghost has tried to box my ears!"

St. Servan's reply came quietly stern.

"I think it were better that Monsieur came with me."

For some reason St. Servan's almost contemptuous coldness fired my blood. I became suddenly enraged.

"I shall do nothing of the kind! Do you think I am going to be fooled by a trumpery conjuring trick which would disgrace a shilling séance? Driven to bed at this time of day by a ghost! And such a ghost! If it were something like a ghost one wouldn't mind; but a fool of a ghost like this!"

Even as the words passed my lips I felt the touch of fingers against my throat. The touch increased my rage. I snatched at them, only to find that there was nothing there.

"Damn you!" I cried. "Funichon, you old fool, do you think that you can frighten me? You see those chessmen; they are mine, bought and paid for with my money—you dare to try and prevent me doing with them exactly as I please."

Again the touch against my throat. It made my rage the more. "As I live, I will smash them all to pieces, and grind them to powder beneath my heel."

My passion was ridiculous—childish even. But then the circumstances were exasperating—unusually so, one might plead. I was standing three or four feet from the table. I dashed forward. As I did so a hand was fastened on my throat. Instantly it was joined by another. They gripped me tightly. They maddened me. With a madman's fury I still pressed forward. I might as well have fought with fate. They clutched me as with bands of steel, and flung me to the ground.

III

WHEN I recovered consciousness I found St. Servan bending over me.

"What is the matter?" I inquired, when I found that I was lying on the floor.

"I think you must have fainted."

"Fainted! I never did such a thing in my life. It must have been a curious kind of faint, I think."

"It was a curious kind of faint."

With his assistance I staggered to my feet. I felt bewildered. I glanced round. There were the chessmen still upon the board, the hanging lamp above. I tried to speak. I seemed to have lost the use of my tongue. In silence he helped me to the door. He half led, half carried me—for I seemed to have lost the use of my feet as well as that of my tongue—to my bedroom. He even assisted me to undress, never leaving me till I was between the sheets. All the time not a word was spoken. When he went I believe he took the key outside and locked the door.

That was a night of dreams. I know not if I was awake or sleeping, but all sorts of strange things presented themselves to my mental eye. I could not shut them from my sight. One figure was prominent in all I saw—the figure of a man. I knew, or thought I knew, that it was M. Funichon. He was a lean old man, and what I noticed chiefly were his hands. Such ugly hands! In some fantastical way I seemed to be contending with them all through the night.

And yet in the morning when I woke—for I did wake up, and that from as sweet refreshing sleep as one might wish to have—it was all gone. It was bright day. The sun was shining into the great, ill-furnished room. As I got out of bed and began to dress, the humorous side of the thing had returned to me again. The idea of there being anything supernatural about a set of ivory chessmen appeared to me to be extremely funny.

I found St. Servan had gone out. It was actually half-past ten! His table d'hôte at the Hôtel de Bretagne was at eleven, and before he breakfasted he always took a *petit verre* at the club. If he had locked the door overnight he had not forgotten to unlock it before he started. I went into the rambling, barnlike room which served us for a *salon*.

The chessmen had disappeared. Probably St. Servan had put them away—I wondered if the ghost had interfered with him. I laughed to myself as I went out—fancy St. Servan contending with a ghost.

The proprietor of the Hôtel de Bretagne is Legitimist, so all the aristocrats go there—of course, St. Servan with the rest. Presumably the landlord's politics is the point, to his cooking they are apparently indifferent—I never knew a worse table in my life! The landlord of the Hôtel de l'Europe may be a Communist for all I care—*his* cooking is first-rate, so I go there. I went there that morning. After I had breakfasted I strolled off towards the Grande Rue, to M. Bobineau.

When he saw me M. Bobineau was all smirks and smiles—he *must* have got those chessmen for *less* than five-and-twenty francs! I asked him if he had any more of the belongings of M. Funichon.

"But certainly! Three other sets of chessmen."

I didn't want to look at those, apparently one set was quite enough for me. Was that all he had?

"But no! There was an ancient bureau, very magnificent, carved"—

I thanked him—nor did I want to look at that. In the Grande Rue at Morlaix old bureaux carved about the beginning of the fifteenth century—if you listen to the vendors—are as plentiful as cobblestones.

"But I have all sorts of things of M. Funichon. It was I who bought them nearly all. Books, papers, and"—

M. Bobineau waved his hands towards a multitude of books and papers which crowded the shelves at the side of his shop. I took a volume down. When I opened it I found it was in manuscript.

"That work is unique!" explained Bobineau. "It was the intention of M. Funichon to give it to the world, but he died before his purpose was complete. It is the record of all the games of chess he ever played—in fifty volumes. Monsieur will perceive it is unique."

I should think it was unique! In fifty volumes! The one I held was a large quarto, bound in leather, containing some six or seven hundred pages, and was filled from cover to cover with matter in a fine, clear handwriting, written on both sides of the page. I pictured the face of the publisher to whom it was suggested that *he* should give to the world such a work as that.

I opened the volume at the first page. It was, as Bobineau said, apparently the record, with comments, of an interminable series of games of chess. I glanced at the initial game. Here are the opening moves, just as they were given there:—

White.	Black.
Queen's Knight's Pawn, one square.	Queen's Knight's Pawn, one square.
King's Knight's Pawn, one square.	King's Knight's Pawn, one square.
Queen's Rook's Pawn, two squares.	Queen's Rook's Pawn, two squares.
King's Rook's Pawn, two squares.	King's Rook's Pawn, two squares.

They were exactly the moves of the night before. They were such peculiar moves, and made under such peculiar circumstances, that I was scarcely likely to mistake them. So far as we had gone, St. Servan and I, assisted by the unseen hand, had reproduced M. Funichon's initial game in the first volume of his fifty—and a very peculiar game it seemed to be. I asked Bobineau what he would take for the volume which I held.

"Monsieur perceives that to part them would spoil the set, which is unique. Monsieur shall have the whole fifty"—I shuddered. I imagine Bobineau saw I did, he spoke so very quickly— "for a five-franc piece, which is less than the value of the paper and the binding."

I knew then that he had probably been paid for carting the rubbish away. However, I paid him his five-franc piece, and marched off with the volume under my arm, giving him to understand, to his evident disappointment, that at my leisure I would give him instructions as to the other forty-nine.

As I went along I thought the matter over. M. Funichon seemed to have been a singular kind of man—he appeared to have carried his singularity even beyond the grave. Could it have been the cold-blooded intention of his ghost to make us play the whole contents of the fifty volumes through? What a fiend of a ghost his ghost must be!

I opened the volume and studied the initial game. The people were right who had said that the man was mad. None but an imbecile would have played such a game—his right hand against his left!—and none but a raving madman would have recorded his imbecility in black and white, as though it were a thing to be proud of! Certainly none but a criminal lunatic would have endeavoured to foist his puerile travesty of the game and study of chess upon two innocent men.

Still the thing was curious. I flattered myself that St. Servan would be startled when he saw the contents of the book I was carrying home. I resolved that I would instantly get out the chessmen and begin another game—perhaps the ghost of M. Funichon would favour us with a further exposition of his ideas of things. I even made up my mind that I would communicate with the Psychical Research Society. Not at all improbably they might think the case sufficiently remarkable to send down a member of their body to inquire into the thing upon the spot. I almost began to hug myself on the possession of a ghost, a ghost, too, which might be induced to perform at will—almost on the principle of "drop a coin into the slot and the figures move"! It was cheap at a hundred francs. What a stir those chessmen still might make! What vexed problems they might solve! Unless I was much mistaken, the expenditure of those hundred francs had placed me on the royal road to immortality.

Filled with such thoughts I reached our rooms. I found that St. Servan had returned. With him, if I may say so, he had brought his friends. Such friends! Ye Goths! When I opened the door the first thing which greeted me was a strong, not to say suffocating, smell of incense. The room was filled with smoke. A fire was blazing on the hearth. Before it was St. Servan, on his knees, his hands clasped in front of him, in an attitude of prayer. By him stood a priest, in his robes of office. He held what seemed a pestle and mortar, whose contents he was throwing by handfuls on to the flames, muttering some doggerel to himself the while. Behind him were two acolytes,

With nice clean faces, and nice white stoles,

who were swinging censers—hence the odour which filled the room. I was surprised when I beheld all this. They appeared to be holding some sort of religious service—and I had not bargained for that sort of thing when I had arranged with St. Servan to share the rooms with him. In my surprise I unconsciously interrupted the proceedings.

"St. Servan! Whatever is the meaning of this?"

St. Servan looked up, and the priest looked round—that was all the attention they paid to me. The acolytes eyed me with what I conceived to be a grin upon their faces. But I was not to be put down like that.

"I must ask you, St. Servan, for an explanation."

The priest turned the mortar upside down, and emptied the remainder of its contents into the fire.

"It is finished," he said.

St. Servan rose from his knees and crossed himself.

"We have exorcised the demon," he observed.

"You have what?" I asked.

"We have driven out the evil spirit which possessed the chessmen."

I gasped. A dreadful thought struck me.

"You don't mean to say that you have dared to play tricks with my property?"

"Monsieur," said the priest, "I have ground it into dust."

He had. That fool of a St. Servan had actually fetched his parish priest and his acolytes and their censers, and between them they had performed a comminatory service made and provided for the driving out of demons. They had ground my ivory chessmen in the pestle and mortar, and then burned them in the fire. And this in the days of the Psychical Research Society! And they had cost me a hundred francs! And that idiot of a ghost had never stretched out a hand or said a word!

A RUBBER OR TWO

"The man's only a visitor—a complete stranger to the club!"

"It's to be hoped he'll remain a stranger."

"To my mind his conduct looks uncommonly like insolence."

"It is certainly presumptuous. I suppose it will be allowed that we have played whist before Mr. Cramp arrived."

"Played whist! Good heavens! I played whist, sir, before I was breeched! The Penfolds have been a whist-playing family for generations. My mother played whist, and her mother! I myself am sixty-three years old, and I beg leave to state that I have lost as much money and made as much money, at whist, as any man of my means in England!"

"I don't pretend to have had your experience, General, but I have always been under the impression that I have some rudimentary notions of the game."

"Of course you have! And so's the Admiral!" General Penfold turned towards Admiral Glover. He raised his voice to a roar. "Haven't you, Admiral?"

The Admiral was sitting in an attitude indicative of dejection. He rubbed his hands together.

"I should like to have a rubber."

Mr. Bowman leaned over towards the Admiral, and explained, in a crescendo scale—

"The General was asking if you had any idea of the rudiments of whist."

"Yes, a rubber at whist. But there are only three of us."

The Admiral looked round the room, as if he were searching for a fourth. The General glared at him.

"The old beggar gets deafer every day." He thrust his hands into his trousers pockets. "It's the craze of the day, the desire to teach your grandmother. But, hang me! if I ever thought it was going to come to whist!"

"Only a visitor too!"

"I've played whist in this club for over fifteen years, and I've never been so sat upon before. Although I say it, in the Pendleton Club I've always been looked upon as an authority on the game. I should like to know how many appeals have been made to me in this room to give my decision upon particular points in the play. Why, if there's any rule in whist which every tyro knows, it is the rule which tells you that you're to return your partner's lead. When, the other night, I had this man Cramp for a partner, he never returned my lead except once! And then, why on earth he did it I don't know."

"When I was playing with him," plaintively commented Mr. Bowman, "he trumped my trick. I have always understood that to trump your partner's trick is not a commendable thing to do. Yet, when, at the end of the hand, I pointed out to him what he had done, he appeared to be quite surprised to find that I thought he had done anything wrong."

"And then the way in which he plays his trumps! When you're strong in trumps, play 'em. Why, I've seen him lead trumps when he had a singleton, and stick to them like glue when he had six in hand."

"Have you noticed how the man's a walking book-case?"

"I should think he's in the trade. Confound him, he's got a book in every pocket. One of these days I expect to see him whip one out of the seat of his breeches. I've played whist all my life, and I never so much as looked at a book. I don't go in for theory, but practice."

"Of course!"

"His long-winded words and scientific balderdash stick in my throat. I play good old-fashioned English whist! I've played good old-fashioned English whist all my life! I mean to play good old-fashioned English whist until I die! It's good enough for me. You can take your twiddly-twaddly new theories, and your American bunkum, to somebody who likes that kind of thing. I don't."

"Just so." A voice was heard on the stairs. "Here's Mills."

"Confound Mills! The man doesn't know a club from a spade." The door opened. Mr. Mills came in. "Hollo, Mills, you're just the man we want. Come and make up the rubber."

Mr. Mills declined.

"Thank you, General. You know I'm no player. But here is Mr. Cramp."

Mr. Cramp came in. He was willing.

"I shall be delighted."

Silence followed. The General and Mr. Bowman looked at each other. Then they looked at Mr. Cramp. Mr. Cramp seemed to be quite unconscious of their scrutiny. He seated himself at a table. He said—

"I am spoiling for a game."

The General and Mr. Bowman advanced towards the table. As they went the General whispered into Mr. Bowman's ear—

"In for it, by gad!"

They seated themselves. The Admiral brought up the rear. They cut for partners. The General and Mr. Bowman cut together.

"As we sit," the General chuckled.

"You remember, General," remarked Mr. Cramp, "that discussion I had with you on leading from five, headed by a series of four. I have here *Bane on the Penultimate*"—

Mr. Cramp produced a little book from an inner pocket of his coat.

"It is my deal," interposed Mr. Bowman. "I think I cut the lowest."

The General assented without so much as a sign. Mr. Cramp went on—

"It is a valuable little work. He says here, on page eleven, referring to the leads from fives, not trumps"—

"Will you cut to me, Mr. Cramp?"

Mr. Cramp cut to Mr. Bowman, and then continued—

"Here is the hand. Hearts trumps. King, ten, five of hearts. Ten, seven of spades. Ace, queen, knave of diamonds. Queen, knave, ten, nine, and four of clubs."

"Knave of clubs." Mr. Bowman faced the trump. "Would you mind taking up your cards, Mr. Cramp?"

"Eh—one—one moment. I—I should like just to tell you what Bane says."

"Couldn't you tell us what Bane says after the rubber?"

"I should very much like to get you one of these little works,

General. Or perhaps I might be able to get one for the club. They are rather expensive, but I think if I were to try"—

"Are you in the book trade, Mr. Cramp?"

"The book trade? What makes you think that?"

"You seem so anxious, sir, that I should purchase books which are absolutely devoid of interest to me."

"It's your lead, Admiral!" roared Mr. Bowman behind his hand.

The Admiral led. The game progressed. Some rather peculiar play was seen. Mr. Cramp and his partner were a little at loggerheads. Mr. Cramp played his game, the Admiral played his. The result was that, though they had a little the best of the cards, their adversaries scored two by tricks. Mr. Cramp endeavoured to observe on this as the Admiral began to deal.

"Didn't you notice my call?" he inquired of his partner.

The Admiral dealt calmly on.

"Didn't you notice my call?" he repeated a little louder.

Still the Admiral dealt. Mr. Bowman's countenance wore a bland smile.

"You'll have to shout if you want to make him hear," he said.

"Didn't you notice my call?" yelled Mr. Cramp.

The Admiral, suddenly alive to the fact that someone was addressing him, fumbled with the cards as he turned his attention to his partner.

"Fall? No, I heard nothing about your fall. Did you hurt yourself?"

Everyone smiled—but Mr. Cramp. That gentleman realised what it is to be afflicted.

"He—he seems very deaf," he said.

No one took the remark as addressed to himself. The Admiral went on dealing. The turn-up fell to Mr. Bowman.

"Misdeal," that gentleman remarked. "You put the Admiral out by shouting at him, Mr. Cramp."

Mr. Cramp looked a little green.

"A man is rather handicapped who has a partner who is as deaf as a post."

The Admiral, who seemed nonplussed at the result of his labours, was staring at the cards as they lay on the table. The General was preparing to take his turn.

"You see, Mr. Cramp," continued Mr. Bowman, "the Admiral has played whist all his life, and, perhaps, thinks he knows a little about it. Possibly he does, if he is left alone."

Mr. Cramp put up his eyebrows. He smiled.

"Don't you think that it is possible for a man to have played whist all his life, and yet to know very little about it after all?"

"Scarcely, if he is an educated man, and has played with educated men."

"But suppose those educated men have been educated in everything else but whist?"

Mr. Bowman shrugged his shoulders. The General laid down the pack of cards with which he was about to deal.

"Excuse me, Bowman, but if we're going to have a discussion on first principles I propose that we adjourn. If we're going to play whist, let's play whist."

"Yes," sighed Mr. Cramp, "let's play whist."

The result of the hand was even more disastrous to himself and his partner than the first had been. By scoring the three odd tricks their opponents were enabled to announce a treble. This dire catastrophe seemed to cause the Admiral some searchings of heart.

"Why," he asked of Mr. Cramp, "didn't you return my lead?"

"What lead?"

For once the Admiral seemed keen of hearing.

"I led a club."

"I wished to establish my spades. I had seven. If you had acted on my signal we should have had the game at our mercy."

The Admiral turned to the General.

"What's he say? If he'd returned my lead I should have made my ace and queen of clubs."

Mr. Cramp leaned over the table.

"I wish you'd let me persuade you to get *Cole on Whist.*"

"Books again!" growled the General.

"My dear General, when a man tells me that he cares nothing for what he calls 'book whist,' I ask myself—and I sometimes ask him—if he thinks it possible to acquire a science by merely getting by heart, poll parrot fashion, a number of obsolete and actually erroneous traditions."

The General seemed to choke back something which was in his throat.

"Whose deal?" he demanded.

"Mine," said Mr. Cramp.

"Then deal."

Mr. Cramp dealt. When the hand had been played, it was found that Pelion had been piled upon Ossa. With three by tricks and the honours the General and his associate scored another treble off the reel. Two trebles and the rub was a pleasant commencement of the evening's play. Nor was the pleasure lessened, from the losers' point of view, by the fact that the cards had not been by any means so one-sided as the result suggested.

By this time several other persons had entered the room. No one attempted to start another rubber, but quite a little crowd clustered round the table to watch the one which was already in progress. The process of cutting for partners was followed with interest, interest which was not lessened when it was observed that the order of the play was disarranged, and that Mr. Cramp was cast with the General.

"Have you been thinking about what I said to you the other night about the call?" inquired Mr. Cramp of his partner, as he took the seat which Mr. Bowman had vacated.

"About what?"

As he put the question the General's bearing was that of a broomstick, with a head on top.

"The call. I have here a very admirable little work, by an American. It is called *The Call for Trumps, with some Remarks upon the Echo.*" Mr. Cramp drew a little paper-covered pamphlet from his waistcoat pocket. The General watched its appearance in a state of apparent speechlessness. "It may seem a little officious on my part to be so continually referring to authorities, but the truth is that whist, as a game, has entirely altered during the last few years. I find here, at Pendleton, such a seeming unconsciousness of this fact, that I hope I may be excused if I venture to call attention to the fundamental difference which exists between whist as it is and as it was."

"Will someone ring the bell for me," observed the General, "and order some brandy neat?"

Mr. Cramp went placidly on, apparently not observing the peculiarity of the General's manner.

"Whist, as it is, has attained to the dignity of an exact science. A whist player is able, by a series of prearranged signals, to inform his partner of every card in his hand. After two or three rounds he should know where every card is lying. So completely is every detail arranged, that it is scarcely an exaggeration to say that he should know exactly what card to play under every possible combination of circumstances. In other words, he should be as entirely at his ease as if the cards were lying face upwards on the table."

"Aren't you going to have any more whist?" inquired, in the innocence of his heart, the Admiral of the General.

The General exploded.

"Good heavens, sir! How the somethinged something should I know? The man's talking to us as though we were an awkward squad."

"Really, General, you mistake me."

Mr. Cramp's manner was mild. The General's manner, as he replied, was anything but mild.

"I would have you not to mistake me, sir! This is the Pendleton Club. We are members of the Pendleton Club. You have done us the honour, while enjoying the Pendleton breezes, to become a visitor at the Pendleton Club. We desire to treat you as our guest. We don't force you to play whist, but for goodness' sake don't try to teach your grandmother if you do."

Mr. Cramp bowed, seemingly in quiet acquiescence. A rather acid smile was on his face. Perhaps he found the General, if a little vulgar, hard to answer. He returned the pamphlet to his waistcoat pocket. Mr. Bowman dealt the cards. The nine of hearts was turned.

Mr. Cramp and his partner ought to have won the odd, but they didn't. This was owing to the difference between their styles of play. Possibly Mr. Cramp wouldn't understand his partner's method, and it was quite evident that his partner couldn't understand his. In consequence of which slight misunderstanding, although they had the honours, their opponents took three tricks.

"I think, General," observed Mr. Bowman, with malicious intent, "that you ought to have had the odd."

"The odd, sir! We ought to have won the game!"

He looked at his partner as if he had a mind to eat him.

"Have you studied the American leads?"

Mr. Cramp put the question to his partner gently.

"The what, sir?"

"The American leads. I have here"—

Mr. Cramp's hand stole towards the tails of his coat.

"Good gad, sir, leave your books in your pocket!"

Mr. Cramp accepted the rebuke.

"It is a little work I have which deals with the American leads. I don't think you have paid much attention to the question which is now so prominent in the circles of pure whist, the question of the penultimate."

"The what, sir?"

"The penultimate."

"I tell you to what you don't seem to have paid much attention, sir. You don't seem to have paid much attention to the fact that you put your ace upon my king."

"I thought you wished me to."

"Wished you to take my trick?"

"In order that I might give you spades."

"Why the something did I want spades?"

"Now that is the question which I put to myself. At the time I could only draw my inferences from your play."

The General took out his bandana. He wiped his brow.

"Hasn't that brandy of mine come yet?"

During the next hand play progressed smoothly—in a sense— and to a certain point. At that point Mr. Bowman picked up a card from the table.

"General, you have revoked."

The General, who had been playing as though he were sitting on hot bricks, turned a beautiful peony colour.

"Never did such a thing in my life!"

"You have done it now. You played a spade when a heart was led, and now you play a heart."

The thing was undeniable. Everyone saw it at once, except the delinquent. He saw it by degrees. Mr. Bowman put up the double.

"That was an unfortunate accident of yours, General." Mr. Cramp said this quite sweetly. "We had the honours and the trumps and the cards. We might have made the odd trick, with luck. I have seen a treble scored with a much worse hand. But that, of course, under present circumstances, we can't expect."

The General leaned upon the table. By stretching out his hand he might have caught his partner by the nose.

"Are you playing with me or against me, sir? If you are playing with me, why do you take all my tricks?"

"I own, General, that I find your lead—no pun intended—misleading!"

The General drew his breath.

"I—I don't want to insult you, sir, but I have played whist for fifty years, and I have never before sat down at a table with a man like you."

"So I should imagine—judging from your play."

The General sat back in his chair. He looked wildly round the room. Again he drew the bandana across his brow.

"Deal, someone! Let's—let's get it over! I—I don't want to make a brute of myself!"

The Admiral dealt. And there was peace for a time. A short time, and then there was a storm. The General brought his fist down upon the table with a crash which appeared to be even audible to the Admiral.

"Why the devil did you put your ace upon my queen?"

Mr. Cramp seemed surprised.

"I don't know if it is the custom at Pendleton to criticise the play while a game is in process."

"I'm not going to sit still and be shot at by my own partner! Why the devil did you put your ace upon my queen?"

"May I explain?" Mr. Cramp turned to Mr. Bowman. That gentleman nodded. "I thought it was an urgent call."

"What the something do you mean by an urgent call?"

"You put your king upon my knave."

"I was third player!"

Mr. Bowman interposed.

"You were wrong, General."

"Wrong!" The General gasped. "Wrong! Upon my soul, I never

thought I should come to this. Let's go on! After this I suppose it doesn't matter what I do."

Whether it mattered or not, he did it. And it did matter, for the result was that Mr. Bowman had the satisfaction—from his point of view—of putting up another treble, off the reel. Mr. Cramp smiled bitterly.

"I think, General, all things considered, that you ought to pay my losses."

The General glared. He clutched the Admiral by the arm.

"Come along, Admiral. Let's get out of this. I—I don't want to misbehave myself in a public room,—a room"—the General stood up—"in which I have played whist for over fifteen years, and in which I have never been insulted till to-night."

He tore the Admiral from his seat. He dragged him with him from the room, which was rather hard upon the Admiral, for he had no cause to find fault with the way in which the game had gone.

"Might I offer my friend and myself as substitutes for the players who are gone?—that is, if no other gentleman cares to play."

The speaker was a tall, slight man, with a long, drooping moustache. Mr. Bowman glanced up at him. He was a stranger to him; but, at that season of the year, there are so many strangers in Pendleton that, at the club, one finds almost as many visitors as residents. Mr. Bowman had no reason to be disagreeable—he had won.

"I am willing."

He glanced at Mr. Cramp. Mr. Cramp made a little gesture with his hands.

"I am at anybody's service. All I ask is—whist!"

The stranger and his friend came forward. They fell together in the cut for partners. The stranger, having cut the lowest, prepared to deal. As he dealt he addressed himself to Mr. Cramp.

"Like you, my friend and myself are students of whist as it is; I might almost say of whist as it might be."

Mr. Cramp rubbed his hands softly one against the other; it was a little trick he had.

"Disciples of Cole?"

"In a degree. In our system of signals we go further than Cole."

"I scarcely see how that can be, unless you have even improved upon the American leads."

"No? Well, I shall be happy to explain to you after the rubber is over."

If the new-comers were not exactly disciples of Cole, they at least appeared to be disciples of the extremely difficult art of getting hold of the cards; and it was charming to see the way in which they handled them. They took trick after trick in the serenest style.

"Book already!" murmured Mr. Cramp.

With a little laugh the stranger shut up the pack. The laugh was not echoed on the expressive features of Mr. Cramp, nor on those of his partner. As yet they had not scored a trick. The new-comers went gaily on. They took the odd trick, and all the rest besides! Or, rather, they stopped at five, since it was scarcely necessary to go further. But there was nothing to show that they could not have taken the whole thirteen had they been so inclined. Silence followed this surprising result; that is, so far as the main company was concerned. The stranger remained quite at his ease.

"You see," he said, "that is what I call whist as it is, or perhaps you would call it whist as it might be."

"It ought to be sent to the *Field*," murmured Mr. Cramp. He seemed troubled in his mind.

"Whist," pursued the stranger, "in its more recent developments, as I understand the thing, becomes simply a question of signals. The most perfect system of signals results in the most perfect game! My friend and I have arranged between ourselves a system of signalling which, I think I may say, is almost perfect."

"It may be made too perfect," said Mr. Cramp.

"How so? You yourself said that whist has been raised to the dignity of an exact science. You can't be too exact. Let's carry the thing to its logical conclusion."

Mr. Cramp was still. Mr. Bowman smiled a ghastly smile.

"I don't like this kind of whist."

"No?" laughed the stranger; "I am sorry!"

"You look sorry," said Mr. Bowman.

One does not mind not making a trick once in a way, though one would prefer to be playing for love even on that solitary occasion; but when the experience is repeated—and in the following hand, a man has fidgets. That is what happened that evening at the Pendleton Club. The new-comers again walked off with the whole of the tricks, and Mr. Cramp had fidgets, and so had his partner! As for the stranger, he, if possible, was more at his ease than ever.

"You see," he cried, "to what perfection a system of signals may be carried! How completely knowledge may eliminate chance!"

"I do," said Mr. Bowman, "I see it plainly. I see it much too plainly. Gentlemen, if this is whist—as it is—in future I shall turn my attention to some other game."

He rose from his seat. Immediately another person, a dapper little man, with shaven cheeks and big black eyes, had his hand on the back of the vacant chair.

"Gentlemen, with your permission, may I complete the four?"

No one offered an objection. The man sat down. He cut Mr. Cramp as his partner. The two friends were again together. The latest comer had the deal.

"Gentlemen," he observed, as he dealt out the cards, "I too am a student of whist, in its latest phase. This is as it appears to me. That a man is bound to acquire a special and peculiar knowledge, either on his own account, or in concert with other men, and that he is entitled to take every possible advantage of a man who knows less than he. As has been said, whist, in a sense, has become a science. Science, in the sense in which in this connection the word is used, eliminates the element of chance. Now, partner, let us see if we cannot command the fortune of war."

He turned the ace of hearts. He took the first trick with a trump—the deuce. He led the ace of trumps in the second trick, the king in the third, the queen in his fourth. At this point the player on his right laid down his hand.

"All trumps," he murmured.

"All trumps," admitted the dealer. With a charming frankness he faced his hand.

"The deuce!" There was an interval for reflection. Then that player delivered himself again. "You're a conjurer," he said.

"I am. So are you and your friend."

"Not conjurers; merely amateurs. Dabblers by the way."

"Oh, that explains it. I'm a professional. And of course in whist, in its latest phase, the amateur is done."

He addressed himself to Mr. Cramp.

"Take my advice. Throw some of those books of yours upon the fire. If their teachings are to be pushed to their logical conclusion, whist will become a game only fit—for conjurers."

MRS. WRIGGLESWORTH'S BURYING

"You don't seem to see that you are placing yourself between two fires—that you will get yourself into trouble either way!"

The chairman brought his hand down on to the table with a gesture which was familiar to the members of the Board—a gesture which was intended to mean that there was an end of it, whatever "it" might at the moment be. Mr. Spurrier, of the "Dixie Arms," added a sort of explanatory postscript.

"You see, Mrs. Wrigglesworth, you have been in receipt of parish relief over thirteen months. That relief you obtained on the strength of your assertion that you were destitute."

"So I were, gentleman; so I were."

"But how can that be, if, as you now state was the case, all the time you were in possession of five-and-thirty pounds?"

"That were for my burying, gentlemen; that were for my burying."

Mr. Spurrier held up his hands. What was the good of talking to such a woman? The chairman tried again.

"Mrs. Wrigglesworth, you elude the point. Either you stated what was false when you stated you were destitute—destitute signifies without means—or you are now stating what is false when you say you have been robbed."

"Not been robbed! Ain't I? What does the likes of you know about it? The money were all right when I went to bed, 'cause I looks and sees—this morning when I gets up it were gone. If there's a law, I'll have it!"

The old lady's voice rose in a thin, quavering crescendo. Her withered form quivered with excitement. Her toothless, nutcracker jaws continued to open and shut after she had ceased to give utterance to audible speech. As the chairman looked at her, he feared that she might be again, as she had been more than once before, a hard nut for the Board to crack. With the fingers of his left hand he softly smoothed his hair.

"I am afraid, if there is a law, it is we who will have to have it, Mrs. Wrigglesworth. What do you know about this matter, Mr. Hibbs?"

Mr. Hibbs was the relieving-officer.

"Mrs. Wrigglesworth came to me in my office this morning and told me she had been robbed. 'Robbed?' I said. 'You? What of?' 'Five-and-thirty pounds,' she said. I didn't believe her, hardly; for the matter of that, I don't believe her now. Mrs. Wrigglesworth, gentlemen, has been on the parish, off and on, for seven years. Thirteen months ago she came on again. I wanted her to go into the House. But it seemed that she was earning a bit now and then, and she had her cottage free, so she was put on the outdoor list. Now, according to her own confession, she's been defrauding the parish all this time. She says that she had a sum of no less than thirty-five pounds hid somewhere in a hole in the wall"—

"It were for my burying—I weren't going to be buried by the parish—not me!"

"You didn't mind living by the parish, though you might object to being buried by the parish, did you?"

As the circumstances were at present, the Board found it difficult to arrive at a decision. Mrs. Wrigglesworth had, unfortunately it is to be feared with cause, such a character for untrustworthiness that it was scarcely safe to believe anything she said merely on the strength of her own assertion. That a pauper should have been in possession of five-and-thirty pounds seemed incredible. No wonder that Mr. Hibbs resented the idea as being a reflection on himself. Where had the woman got it from? On that point she was dumb; she either could not or would not vouchsafe information. Her husband had been an agricultural labourer—he had been buried by the parish. It was not likely he had left a fortune behind. She had had no children. So far as was known, and according to her own statement, she had not a relation in the world.

"It were mine," she repeated, when pressed to explain how she came to be in possession of such a sum. "It were for my burying. If there's a law, I'll have it."

"What was it in?" inquired the chairman, when all attempts at ascertaining how she had become possessed of it had failed; "gold or silver?"

"Eh?" The old woman looked at him with her blurred yet cunning eyes. "It were in money."

"Yes, you've told us that already, but what sort of money? Was it in gold?"

"That's my affair; that's naught to do with you!"

"But, you silly woman, how can we help you if you don't describe your property? Was the thirty-five pounds of which you say you have been robbed in notes or in gold—or in what?"

But she was as unmanageable upon this point as upon the other; she either could not or would not say. She would only persist in the repetition of what, with her, seemed to be a sort of formula—

"It were mine—it were for my burying—if there's a law, I'll have it."

The Board felt that at present nothing could be done. If any evidence were to transpire which would go to prove the truth of the woman's story, then steps would have to be taken—of a sort which she might find disagreeable. In the meantime information, such as it was, had been given to the police. They could but wait—time would show. When Mrs. Wrigglesworth had withdrawn, or, rather, when she had been withdrawn, the chairman did make one suggestion to Mr. Grey.

"By the way, Mr. Grey, you don't live far from the woman, do you?"

"Within a stone's-throw."

"Perhaps, at your convenience, you would not mind calling at her place, examining this hole in the wall of which she speaks, and looking into the thing all round. You may be able to do more with her in private than we have been able to do in public."

Mr. Grey had no objection. He expressed his willingness to act on the chairman's suggestion.

"Her cottage is close to my place. I have to pass it on my way. I'll look in as I go home."

The Board sat till four. Several squabbles took up a good deal of time. Mr. Martin had his usual passage of arms with Mr. Spurrier; there was a heated discussion about the state of the road in which an esteemed member of the Board happened to reside, and so on.

A good deal had been said which might much better have been left unsaid, before the chairman declared the meeting closed. As they were leaving the building, Mr. Martin buttonholed Mr. Grey.

"By the way, Mr. Grey, you won't forget that that bill of yours falls due to-morrow?"

"I was going to ask you if you could let me have, in case of accident, a day or two's grace. A payment which I have expected to receive is overdue."

"Sorry I can't, sir! You have had due notice. The bill will be presented in the usual course. I want the money!"

Mr. Martin walked away without giving Mr. Grey a chance to add a word. This was one of the results of the things which had been said at the meeting. Mr. Martin had been worsted in his passage of arms with Mr. Spurrier. He had challenged a division; had been beaten badly—Mr. Grey had voted with the majority.

Mr. Grey turned homewards with knitted brow. Things had not been going over well with him of late. This little affair of Martin's might do him vital harm. If he had had the faintest notion that the man would have taken his action as it seemed he had done, for once in a way he would have voted with him, in his everlasting quarrel with Spurrier, though his doing so might have involved a slight strain upon his sense of right and wrong. Martin must be quite well aware that he was solvent; the bill was only for a paltry fifty pounds; he had expected to receive payment of a large amount for days, only the mischief was, that if that payment did not turn up to-morrow—and he had reasons of his own for suspecting that its arrival might be delayed for a day or two—he was without the actual cash in hand with which to meet the bill; and if Martin chose to be nasty, it might go hard with him. Hang Martin! Confound Spurrier! Bother the Board! He wished he had never allowed himself to be nominated! He had been mixed up in other people's squabbles ever since.

As he was mentally engaged in dealing out hearty all-round anathemas, he suddenly remembered that he had been deputed to visit Mrs. Wrigglesworth. Here was fresh cause for objurgation. What had he to do with the shuffling, lying old jade? He was actually at his own gate before he thought of her. To visit her would necessitate retracing perhaps twenty or thirty yards. Still, he had promised—he had better go. He need not stay a moment; in his present mood he told himself that he would be able to see all that he wanted to see in much less time than that

Mrs. Wrigglesworth's cottage stood by itself, in a piece of garden ground which had run all wild. It was a very little and very ancient cottage, the property of the lord of the manor; she lived in it rent-free, on the understanding that when she died it was to be razed to the ground. Mr. Grey hammered with his stick against the door. The ramshackle condition of the place struck him forcibly.

"It strikes me that if three or four strong men were to put their shoulders against the wall, they might shove the whole place over. I wonder if the old girl's in."

He knocked again. No answer. He turned the handle; the door was open. He stepped inside.

"Mrs. Wrigglesworth!" All was still. "Mrs. Wrigglesworth!" Still not a sound. He looked about him. The room in which he found himself was larger than might have been expected. The ceiling was low, the floor was paved with brick. The walls were wainscotted here and there; the wainscot seemed to be rotting away. By the fireplace an upper panel seemed to have been recently removed; it was lying on the floor.

"I wonder if that's the famous hole in the wall?"

Closing the door behind him, he crossed to see. The displaced panel had left a cavity about eight inches wide. There was a considerable space between the wainscot and the outer wall. It seemed full of dirt and cobwebs, and from it there proceeded a musty, fusty smell. Four inches below the level of the panel which was missing was what appeared to be a kind of shelf. It was a makeshift affair: a piece of rough board about a foot long had been inserted between the wainscot and the wall. It was too wide for the intervening space; it had been placed carelessly enough upon the slant. Without intending any exertion of strength, Mr. Grey pressed upon it with his hand. It gave way beneath his touch. Mr. Grey had a small head: he could almost insert the whole of it within the panel. He looked to see where the board had fallen. He could see nothing of it; apparently it had passed from sight—but he could and did see something else. Not six inches below the place where the board had been, caught by some inequality in the exterior wall, was a pocket-book. Not a common, thrown together sort of thing; not even an article designed for service rather than for show—a costly, apparently brand-new pocket-book, of handsome and indeed unusual design.

Mr. Grey understood, or thought he understood, exactly what had happened. This was Mrs. Wrigglesworth's treasure case, though how an old woman in her position came to be in possession of such a piece of personal property he never stopped to think. She had placed it on the makeshift shelf; either the board itself had slipped, or in some way it had slipped from off the board, and lodging beneath the board it had been effectually concealed from sight. Missing it from its accustomed place, taking it for granted in her haste that she had been robbed, the old lady had raised the hue-and-cry.

Unbidden thoughts crowded into Mr. Grey's brain. The pocket-book contained five-and-thirty pounds; the woman was a fraudulent old sinner; the money would not be of the slightest use to her; according to her own statement she only intended to use it for her burying; that bill of his would fall due to-morrow. In the first place, no one believed that the woman had ever been in possession of such a sum; in the second, not even she herself had the faintest notion of whereabouts it really was—where would be the harm? Thrusting his arm into the aperture, snatching up the pocket-book, it was in the inside breast-pocket of his coat before he had really realised what it was he thought of doing. When it was inside his pocket, he looked about him as if reflecting what was the next step it might be advisable for him to take. There was a sound of someone moving overhead. He glanced at the dilapidated staircase which led to the room above. Someone was beginning to descend it—Mrs. Wrigglesworth! Mr. Grey was conscious that the sight of the ancient female filled him with a sense of curious discomfort. Confound her! what had she been doing? Why had she not answered when he called? He stood staring at her, tongue-tied. She tottered from step to step feebly and very slowly. He watched her as if she had been some dreadful thing; he felt, rather than saw, that her eyes were on him all the time. At the foot of the stairs she paused. Stretching out her shaking hand, she said in that shrill, quavering voice of hers—

"Give it me."

What did the old hag mean? A damp moisture seemed to steal all over him.

"Give it me," she repeated.

"Give you what?" He was startled to perceive how husky his voice seemed to have suddenly become.

"My money!"

"Your money, you old fool!" In his natural indignation at this fresh exhibition of her irritating imbecility, he was scarcely courteous. Trying to get the better of the feeling, which positively almost amounted to terror, which so unexpectedly had overtaken him, he endeavoured to assume towards her that manner which he considered it right that a member of the Board of Guardians should assume towards a person in her position. "I have been deputed by the Board to make further inquiries into this story of yours about the sum of money which you say you have lost. Now, where do you say you used to keep it?"

"Give it me."

"Is this the hole in the wall of which you spoke?"

"I see you take it."

"What!" He turned to her again. In spite of himself, he felt that his face had gone a ghastly white. "Woman, you've been drinking!"

"Not me! No such luck! I ain't been a-drinking this week, I ain't; nor yet last week neither. I were a-lying on my bed, a-thinking where my money were. I see you a-coming in, I see you a-going to the hole in the wall, I see you a-pushing of the shelf, I see you a-taking of the pocket-book, I see you a-putting it in your pocket— it's in your pocket now—you give it me!"

On the face of it, the woman's story was incredible. If, as she stated, she had been lying down on her bed upstairs, and it was certain that she had been nowhere in the room below, how could she have seen what she said she had? No judge or jury would believe her for a moment. At the same time, and purely as a matter of fact, her story bore such an amazing resemblance to what had really taken place, that Mr. Grey was conscious of a threatened weakness about the region of the knees. He tried to be stern.

"If you are not more careful, Mrs. Wrigglesworth, of that scurrilous tongue of yours you will get yourself into serious trouble with the police."

"The police!" She raised her voice to a quavering shriek. She advanced towards him with a degree of agility of which he had not supposed her capable. "I'll have the police for you! If there's a law, I'll have it! Give it me!"

She stretched out her hawk-like talons as if she would seize him by the collar of his coat. He put out his hand to keep her from him. She was too beside herself with excitement to be easily eluded. Grasping his coat with one hand, with the other she actually began feeling for his pocket. He had to exercise considerable force to thrust her from him; possibly because he could not find it in his heart to prolong a painful scene, before she could assail him again he was out of the house. He hurried across the garden. At the gate he encountered Patten, the blacksmith.

"Well, and have you found out anything about her five-and-thirty pound?"

Mr. Grey looked at him almost as if he did not know him. His faculties seemed, for the moment, to be numbed. It was with an effort he roused himself.

"Nothing! There's not a word of truth in anything she says; it's a cock-and-bull story altogether."

"I should say it was something of a cock-and-bull story. She's the sort to have five-and-thirty pound, she is. I should say it was many a year since she had five-and-thirty pence to call her own, let alone five-and-thirty pound."

Patten grinned, as if he had been guilty of a joke. Mr. Grey took off his hat to wipe his brow. It was not a warm day, nor was he a man given to perspire even when the day was warm. But, as he removed his hat, one could see that, for some reason, his brow was damp with sweat.

"It strikes me that the woman is not quite right in her head. That is the impression which her manner leaves on me."

"No," said Patten, "I shouldn't be surprised if she was a bit queer, Mr. Grey."

A horseman reined up close beside them; it was Sir John Stoton, the largest landowner in the countryside.

"Ha—what's this I hear about the Wrigglesworth woman being

robbed of five-and-thirty pounds? It's occurred to me, Mr. Grey, as being just possible that the money, of which she says she was robbed, was mine."

Mr. Grey stared at him askance. What was coming now? Sir John continued, in that loud and slightly raucous voice, which was apt to have such an awe-inspiring effect upon the representatives of local crime at Petty Sessions—

"Ha!—about five months ago, Mr. Grey, I lost a pocket-book."

A pocket-book! Mr. Grey's hand moved mechanically towards the inside breast-pocket of his coat.

"Ha!—my impression was that I lost the thing on the way to town. Under that impression I communicated with the railway people, and with the police, and ha!—I offered a reward. But on reflection I think it quite possible that I lost the thing between my place and the station. I shouldn't have thought of it—ha—if I hadn't been told that the woman says she's lost five-and-thirty pounds, and that was exactly the sum my pocket-book contained,—seven fives."

Mr. Grey's lips were parched and dry. He had to moisten them with his tongue before he could speak.

"I'm very much obliged to you, Sir John. About the pocket-book—what sort of a pocket-book was it?"

"Ha!—rather a remarkable pocket-book—ha!—in fact, it was a present from my wife—made of crocodile skin, bound with gold, and in one corner a piece of red leather had been inserted, and on this piece of red leather were my crest and arms."

Sir John paused. But, although given the opportunity, Mr. Grey could not have spoken for a good deal just then. He had not closely inspected it, but he had seen enough of it to be convinced that the identical article which Sir John described was at that very moment in his pocket. Sir John's horse chanced to be taken with a fit of the fidgets, which afforded Mr. Grey an excuse for silence. While the animal was still showing signs of restlessness, its rider went on—

"Of course—ha!—there may be nothing in it, and what the woman says may be all right, but as I saw you here I thought I'd mention it. I'll send you the numbers of the notes in case anything turns up."

"Thank you, Sir John."

Mr. Grey managed to articulate so much, as saluting with his whip, the baronet rode off. Directly he was out of hearing Patten delivered himself of a piece of his mind—

"I shouldn't be surprised if the old cat found the very pocket-book Sir John lost—she's got eyes what can see through a brick wall; she can see anything, she can; there never was such a one for finding things; though she's turned seventy she could find a needle in a bundle of hay, it's the common talk; and she's trying to make out that the money what was in it was her own."

Mr. Grey was solemn.

"I'm afraid she's a woman of indifferent character—I'm afraid she is."

He crossed to his own house. On entering the small apartment which he dignified by the name of study, he found on the table, awaiting him, a letter. He stared at it; he snatched it up; he tore it open with trembling fingers. It was the remittance he had been expecting, which, though tardy, still had come in time. Instead of welcoming its arrival in a spirit of thankfulness, a stifled execration escaped his lips.

"I've done it for nothing, after all!"

He sat down at the table, glaring at the open letter he was holding in his hand. His wife came in. She wanted to know why he was so late. She, also, was full of the robbery of which Mrs. Wrigglesworth maintained she was the victim. Mr. Grey did what he had never done before in the presence of his wife—he swore.

His wife started as if he had struck her. He was, in his way—which was not by any means a bad way—a model husband; just as, to do him justice, he had hitherto, according to his lights, con-scientiously endeavoured to be a model man. He was ashamed of himself directly he had spoken. He made a lame attempt at apol-ogy. "I beg your pardon, my dear, but the fact is I've had nothing but worry, worry, all day long; and as for Mrs. Wrigglesworth, I've heard enough about her to last me for the rest of my life. If you don't mind excusing me, my dear, there are one or two things I must attend to—don't wait tea—I'll join you directly I've done."

Mrs. Grey withdrew. Apparently he had shocked her into speechlessness; though he felt that in all probability she would favour him with her views on his behaviour when, later on, her faculty of speech returned. When she had gone he locked the door. So far from evincing a proper spirit of penitence, he swore again. What a mess of things he had made all round! Why had he not come home before calling at that wretched woman's? If he had received his letter, there would have been no temptation for him to do the thing he had done. Why had he not given the woman the pocket-book when she had asked for it? Why had he been idiot enough to tell Patten that he had found out that there was no truth in the story the woman had told? Why, above all else, had he not whipped out the pocket-book the very instant Sir John had mentioned the word?

Yes, a pretty mess he had made of things all round. To have robbed Mrs. Wrigglesworth would have been—something, perhaps, but still not much. It was absurd to suppose that she could live at the expense of the parish while all the time she was in possession of a considerable sum of money, which after her death was to be devoted to the ridiculous purpose of providing her with a handsome funeral. Such a woman, in a sense, deserved to be robbed. But, when it came to robbing Sir John Stoton, it was a different pair of shoes entirely. The baronet was his—Mr. Grey's—chief patron. By profession Mr. Grey was a veterinary surgeon; Sir John was master of the local hounds. To fall under the ban of his displeasure would, for all practical purposes, mean ruin to Mr. Grey.

Although he knew that the door was locked, Mr. Grey looked at it again, to make quite sure. As gingerly as if it had been red-hot, Mr. Grey withdrew the pocket-book from its place of hiding. It was Sir John's. Any lingering doubt he might have had upon that point vanished as he looked at it. If he had only had the chance of examining it before Mrs. Wrigglesworth had appeared upon the scene, he would at once have recognised the arms and crest, which were stamped in gold on the piece of red leather in the corner, and he would not have made of himself the fool he had done. Now, what was he to do? Since the remittance had arrived, the contents of the pocket-book were really not required. He was solvent enough; it was only the moment's pressure he had feared. In any case he would not have been able to use the five-and-thirty pounds—seven five-pound notes, and the baronet had their numbers.

He had an odd feeling of being overlooked; he felt as if Mrs. Wrigglesworth was watching all he did. She had already professed to see what was taking place in one room while she was in another. And what was that Patten had said, about her being credited with extraordinary powers of vision? It was absurd; but, with recurrent fits of queer self-consciousness, he kept slipping the pocketbook out of sight, as if someone had been present with him in the room—someone who kept trying to see what it was that he was holding in his hand. It was with feelings of unmistakable perturbation that he opened it to examine the notes which it contained.

It was strange—he could not find them. In which of the pockets were they? He hurriedly examined them, one after the other. He realised the truth. It was empty!

It was: he had stolen an empty pocket-book. He had risked his all, not only for nothing, but for less than nothing—for something which was not only worthless, but the mere possession of which meant infinite danger. He sank into his chair with a gasp of stupefaction. He ransacked the thing again, this time carefully, searching for some hidden aperture. It contained nothing—absolutely nothing—not even a pencil nor a line of writing; it looked as if it had just come from the maker's shop. Had he been tricked? What did it mean?

For this he had placed himself in the woman's power. He did not doubt that she would do her best to raise a nest of hornets about his ears. She might even be moved to confess to the finding of the pocket-book, charging him with having stolen it from her. Not everyone would believe her: his reputation was too good for that; but some of the mud might stick. He had enemies—rivals, even—who, he felt confident, would be glad of any weapon of assault. There was no knowing where the thing might end. Should he play the man—should he go and tell her, not only that he had found the pocket-book, but also that he had found its owner? Suppose she charged him with having stolen its contents? His latter state might be worse than his first.

He sat, doing his best to face the situation, to perceive in it somewhere a path of safety. The darkness was gathering; the room was in shadow. There came a sudden knocking at the door. The start with which he sprang to his feet did more to show the state of his nerves than any words could possibly have done. He clutched at the open pocket-book, endeavouring to manipulate its ingenious fastening with fingers which shook as with the palsy.

"Who's there?"

He scarcely knew his own voice—it sounded so strange to him. His wife replied—

"It's Mr. Packham. He wishes to speak to you."

Packham, the village constable! He reeled, as if someone had struck him a blow. Was it possible that the woman had already carried to him her tale, and had he by any possibility believed her? He had not a moment to spare for thought; to keep him outside the door might aggravate the man's suspicions. What was he to do with the pocket-book? If, as though it was hard to believe, was at anyrate conceivably possible, on the strength of Mrs. Wrigglesworth's information, the man had come to effect his arrest, to be found with that upon him would mean complete destruction. Unlocking the bookcase he dropped the pocket-book behind a row of volumes.

"Half a second; I'm just finishing something. Tell Packham I'll see him in a moment." He opened the door. His wife was outside. Behind her was the constable. "Well, Packham, what's the matter?"

"I've come to speak to you, sir, about this here Mrs. Wrigglesworth."

Mr. Grey had returned to his writing-table. He was clutching at its edge. "Well, what about her?"

"It's about this here money of hers."

"Yes, I know; I saw her not very long since."

"So I hear." Mr. Packham paused.

What was coming next? Mr. Grey was thankful that the room was in partial darkness, or the man could scarcely have failed to see how the muscles of his face were working.

"It's all true what she says about this here robbery."

Another pause. Why did not the man go on? Slow-witted lout.

"We've got the chaps as done it."

Mr. Grey made an involuntary forward movement

"You've got—what?"

"We've got the chaps as done it."

Mr. Grey turned away. A rush of blood to his head made him

suddenly giddy. "You've got the chaps as done it? What do you mean?"

"Oh, we've got them safe enough; there's no mistake about that. It seems that a couple of chaps have been drinking all day over at Haughan, at the 'Dun Cow.' They changed a five-pound note, though they didn't look as if they were the sort to have a five-pound note about 'em. They got drunk, and they fell to quarrelling; then one of them accused the other of putting him up to this here robbery, and t'other gave him as good as he sent, and there was a row; then Mr. Miles, the landlord, he sent for us. Then the inspector he sent some of our fellows over, and they took 'em; and though the pair was pretty drunk, they made a clean breast of it, in a kind of way. It seems that they're a couple of tramps. They called at Mrs. Wrigglesworth's, and they saw her taking something out of a hole in the wall. They went back later, when the old lady was in bed, and they looked where they'd seen her looking, and hidden in the wall they found a pocket-book. They cleared off with what was in it, the book itself they left behind them—at least, so they say."

Mr. Grey was seated at the table. He was bending in the partial darkness over some papers which were in front of him. He had never felt so strange in his life.

"About the money—has any been recovered?"

"Six five-pound notes, four pounds in gold, and some odd shillings. They'd spent the rest."

"It seems that the money may not be the woman's after all. I just saw Sir John Stoton. He tells me that a little time ago he lost a pocket-book, in which were seven five-pound notes. You had better tell the inspector to send and ask him for the numbers. Those you have recovered may turn out to be some of them."

"I will, sir. I heard about Sir John speaking to you,—that's why I thought I'd come and have a word with you first, before I went and had a word with Mrs. Wrigglesworth."

"Mrs. Wrigglesworth! Are you going to her now?" An idea occurred to him. "I'll come with you, if you'll wait. My dear, take Mr. Packham into the front room, and give him something to drink."

"Won't you have the lamp?" asked Mrs. Grey.

"No, thanks; what I have to do I can do quite as well in the darkness."

Quite as well—perhaps better. When they had gone he rose from his chair. He stood straight up. Then, kneeling down, he hid his face in his hands, and his hands he laid upon the table. He remained like that for more than a minute, probably in a somewhat curious frame of mind. When he regained his feet, taking the pocket-book from behind the row of books, he once more put it back into his pocket. Then he went into the front room to his wife and Mr. Packham.

"I think I'll have a little something to drink, dear." He had a little something, nearly neat. He spoke to the policeman. "It's been a worrying day up at the Board."

"I shouldn't be surprised, sir, if you gentlemen on the Board have a deal of worry now and then. Them paupers is a fractious lot."

"We have, Packham—a deal of worry—more than people think. Now, if you're ready."

Mr. Packham was ready; they started off together to visit Mrs. Wrigglesworth. Quite a small crowd of people had assembled in the roadway in front of the old lady's cottage. Some of them were indulging in sounds which were not intended to be complimentary to its occupant. These advanced representatives of the popular feeling might have done more than make a noise if Mr. Packham had not appeared upon the scene. They might, and probably shortly would, have visited the cottage personally, and in a fashion of their own. Mr. Packham's advent, however, was immediately productive of good order.

"Now, then, none of that, if you please! What d'ye mean by making that noise?"

He caught a youngster by the ear.

"If you please, sir, it weren't me. I weren't a-doing nothing—it were Bill Perkins."

"I saw you a-doing of it!—don't tell me!—I know! Now, then, off you go—all the lot of you!"

Some of them did go—perhaps a dozen feet farther down the road. There, for a moment, they stayed, to edge their way, a foot at a time, back to where they were before. Mr. Grey and the policeman passed together up the cottage garden. Mr. Packham knocked at the door. No answer.

"Perhaps she's in bed."

Mr. Packham knocked again.

"I daresay—she was in bed when I came before."

"Ah, she's a lazy lot! She may be old, but it isn't only her age what's the matter with her."

Another clattering at the panels of the door.

"See if it's fastened."

"I was just thinking of doing that. She'll never hear—not if she don't choose she won't."

The door was not fastened. Mr. Packham threw it open.

"Mrs. Wrigglesworth! Why, it's pitch dark." He stepped inside. "Mrs. Wrigglesworth!"

Mr. Grey stepped in after him. By now it was dark enough outside; within that ill-lighted, low-roofed chamber was darkness which might have been felt. Passing the constable, who stood hesitating on the threshold, Mr. Grey went right into the house. He made no complaint of the darkness; possibly because for the moment it was welcome. As he moved, he withdrew something from the pocket of his coat; with his hand he felt along the wall: there was a sudden sound.

"What's that?" asked Mr. Packham, standing at the door.

Mr. Grey's voice came out of the depths, "It was something falling."

It was—it was Sir John Stoton's pocket-book falling back into its former hiding-place in the hole in the wall.

"I never see anything so dark. Mrs. Wrigglesworth! I shouldn't be surprised if she's listening to us all the time—I know her games! I'll strike a match. What's the matter, Mr. Grey?"

Something was the matter. Mr. Grey came rushing to the door. The policeman could feel that his hand was trembling as he laid it on the sleeve of his tunic. He was breathing in gasps.

"Packham, there's—there's someone lying on the floor."

"Is there? How do you know?"

"I—I felt with my foot—Packham!"

"It strikes me we shall want a light for this here job." He called into the road. "One of you men fetch me a candle or a lamp or something. It's all right, Mr. Grey; if you'll let go of me I'll strike a match." Mr. Grey was clinging to him so closely as to impede his movements. "Now, let's have a look." The match was struck.

"There is someone there, sure enough. Why, it's the old lady."

He moved forward, holding the flickering match in front of him.

"Mrs. Wrigglesworth! What's the matter with her? Is she asleep or drunk, or what?" He stooped over the recumbent figure. "I believe she's dead."

The match went out. "Hurry up there with a light, someone! I believe it is a case, sir; she's not breathing, nor nothing, and she's as limp as a rag. Mrs. Wrigglesworth!"

But Mrs. Wrigglesworth had gone to where, if sounds reached her, she was not able to communicate to them the fact that she heard. The light was brought. The villagers streamed in, men, women, children. With scared, excited faces they stared at Mrs. Wrigglesworth, lying in a heap, dead, on the floor. Mr. Grey was himself as white as death. Had he, after all, passed from the frying-pan to the fire? Had he had anything to do with this? He had had to use considerable violence to free himself from her grasp. He had not waited to see what had become of her. Had she fallen and struck against something, and been killed? If so, for what had he to answer?

"Someone run and fetch Doctor Baker," cried Mr. Packham. "We mustn't meddle with this until he comes."

There was a suggestiveness about Packham's words and manner which almost made Mr. Grey's heart stop beating. But he was to escape again. The doctor's first words relieved him of the burthen of a hideous fear,—the second burthen of which, owing to no deserts of his own, he had been relieved within that house. The woman had died of heart disease. The thing was simple enough. Doctor Baker was the parish doctor: in that capacity he had been aware that she had had a weak heart for years. The mystery to him was, not that now she had died, but that she had lived so long.

Mrs. Wrigglesworth had her "burying,"—the "burying" for which her soul had longed. She was not buried by the parish, not she! She had as fine a funeral as she could have herself desired, at Mr.

Grey's expense. People wondered. What was Mrs. Wrigglesworth to him that he should spend so much money on a pauper's burying? Probably the answers they received were not entirely to their satisfaction. Though it may be surmised that, at least in one quarter, an explanation was given, which was full and complete. Because, while the chief mourner was the guardian who footed the bill, at his side, in the first carriage, sat Mrs. Grey.

THE DISAPPEARANCE OF
MRS. MACRECHAM

CHAPTER I

"TO TRANSFORM A WOMAN INTO A CAT—A SIMPLE METHOD"

DIRECTLY I entered Waller's room I perceived that there was something the matter. Hereward Waller is one of those cold-blooded, self-possessed individuals who, with unfaltering hand, would continue to light and wrestle with a troublesome cigar in the presence of an earthquake.

Knowing him to be this kind of person I was the more surprised to perceive in his demeanour unmistakable signs of discomposure. He greeted me with a degree of effusion which, in Hereward Waller was really quite unnatural.

"You had my note?"

I told him that I had. And that its peremptory, and even mysterious tone had brought me off to him at once.

He regarded me, when I said this, with curious intentness. With his left hand he softly smoothed his shaven chin. Opening the door, he looked outside as if to learn if anyone was listening. Then, returning into the apartment, he began to fidget about the room in a manner which was so foreign to his usual habits that I became more and more amazed. He took up his position on the hearthrug. Even in the tone of his voice I noticed that there was something strange.

"Durrant, I have always looked upon you as that increasingly rare product of modern civilisation, a level-headed man." I felt flattered. I told him so. "I have also looked upon you as that even rarer article, a friend. And, in the dual capacity of level-headed man and my friend, I have sought you for what one man seldom does seek from another man, with the least intention of acting on it—advice. But if under the very—very peculiar circumstances you are able to proffer me advice of—of almost any kind, I assure you, Durrant, I will act on it."

This was such a remarkable speech to proceed from Hereward Waller that I was really at a loss for an answer. While I hesitated, he addressed to me a question—

"Have you—have you heard the news?"

"To what news do you refer?"

He gave what seemed to me to be a sigh of relief. I wondered more and more.

"I see you haven't. I thought you might have done. I suppose a great many people have. I believe advertisements have appeared in the newspapers. I know the police have been communicated with, and I have reason to think that notices have been posted up outside the various station houses."

"My dear Waller, I have not the most remote idea what you are talking about."

He lowered his voice. He even glanced furtively about the room.

"Mrs. Macrecham has disappeared."

"Mrs.—who?"

"Mrs. Macrecham—my landlady."

"Do you mean that cantankerous, narrow-minded old Scotchwoman who made such a fuss about your having a game of chess in her house on Sundays?"

To my amazement, Waller seemed to be positively agitated.

"S-sh! I would rather you did not talk like that, under the—the peculiar circumstances."

I stared.

"You don't mean to say that you contemplate going into mourning for the old cat?"

Unless I am mistaken, Waller actually jumped.

"Durrant, don't! I beg you won't! You—you don't understand. I am about to explain. Indeed, I sent for you here for the especial purpose of making to you an explanation. With your permission, I will take a chair."

I did not see that he required my permission to take a chair in his own room—but I did not say so. He sat down. He took out his handkerchief and wiped his brow. I had never seen him do such a thing before,—he had always prided himself on his constitutional Arctic coolness. A curious and, to me, incomprehensible change had suddenly taken place in Hereward Waller.

"This is Tuesday. Last Thursday afternoon I was left alone in the house with Mrs. Macrecham." Again he glanced furtively about the room. "Polly Macrecham, Mrs. Macrecham's niece, had gone on an errand to a tradesman. When she returned she could not find her aunt anywhere about the house. She came up to ask if I had seen her. I—I said"—his voice distinctly trembled—"I said that I had not. Miss Macrecham supposed that her aunt had taken a sudden fancy into her head, and gone and paid a visit to a neighbour. About—about midnight"—Waller's voice again distinctly trembled—"Miss Macrecham came up to me again, and told me that not only had her aunt not yet returned, but that she had run into all the neighbours of whom she could think, and that none of them had seen her; and that, moreover, Mrs. Smithers, who lives across the road, had been sitting at one of her front room windows, and had seen Miss Macrecham depart upon her errand to the tradesman. She said that she had not moved from the window until Miss Macrecham returned, and was positive that the aunt had not left the house during the niece's absence: if she had she must have seen her. I endeavoured to assure Miss Macrecham that Mrs. Smithers must be mistaken. But Miss Macrecham would not have it. She insisted that something dreadful had happened to her aunt, and that she was somewhere about the house. With a view of reassuring Miss Polly, I assisted her in minutely searching the house from attic to basement. We saw nothing of Mrs. Macrecham. Nothing has been seen of her unto this hour. She—she has disappeared."

"Well?" I asked. For I failed to perceive what the fact of Mrs. Macrecham's disappearance had to with Hereward Waller's evident and momentarily increasing agitation.

"Well, you see, I—I am placed in rather an unpleasant situation."

"What on earth do you mean? You don't mean to say that you are suspected of having taken advantage of the fact of having been left alone in the house with her to murder her? though, if you had done so, for my part I should have held you justified. Cross-grained old witch!"

She had come upon me, one wet Sunday afternoon, playing a game of chess with Waller in his rooms, and had preached at me for an hour on what she called the desecration of the Sabbath, in a manner which I am not likely to forget. Hereward, in his cold, dry manner, had been wont to speak of her to the full as unkindly as ever I had done. But now, to my surprise, he adopted an entirely different tone.

"Hush! I would rather you did not speak of her like that. Under the—under the peculiar circumstances, I really would." Again he wiped his brow. "I won't say that I am suspected of actual murder, but, by certain people, I am certainly suspected of something. And that the police have their eyes upon me, I'm assured."

"Hereward!"

"It's—it's in this way. When Miss Macrecham asked me if I had seen her aunt during her absence, I said that I had not. When, later, she asked me more than once again, I still said that I had not. But it appears that the observant Mrs. Smithers, sitting at her window across the road, had seen Mrs. Macrecham open the door to a boy who brought a parcel. She had gone so far as to recognise the boy as being in the employ of Thorpe, the stationer. Inquiry at Thorpe's elicited the fact that his boy had brought a parcel; that the parcel was for me; that it contained half a dozen packs of playing-cards; and that the boy had given it to Mrs. Macrecham, who had informed him that she would take it up to Mr. Waller. Now, unknown to me, when Miss Macrecham had come to my room to ask if I had seen her aunt, she had noticed this identical parcel lying on my table. When, later, I was asked who had brought it to my room if Mrs. Macrecham hadn't, I—I am afraid that I exhibited confusion."

"Had the old woman been to your room while the niece was out?"

"She had; and, what's more, she's in it now."

"In it now?"

As I echoed his words, I stared. I had not the faintest notion of his meaning.

"Yes, Durrant, it's an incredible and—and an appalling fact, that while her niece is torn with doubts, and the police are searching for her, dead or alive, in all directions, Mrs. Macrecham is, at this present moment, in this room. She has not quitted it, even for a single second, since she entered it on Thursday afternoon."

Beads of perspiration were standing on Hereward Waller's brow. I began myself to be conscious of a sense of vague discomfort. What did he mean?

"Allow me to explain." As he rose I perceived that he was positively trembling. "She's in this sideboard." He pointed to a piece of furniture which occupied a corner of the room. "Just come—just come and see."

I followed him across the room with feelings which I experience some difficulty in describing. As he produced a key from his waistcoat pocket, and, with shaking fingers, fitted it into the lock of the sideboard, I regarded him with a sort of shuddering aversion. Was it possible that I was about to gaze upon the evidences of some hideous tragedy? I knew Hereward Waller to be a cool, calculating, and almost, in a certain sense, an unprincipled man,—a man who, under certain circumstances, would stick at nothing. I knew, too, that he had had more than one passage of arms with Mrs. Macrecham. Was it possible that, in a fit of sudden anger—and I knew how nasty he could be when he was in a nasty frame of mind—he had slain his landlady? And had he actually gone so far as to conceal all that was left of her in the sideboard in which he kept his wines and spirits? Did he propose to treat me to a private view of the ensanguined corpse, and so make of me a confidant of his horrid crime?

I was about to explain to him that anything which he revealed to me he revealed at his own risk, and that I should allow no ties of friendship to stand between me and the police, when—he opened the sideboard door.

"Look!" he said. I looked, with half-unwilling, half-fearful eyes. I saw nothing unusual, except that he seemed to have cleared the bottles upon one side, in order to make room for a large tabby cat, which was lying asleep on the top of a heap of what appeared to be Waller's underclothing. "That is Mrs. Macrecham."

I supposed that there was something at the back of the cupboard which I could not see, so I stooped still lower down. There proved, however, to be nothing there. I felt a trifle nettled.

"I don't know, Waller, if you are trying to play off on me some idiotic little joke of yours."

"Joke! I wish it were a joke!" I looked at him. I had never supposed it possible that a man could show such signs of physical and mental agitation. The sweat was gathered in great drops upon his forehead. He pointed to the open sideboard. "I tell you that that is Mrs. Macrecham."

"Which is Mrs. Macrecham? There's nothing but a cat, you ass!"

Never shall I forget the tone of voice in which he uttered his next words, as though they were wrung from him in his agony—

"The cat is Mrs. Macrecham!"

"The cat! Waller!"

As he said that I gazed at him in horrified amazement. In an instant it flashed across my brain that the cause of his unusual agitation was now made plain—too plain. My boyhood's friend had lost his mental equilibrium. He had joined, what statistics assure us, are the increasing ranks of the insane. I eyed him with an expression of countenance which, I have no doubt, was eloquent with meaning.

He immediately detected what was passing through my mind.

"You think that I am mad. Sometimes I think so too. I think that I must be mad. But reflection shows that such is not the case. The circumstantial evidence which goes to prove my sanity is overwhelming. At times I am almost tempted to wish that I, in truth, was mad."

I made a strategic movement in the direction of the door,—a madman's logic is proverbial.

"Excuse me one moment, I just"—

He perceived my intention. He sprang between the door and me.

"Durrant, what are you going to do? You won't desert me! For God's sake, man, don't do that! There never was, in the whole history of the world, a human creature in such frightful need of the guidance of a faithful friend as I am now. I give you my word of honour, I'm not mad. If—if you'll allow me, I'll explain."

THE DISAPPEARANCE OF MRS. MACRECHAM 199

I allowed him to explain, because I could not very well see my way to help it. I deemed it better policy to humour him. As he explained, I glanced round the room in search of a weapon of defence in case of a sudden outbreak. I decided that there was no better defensive weapon available than one of the heavy, leather-covered chairs. So I firmly grasped the back of one—in case of need.

He explained.

"Durrant, I—I have been the victim of an unparalleled experience,—of so unparalleled an experience that, were it not for the undeniable evidence of a hundred various details, I should be persuaded that I have been the nightmare-haunted dreamer of some amazing dream."

He wiped his forehead with his pocket-handkerchief. Directly he had done so I perceived that it had become immediately damp again with sweat.

"Last Thursday morning I had business in the neighbourhood of Fleet Street. I strolled homewards by way of Bookseller's Row. I glanced at the bookstalls. In one of the fourpenny boxes I saw a moth-eaten, tattered, marble-covered duodecimo. I picked it up. I found that it was a work which was entirely strange to me, even as regards its title. It was entitled *The Art and Theory of Magic*. I bought it,—I really don't know why. I wish to Heaven a thousand times I hadn't."

Again he paused to wipe his brow. His manner certainly was most singular, especially for a madman. I found myself staring at him with renewed perplexity.

He continued to explain.

"When I returned home I threw the book aside. I forgot all about it till after I had lunched, when I chanced to light upon the thing as it lay upon the sideboard, half hidden among a heap of newspapers. I—I opened it."

Waller was speaking now as a man might speak whose mouth was parched and dry.

"I—I began to read it. It was full of some of the most—most amazing rubbish I ever remember to have seen. It was arranged like a cookery book, only, instead of containing recipes for cookery, it contained what purported to be recipes for the performance of feats of magic. I—I never read anything so absurd."

I was driven to ask a question.

"Why did you read it if the thing was so absurd?"

"Durrant, you will laugh at me, but—but the thing exercised on me the—the most extraordinary fascination,—a fascination which I verily believe was in proportion to its absurdity. One—one recipe in particular, which, on the face of it, was perhaps the most absurd of all, affected me to a quite inconceivable extent."

"Which one was that?"

"The recipes were headed as the recipes are headed in a cookery book. This one was entitled 'To Transform a Woman into a Cat—a Simple Method.'"

When Waller said that, I started. I instinctively glanced towards the open sideboard. I saw that Waller started too, even more than I had done, and that his glance followed mine. My doubts as to his sanity returned. I said, to humour him—

"I see,—a simple method. It is as well, when one has to do a thing like that, that the way to do it should be made as simple as possible."

"This—this was simplicity itself. In its simplicity lay its acute absurdity. One had only to go through certain elementary formulæ, and to utter certain rubbish, and, according to the book, the thing was done."

"In what then lay its fascination for a mind like yours?"

"Durrant, I cannot tell you—I cannot tell you! I do not know myself. I only know that it did fascinate me, and that to an indescribable degree. I read it and re-read it, and was still re-reading it when the door opened, and Mrs. Macrecham entered."

Again Waller paused to wipe his brow. I was becoming more and more uncomfortable. Whether the man was mad or sane, it seemed to me that the situation was almost equally unpleasant.

He went on in a tone of voice and in a manner which did not tend to increase my peace of mind.

"She had in her hand the parcel of playing-cards which had just come from Thorpe, the stationer. She had either guessed at the contents, or inquired what they were from the boy who had brought the parcel. 'More devil's pictures, Mr. Waller,' she said. And then she started off in the style which, as you are aware, has caused me more than once to wonder why I suffered such a woman to be my landlady. She—she had her good qualities, and even her bad ones had sometimes been to me a source of amusement, but—but I suppose that—that just then I—I was in—in a very peculiar frame of mind. I know that what she said stung me to an unusual degree of anger."

His voice sank to a whisper—a whisper, however, which was of a singularly penetrating kind.

"I had that—that wretched little book in my hand. The words of that—that preposterous recipe were dancing before my eyes. Mrs. Macrecham stood in front of me. Almost before I knew what I was doing, in the midst of one of Mrs. Macrecham's diatribes, I began to repeat the formulæ as they were set down in the book. The effect upon Mrs. Macrecham was extraordinary. She instantly ceased speaking, and—she looked at me! How she looked at me! Something urged me to go on. I went on. I repeated the gibberish as the book directed. Durrant"—

Waller sank into a chair. His head sank forward on to his chest His attitude was that of a man who had been overwhelmed by some sudden, overpowering shock.

I encouraged him to go on,—only to find that my own voice had become a trifle shaky.

"We-ell?"

"Durrant, hardly had the last syllable escaped my tongue, than Mrs. Macrecham disappeared, and on the floor where she had just been standing was a tabby cat. I never saw such a thing before in all my life—never! The change was so instantaneous that you could scarcely follow it with the eye, and yet I saw her change into a cat—a monstrous tabby cat! You know that I have a constitutional dislike to cats. When I saw this creature, purring, wagging its tail, and looking up at me, I gazed at it with unspeakable disgust. As I did so I heard someone running up the stairs. I guessed that it was Miss Polly coming to inquire for her aunt. I kicked the cat into the cupboard, I turned the key, and—I lied to Miss Macrecham."

He paused—it was about time he did! I stared at him, scarcely knowing whether to deem him mad or sane. He sat staring, as it seemed to me, into vacancy.

"Granting that this amazing legend of yours is, at anyrate,

founded upon fact, did that fourpenny treasure contain no directions for retransforming a cat into a woman?"

"I saw none."

"Where is this wonderful volume?"

"Durrant, when I had lied to Miss Macrecham, in the first horror of that dreadful moment, tearing the book into a dozen fragments, I threw them, one by one, into the fire"—

I interrupted him.

"That was scarcely a wise thing to do."

He went on.

"All but the last half of the cover. I was about to throw it after the other portions of the book, when I saw, written on the inner side of it, some words which caught my eye."

"What were the words?"

"Here is the piece of the cover to which I refer. I have kept it. You shall see what is written on it for yourself. It may, or it may not, contain the secret of the retransformation. After what I have seen, I cannot, I dare not, say. You will yourself perceive that the suggestion it conveys is of an extremely hazardous kind,—a veritable case of kill or cure."

From an inner pocket of his coat he produced what purported to be the only remaining portion of that "fourpenny treasure." It was, as he said, half the cover. The book had apparently been a cheaply-got-up duodecimo, and had been bound in the days when "marble backs" were all the rage. The cover had seemingly been lined with coarse whitey-brown paper. On this whitey-brown paper were written the words to which Waller had alluded.

They were written in a bad hand, with a bad pen, by a person whose education, on the face of it, had distinctly been deficient.

"To tern a cat bak into a woman, cut her throte."

That was what was written on the cover of Hereward's "fourpenny treasure."

"You see," he said, "the hazardous nature of the suggestion."

"I don't quite understand the thing. Whose throat are you to cut,—the cat's or the woman's?"

"I presume the cat's. You see, to cut a cat's throat would be to kill it—at least, such would be the ordinary inference."

As he seemed to pause for me to speak, I spoke.

"Just so," I murmured

"To kill the cat would be to kill Mrs. Macrecham. Although, under the circumstances, it would be a moot-point as to whether that was, or was not, murder, still, you understand, I should not care to run the risk,—the more especially as I should always be haunted by a doubt as to whether I had, or had not, the brand of Cain upon my brow."

As he seemed to pause for me to speak again, I spoke again.

"I see," I muttered

Rising from his seat he began to pace about the room. He spoke as if he were torn and racked by a thousand dreadful doubts.

"You plainly perceive, then, what is the truly incredible nature of the position in which you find me placed. Mrs. Macrecham has disappeared. Her niece is tortured with anxiety. Her creditors are dubious. Her neighbours are filled with a morbid curiosity. The police are moving heaven and earth to find her, dead or living. Already a whisper of crime is in the air. Wagging fingers point my way. Searching eyes see guilt upon my brow. If I move abroad, my steps are dogged. To all intents and purposes, the avengers of blood are already upon my heels. I am a marked man! Nor is it strange, for, all this time, Mrs. Macrecham is hidden in the cupboard of my room. And yet I cannot take Miss Polly to the cupboard, and show her the tabby cat, and say, Miss Macrecham, this is your aunt. She would exclaim, as you exclaimed, that I was mad. And even if I succeeded in convincing her of the truth of what I said, she would still not be content. You would with difficulty persuade a right-minded young woman to accept a monstrous tabby cat as an in any way satisfactory substitute for a venerated aunt. No! she would straightway denounce me to the officers of the law. I am not sufficiently a lawyer to be able to say of what crime I have been guilty, but I cannot doubt that I have been guilty of some crime. It is ridiculous to suppose that one person is to be allowed to turn another person into such a creature as a cat with complete impunity. And, Durrant, to add to my distresses, which, as you see, are already manifold, I have been carrying about with me, in the pocket of my coat, the back cover of that fateful volume, on which is written—what shall I call it?—that sanguinary recipe. And, night and day, in consequence, I have been asking myself the question,

Shall I improve the situation by slitting the animal's throat from ear to ear? And—and, Durrant"—

Waller came closer to me. He laid his trembling hand upon my arm. He looked at me with fevered eyes.

"There's another thing. I—I am afraid that Mrs. Macrecham's ill. I—I am not an authority on cats, but I fear that either the food which I have given her has disagreed with her digestion, or else the close confinement has proved trying to her constitution. I dare not let her loose; think—think of the long chain of possibilities if Mrs. Macrecham should go philandering on the tiles!—certainly she appears unwell. She refuses all food, and appears to be possessed by a constant lassitude."

He tightened his grasp upon my arm. His eyes seemed to scorch me.

"If she should die!—Durrant, what shall I do? You see that there never was a man in more pressing need of the faithful advice of a faithful friend. Give me, I implore you, your advice!"

I hesitated,—it was a case in which a good deal of hesitation appeared to me to be required. When I spoke, I do not think he derived much comfort from my words.

"Waller, I don't know whether you're mad, or whether you aren't; I don't know whether you are having a little joke with me, or whether you aren't; I don't know whether you are telling the truth, or whether you aren't. But, in any case, the situation is more than I can manage. I am an authority neither on cats nor women. You have got into the muddle by yourself. I am afraid, so far as I am concerned, that you will have to get out of it by yourself."

Possibly he took my words to convey an intimation of immediate retreat. He grasped me still tighter by the arm.

"You won't desert me!—Durrant!—Hush!—There's someone coming up the stairs."

CHAPTER II

WILLIAM BROOKER

His hearing must have been unusually acute,—possibly recent circumstances had made it so. I heard nothing. But, after some moments of the intensest listening, he proved to be right. Someone tapped at the panel of the door, and, without waiting for an invitation to enter, someone came into the room.

This someone was a man. A tall, loose-limbed, beefy-looking man, with sandy whiskers, sandy hair, and, if I may be allowed to write it so, a sandy nose. He closed the door behind him, and, with a billycock hat in one hand and a stick in the other, he stood looking at us in what seemed to me to be rather an impertinent manner. I do not know why it should have been so, because, although large and bulky, he was not a formidable-looking individual, and he was a complete stranger to me; but something about the man, his looks or his manner, or something, made me wish that he had postponed his call on Hereward until after I had gone away. I felt an inward conviction, as he stood there eyeing us, that our demeanour, both Hereward's and mine, struck him as curious. He looked at Hereward, and then he looked at me. And then he said—to me—

"Mr. Waller?"

"No." I motioned towards Hereward. "This is Mr. Waller."

"Ah!" The man's tone was peculiarly significant,—though significant of what is more than I can say. He took a good long stare at Hereward. Then he observed, "I am William Brooker."

"Indeed?" stammered Hereward.

"Perhaps you have heard that name before?" Hereward stammeringly doubted if he had ever had the pleasure. "It's a name that's been before the public a good many times, and in some good big cases too. I'm a private detective."

When he said that I know that I turned rightabout face, so that I am not able to say exactly what Hereward did, but I feel sure that he did not look happy. When I again looked round Mr. Brooker had laid his hat and stick upon a chair. He held an open pocketbook and a lead pencil in his hand.

"I've come to ask you a few questions, Mr. Waller, about the disappearance of Mrs. Macrecham."

As he said this, he regarded Hereward with what struck me as being a disagreeably inquisitorial stare. Possibly Hereward himself felt it to be so. He repeated Mr. Brooker's words in a sort of arid echo.

"The disappearance of Mrs. Macrecham."

Mr. Brooker continued. "Now, I'm a second cousin of Mrs. Macrecham's, and although I differed from her on about eleven subjects out of every ten, it is not, therefore, to be supposed that I'm going to allow anybody, no matter who it is, to play hankey-pankey tricks with her, and never say a word."

"Just so," stammered Hereward. "Quite—quite natural. Will you"—

"One moment, Mr. Waller. Now, with regard to the disappearance of Mrs. Macrecham, it is felt by certain persons, and, among others, I tell you frankly, it is felt by me, that you know more about the matter than, up to the present, you have chosen to say."

When Mr. Brooker said that, Hereward did as I had done,—he turned rightabout face. It was a foolish thing to do, with that man's inquisitive eyes fixed intently on him,—but he did it. I could see that his face had become of a sickly pallor, and that the muscles of his countenance were working, as it seemed, convulsively.

"Will you," he stammered, "will you—will you have something to drink?"

Mr. Brooker's gaze was still intently riveted on the back view which he presented. Perhaps, to Mr. Brooker, that back view was eloquent.

"Thank you. It's all the same to me. I don't mind if I do."

Hereward moved to the sideboard. Although it appears incredible, it really almost seemed as if he had temporarily forgotten the existence of the tabby cat. For, when he reached the cupboard, and, stooping down, perceived the creature lying there asleep, starting back, he stared in what seemed to be speechless amazement. Just at that moment the cat awoke, and, after the manner of cats, began to stretch itself and arch its back.

Mr. Brooker's eyes, hitherto centred upon Hereward, were now turned towards the cat.

"That's a fine animal you have there, Mr. Waller."

Hereward seemed to experience some difficulty in inducing his voice to perform its office. "Ye-es," he stammered.

"I suppose that you are fond of cats, or you would not make a bed for one inside your wine cupboard. Are you very fond of cats, Mr. Waller?"

Hereward gave painful utterance to another faintly stammered affirmation. Mr. Brooker was regarding him with evidently increasing interest. His bearing was not by any means that of an enthusiastic lover of the feline race. He stood glaring at the tabby cat as though the creature exercised on him some hideous fascination. Apparently he had forgotten his offer of refreshment. Mr. Brooker ventured to recall it to his mind. He drew his hand across his mouth.

"I've come some distance, and I think you were kind enough, Mr. Waller, to say something about a drink."

Mr. Brooker's, unless his nose belied him, was a thirsty soul.

Hereward, thus gently reminded of his proffered hospitality, stretched out his hand to take a bottle from the shelf. As he did so, the cat, as cats will do when they are disagreeably inclined, spat, and struck at him with its paw. The effect upon Hereward of the animal's unfriendly behaviour was absolutely ludicrous. The man, whom I had supposed to be the least nervous person of my acquaintance, sprang back with what was unmistakably a cry of terror, and stood actually trembling with agitation.

Mr. Brooker seemed to be both amazed and amused.

"If you are fond of cats, Mr. Waller, cats don't seem to be fond of you."

Hereward said nothing. He stared at the cat. In return, the tabby stared at him. It not only stared, but, coming out of the cupboard, it advanced towards Hereward. As it advanced, Hereward retreated. The animal went forward; Hereward went back. It was a ridiculous and yet a painful scene. Waller's distress was so wholly undisguised. There was nothing unfriendly about the animal's demeanour, so far as I could judge. And yet, as the cat came on, Hereward shrunk back, with a degree of shuddering aversion which it almost gave one the "creepy crawlers" merely to look upon. When he had backed against the wall, so that he could get no farther, Hereward turned his face away, and, raising his arm as if to screen his eyes, he actually called to me for help.

"Durrant! Durrant! Take her away!"

Mr. Brooker and I looked on with what, I have no doubt, were mingled feelings. The man crouching against the wall, the cat looking up at him with what seemed very natural surprise, was a sight not often witnessed. Mr. Brooker turned to me, and asked—

"Has he"—he made a significant gesture with his hand—"been drinking?"

The fellow was suggesting that Hereward was suffering from delirium tremens. I indignantly repudiated the suggestion.

"What do you mean, sir? My friend is almost a teetotaller."

The detective smiled. I believe he was incredulous.

"He doesn't look as though he were very fond of cats at any-rate," he said. "Pussy! Pussy!"

He called the cat. Without a moment's hesitation, the creature came running towards him. Mr. Brooker took it in his arms. Seating himself, he placed the cat upon his knee.

"There doesn't seem to be much the matter with the cat, Mr. Waller. It seems to be rather an affectionate sort of beast."

It did seem to be so just then. Mr. Brooker made a fuss with the cat, and the cat made a fuss with Mr. Brooker. The detective stroked and tickled the tabby. The tabby purred, and rubbed itself against the detective's waistcoat. Moving away from the wall, Hereward stood silently looking on. Mr. Brooker eyed him with a curious smile.

"Do you know, Mr. Waller, that you remind me of a story which I was reading some little time ago. It was written by a man who seemed to fancy himself as an authority upon detectives. I think the story was called 'The Black Cat.'"

Hereward started. I believe I started too. Mr. Brooker went on, apparently taking it for granted that we neither of us were students of Poe.

"It wasn't a pretty story, but it was a strange one. It was about a man who murdered his wife. The only witness of his crime was a cat. Not a witness, one would think, greatly to be feared. And yet, ever afterwards, the man, victimised by his guilty conscience, regarded that cat with, among other things, an unspeakable horror,—almost as you seem to regard this cat, Mr. Waller."

Hereward still said nothing. He continued to look at Mr. Brooker and the cat, like a man who, though wide awake, mentally struggles with some dreadful dream.

Perceiving him to be still silent, the detective went on—

"Since there seems to be no prospect of that little refresher, I think, Mr. Waller, if you have no objection, we will return to the subject of Mrs. Macrecham. There are one or two questions which I wish to ask you."

With what seemed to be an effort, Hereward managed to find his voice. His words came out with a rush. He was as voluble, all at once, as he had been taciturn before.

"Excuse me for one single instant, Mr. Brooker. You must really forgive my unpardonable remissness, but I—I have been very far from well just lately. What can I offer you to drink—brandy? whisky? rum? Or can I tempt you with a glass of champagne?"

He moved rapidly across the room. But, as he neared Mr. Brooker and the cat, he hesitated,—and he glanced at the cat. Unless I greatly err, at the mention of those various liquids, Mr. Brooker's eyes grew dim. Like the proverbial sailor, he seemed to be divided in his mind.

"Well, I—I think I'll have a glass of champagne; it isn't often that champagne does come my way—thank—you."

Mr. Brooker—and the cat—were on Hereward's right,— between him and the cupboard. Just as Hereward moved, the cat moved too—that is to say, it raised itself on Mr. Brooker's knee and looked at Waller, it seemed to me, in the most peaceful way imaginable. But, had it sprung in wild frenzy at his throat, he could not have exhibited more concern.

"Hold her! hold her!" he screamed. He was trembling as with ague. Mr. Brooker and I stared at him in amazement. He stammered out a sort of explanation. "How—how am I to get to the cupboard if she's in the way."

Mr. Brooker was circling the cat with his arms.

"I don't know what's the matter with you, Mr. Waller. The cat is not in your way. She seems to me to be the nicest tempered cat I ever saw."

Hereward's trembling fit continued for a moment longer. Then, still keeping one eye fixed upon the cat, and giving her as wide a berth as possible, he went to the cupboard. He took out a bottle of champagne, the nippers, and a glass.

"None for me!" I said.

Judging from the glance which Hereward cast in my direction, my refusal was unnecessary,—he had apparently forgotten I was there. Drawing the cork, he poured the creaming liquid into the glass. He held the bottle and glass out towards Mr. Brooker.

"Take care of her," he said, with an eye upon the cat.

"I'm taking care of her—if you'll put it on the table—thank you, sir."

Hereward put the bottle and the glass upon the table,—going half round it to avoid the cat. When the bottle was opened, Mr. Brooker observed that there was but a single glass.

"Won't you join me, sir?"

Hereward declined.

"I'm—I'm going to have some brandy."

Mr. Brooker raised his glass to his lips. He nodded to Hereward and then to me.

"Your good health, Mr. Waller,—and yours, sir." Mr. Brooker took a sip,—a copious sip. "A very nice glass of wine, Mr. Waller."

Hereward had returned to the sideboard. He took out a decanter of brandy and a tumbler. He half filled the tumbler with the raw spirit arid drank it, at a gulp, neat. Mr. Brooker winked at me.

"Almost a teetotaller," he whispered.

Hereward was almost a teetotaller, as a rule. I had never seen him do that kind of thing before. Not himself a lover of ardent spirits, he had always maintained that a person who resorted to their use, with a view of sustaining his courage, or in any way rehabilitating his disorganised nervous system, was a cur, and worse. He seemed to have forgotten, just then, the cold logic with which he had been wont to press his point. Not content with one half tumbler, he three parts filled the glass again, and sent it, as before, with a single gulp, after his former draught. Taking the decanter and the glass with him, he placed them beside him on the mantelshelf, and took up his position in the centre of the hearthrug.

Having refilled and re-emptied his own glass, Mr. Brooker returned to the subject which was supposed to be in hand.

"That's a very nice glass of wine, Mr. Waller,—a capital glass of wine! Now, with your permission, we will return to the subject to which I am indebted for the pleasure of this interview,—the disappearance of Mrs. Macrecham. I understand from Polly Macrecham that you did not see her aunt during her absence from the house on Thursday afternoon. May I ask you, Mr. Waller, confidentially as between man and man, if that really is the case?"

Hereward, in the centre of the hearthrug, was looking more like his usual self,—dogged and cold. I could see that the brandy had had its effect; but I was not prepared to find that it had done its work so completely as it really had done.

"Mr. Brooker, there is one remark which I wish to make to you."

"I shall be very happy to listen to anything you have to say, Mr. Waller. Indeed, it is for that especial purpose I am here."

Mr. Brooker affably refilled his glass.

"The remark which I have to make, Mr. Brooker, is to the effect that you are an impertinent fellow."

I scarcely imagine that that was the kind of thing to which Mr. Brooker had come to listen. He glanced up in apparent surprise.

"Sir?"

"I say, Mr. Brooker, and I repeat it, that you are an impertinent fellow,—an impertinent, presuming, ill-mannered, ill-conditioned fellow. I am prepared to say more, if you wish to hear it. I shall say more, if you do not take care. Uninvited, you have intruded yourself into my apartments, with the ignorantly avowed purpose of asking me insolent questions about a subject in which I take not the slightest interest. Such being the case, you will be so good, upon my invitation, as to take yourself instantly outside my rooms."

Mr. Brooker's glass had paused half-way to his lips. There could be no doubt that he was surprised. There had been nothing till then in Hereward's manner to lead him to suppose that this was the kind of man he was. His countenance became quite rubicund. He evinced an inclination to splutter.

"Am I to understand that you decline to give me any information about Mrs. Macrecham?"

"You are to understand that you are instantly to leave my room. You are a bigger man than I am, Mr. Brooker, but there have been instances of the bigger man being thrown by the smaller man down two flights of stairs."

Mr. Brooker chose to interpret Hereward's words as conveying a threat of personal violence. He rose from his chair,—the tabby in his arms.

"You touch me!" he exclaimed.

"I very shortly shall touch you, to the extent of ejecting you from my apartments, if you don't at once vacate them of your own accord,—rest assured of that, Mr. Brooker."

Mr. Brooker hesitated. I have seldom seen a man so suddenly demoralised. It was hard,—one moment to be enjoying, all to himself, a bottle of really good champagne, and the next moment to be threatened by his host with being kicked from the room. He seemed suddenly to remember that he had the tabby in his arms. With almost feminine spite he tossed her in Hereward's direction.

"Perhaps you would like your cat, Mr. Waller?"

The unfortunate animal alighted at Hereward's feet. With a dexterous kick he sent it flying into the far corner of the room. No wonder the ill-used creature emitted in mid-air a scream of mingled pain and terror. Hereward advanced to Mr. Brooker.

"Are you going, sir?"

Mr. Brooker still hesitated,—for one second, not for more. When he saw the look which was on Hereward's face, and perceived the sort of mood he was in, he deemed discretion to be the better part of valour.

"I am going, sir,—oh yes, I'm going." He glanced down at the table. The spirit, perhaps, was almost willing, but the flesh was decidedly weak. "I suppose I may be allowed to drink my glass of wine before I go."

"Certainly. You may take the bottle with you if you like. It occurs to me, my man, that it was on the off chance of getting something of that sort you came."

I fancy Mr. Brooker would have dearly liked to have taken the bottle with him,—but he could not, for very shame. A cruel, remorseless sense of dignity compelled him to treat with contemptuous scorn the liquor he so fondly loved. Mr. Brooker went to the door. He took his hat and stick from a chair. Being as he deemed at a safe distance, he had a parting shot at Hereward—

"You will hear from me again, sir,—make no mistake about that! I believe that that poor, dumb cat, if she could only speak, could reveal a tale of horror which would make the blood run cold. And it shall be revealed to the world, sir,—by me!" Mr. Brooker put his hat upon his head. "I will not say good-bye, Mr. Waller, but—*au revoir.*"

And Mr. Brooker went.

CHAPTER III

THE BUTCHER BOY

HEREWARD stood still for a moment or two after the detective's departure. It struck me that he was listening, to make sure that he was descending the stairs. Then he turned to me. He spoke with a peculiar intensity of passion—

"You hear what he says? He suspects me,—even that dull-witted fool! He perceives—even that dullard!—that the secret of the mystery is hidden in the bosom of the cat,—that mottled beast!"

The ill-used tabby had prudently remained in the corner into which she had been kicked. She sat licking her paws with an air of forgetfulness of injuries which was almost sublime.

I hardly knew what to say to Waller. Indeed, I felt that it would be to follow the path of wisdom to say nothing at all. This little affair of his was altogether too much for my limited capacities. I had always liked fairy tales, but I had hardly expected that I should ever be called upon to breathe into my lungs, and at the same time to scientifically analyse, the atmosphere of the Arabian Nights.

When Hereward perceived that I did not speak, and that I evinced no intention of speaking, he turned to the decanter and the tumbler which he had placed upon the mantelshelf. On the whole, I wished that he would not,—the situation, in my judgment, was already sufficiently intoxicating,—but at the same time I scarcely felt called upon to tell him so. He half filled the tumbler with brandy,—this is a sober narrative of sober facts,—and, again at a single gulp, he sent it after his other two potations.

Then once more he turned to me.

"I have made up my mind. The other recipe was successful,—

too successful!—why should this one not be successful too? I will do it!"

"You will do what?" I ventured mildly to inquire.

"I will slit Mrs. Macrecham's throat from ear to ear!"

He pointed with almost fiendish malignity to the tabby cat, who was quietly licking her paws in a corner of the room. I felt uneasy.

"Hush! If I were you, Hereward, I wouldn't speak so loud. There may be someone listening, and a listener might misunderstand the meaning of your words."

"There had better not be anyone listening! There had better not!"

He strode to the door. He threw it open. Fortunately for all concerned no one was outside. Shutting the door again, he returned into the room. He put his hand up to his brow.

"If I don't do something, Durrant, I shall go raving mad!—There's a butcher in the street!"

I did not see the inevitable connection which existed between his mental condition and a butcher, but, as he looked out of the window, I looked too. A butcher boy was on the opposite side of the road, whistling and swinging an empty tray. Hereward threw up the window. He hailed the butcher boy. I felt that this was a new phase in the disease from which, I could not conceal from myself, he must be suffering.

"Butcher! butcher!" The butcher boy looked up. "Come here— I want you!" The butcher boy crossed the road. Hereward turned to me. "Wait,—I shan't be a moment! I'm going to let him in. See—see that Mrs. Macrecham doesn't leave the room."

It scarcely was more than a moment before he reappeared in the room with the wondering butcher boy. He came at once to the point—

"Butcher, would you like to earn half a sovereign?"

The butcher boy grinned.

"I wouldn't mind, sir."

"Cut that cat's throat and I will give you half a sovereign."

Hereward pointed to the unconscious tabby, who still was quietly licking her paws in a corner of the room.

"If I was to take her home I'd do for her in a better way than that, sir."

Hereward did not relish the butcher boy's suggestion.

"You will either cut her throat, or you will do nothing at all."

The butcher boy did not seem to quite know what to make of Hereward's manner.

"Is it your cat, sir?"

"Of course it's my cat. What do you mean?"

"Well, sir, the other day a party give me a cat and half a crown to do for it, and when I'd done for it I found that it was the party's cat what lived next door to this here first party,—a old lady's cat it was. And didn't she go on when she found out I'd done for it. She come round to my master—she's a customer of his—and he almost give me the sack, though it wasn't no fault of mine. I didn't know whose cat it was."

"This cat is mine all right. Take it into my back yard, and cut its throat at once, and I'll give you a sovereign."

"A sovereign!" The butcher boy's eyes glistened. "I'll do it. I've got a sharp knife in my pocket."

He produced the knife. It *was* a knife,—a murderous-looking weapon. That perfidious butcher boy, with soft allurements, enticed that trustful tabby. He held out his hand invitingly.

"Pussy! Pussy!" he murmured.

The unsuspecting cat came trotting towards him across the room. Possibly she thought that he smelt of meat. She little dreamed that he intended to make meat of her! The butcher boy took her up into his arms.

"If you go downstairs you will easily find your way to the yard. When you've done it, come back to me for the sovereign."

The butcher boy left the room with his unconscious burden in his arms. Directly he had gone, Hereward turned again to the decanter and the tumbler. This time I did interpose.

"If I were you, Hereward, I would leave that brandy alone. It strikes me that you have had more than enough of it already."

The only notice he took of what I said was to gulp down another half-tumblerful.

"I must! I must!" he declared. "Durrant, if—if he were to kill her!"

It struck me as extremely probable that he would kill her,—if "he" meant the butcher boy and "her" meant the cat. I did not see what else could reasonably be expected. To cut a cat's throat is not generally supposed to be the best means of prolonging the animal's life. However, I said nothing,—it was a matter between the butcher boy and Hereward.

Waller's sitting-room and bedroom adjoin each other. They communicate by means of folding-doors. The bedroom window overlooks the yard which was to be the scene of the approaching tragedy. Opening the folding-doors, Hereward entered the bedroom with the evident intention of being a spectator of the coming drama. I preferred to remain where I was.

However, Hereward, at the bedroom window, managed to give me, at the sitting-room window, a sufficiently lively idea of what was going on.

"Here he is!—He's got her!—He's opening his knife!—He's—he's going to cut her throat!" Hereward's voice, coming to me in quick, eager, almost frenzied tones, made me feel as though I were witnessing—and aiding and abetting in—a murder. "He's cut her throat!—Oh-h!—Oh-h!" Hereward began screeching in a manner the like of which I never heard before or since. "Mrs. Macrecham!—Mrs. Macrecham!"

I had not at the moment the faintest notion of what it was he meant,—but I knew that, whatever it was, I wished he wouldn't There was a sound below as of someone making a tumultuous entry from the rear of the house. I heard the area door thrown frantically open. I saw the butcher boy come tearing up the area steps. When he reached the top he went rushing down the street, hatless, trayless, sovereignless, as if Satan was at his heels.

And a moment afterwards I heard, downstairs, a voice,—a well-known voice. It was the voice of Mrs. Macrecham. She was addressing herself to Mr. Brooker, who had apparently delayed his departure from the house for the sake of pursuing his inquiries. Judging from her tone, she was addressing him on one of those eleven subjects out of every ten on which, as he himself allowed, they were wont to differ.